After Lise

Denise Pattiz Bogard

Finalist
Faulkner-Wisdom
Competition

Also by Denise Pattiz Bogard
THE MIDDLE STEP

Visit Denise Pattiz Bogard's Author Page
at
www.ArdentWriterPress.com

To have the author join your bookclub or to learn more contact:
www.denisebogard.com

The Ardent Writer Press
Brownsboro, Alabama

For general information about publishing with The Ardent Writer
Press contact *steve@ardentwriterpress.com* or forward mail to:
The Ardent Writer Press, Box 25, Brownsboro, Alabama 35741.

This is a first edition of a novel, *After Elise*, by Denise Pattiz Bogard, St. Louis, Missouri. *After Elise* is a book about how unexpected tragedy changes the lives of a dysfunctional family while demonstrating that patience, understanding and forgiveness bring hope. All rights reserved by Denise Pattiz Bogard. Excerpts of text may be posted online only for a noncommercial use, provided quotations do not exceed a total of over three hundred (300) words.

Cover Art by The Ardent Writer Press using a photograph from Robert Bogard augmented with public domain photographs and Photoshop techniques. Cover composition by The Ardent Writer Press. Composition and cover are covered by the same grant for noncommercial use noted above.

Photo of Denise Pattiz Bogard is from the author.

Library of Congress Cataloging-in-Publication Data

Denise Pattiz Bogard, St. Louis, Missouri
After Elise by Denise Pattiz Bogard

p. cm. - (Ardent Writer Press-2017) ISBN 978-1-64066-051-9 (pbk.); 978-1-64066-053-3 (eBook mobi)

Library of Congress Control Number 2018938004

Library of Congress Subject Headings
- Fiction/General
- Fiction and reality
- Fiction/Jewish

BISAC Subject Headings
- FIC045000   FICTION/Family Life/General
- FIC046000   FICTION/Jewish

First Edition (Copyright Denise Pattiz Bogard © 2017)

Dedication

*Dedicated with love
to my children and grandchildren:*

Daniel & Karen

Tenzin Yidok&Gonpo

Jonathan & Vanessa

Gavi, Noa, Yaeli&Namkha

"The changes wrought by death are in themselves so sharp and final, and so terrible and melancholy in their consequences, that the thing stands alone in man's experience, and has no parallel upon earth. It outdoes all other accidents because it is the last of them. . . And when the business is done, there is a sore havoc made in other people's lives."

Robert Louis Stevenson, "Aes Triplex"

"Forgiveness is meaningless without tshuvah, an honest and true change for the better."

Rabbi Ben Feldman

Prologue

YEARS LATER, when the gift of time allowed her to finally step away, Terianna Meyer Berger came to realize that in many ways the line dividing before and after was not the accident, but the eventful week when all their lives could have gone one way or another.

Carly said as much at her college graduation. During a lull immediately after the commencement ceremony, she grasped Teri's hand and squeezed so hard Teri winced.

"I did the right thing, didn't I, Mom?"

Teri hesitated and for a moment it all fell away—the gowned grads, the clicking of cameras, the din of success—and Teri was once again racing up the stairs and banging on Carly's locked door pleading to be let it. Then she snapped back. Carly's face had grown tight and wan.

Teri nodded, yes, of course she'd made the right decision. There was no need on this special day to remind Carly of the narrow distinction between chance and choice. Celebration permeated the air; the country was still on a high from electing the first African American president to the White House and the New York University graduates had just been inspired by Secretary of State Hillary Clinton's keynote address. It was a day when all things seemed possible, not a time to ruminate on the what should have been.

So Teri flashed her most reassuring smile and clasped Carly close. "You absolutely made the right decision."

She owed her daughter that much.

1

TERI

ON WHAT COULD HAVE BEEN an ordinary Wednesday in November, Teri Berger awoke to the insistent honking of a car outside their bedroom window. She peeked through the blinds as the Rubins' oversized, black van pulled away from their driveway.

She hurried to Jimmy's room. His lanky, eleven-year-old body created a pencil-shaped lump under the comforter. His arm was draped over the nearby alarm clock, a snooze button gone silent.

"Jimmy, get up."

"What … huh?"

"You overslept again."

He bolted up in a tangle of bed sheet and blanket. "Uh oh. Sorry, Mom." He slid out of bed, taking care first to shove a one-eared, black and white stuffed dog under the blanket.

Teri bit back a smile acknowledging neither the stuffed animal nor the apology. Just recently, Jimmy had grown sheepish about his inability to fall asleep without "Dawg" tucked between arms that were beginning to darken with fine black wisps of hair.

"You've got three minutes to get ready," she said and stepped into the hallway where she collided with Len as he was scurrying to the kids' bathroom.

"Our shower head is loose and leaking water all over the floor," he said. "I thought you called the plumber." His hair was matted down in front and dripping in back and in his rush to switch bathrooms he'd pulled on a pair of red and yellow, smiley face boxers that were nearly as old as their marriage.

Teri couldn't hold back a snort of laughter, which elicited a scowl, and then a grudging smile from Len. He opened his arms and she rested her head against his chest for a moment.

"Hey, both the kids have plans for later tonight," he whispered against her ear. "Wanna be my little Thanksgiving turkey?"

"Mom," Carly shouted from across the hall. "Did you wash my new jeans?"

"Oh, hi, Pop," Jimmy said, hurrying past, still in his pajamas.

Teri rolled her eyes, detached herself. "Mornings," she grumbled then shouted, "Kids, you need to get going!" as she headed down the stairs in pursuit of coffee.

She was just pouring her first cup when Jimmy tumbled in wearing yesterday's clothes, toothbrush sticking out of his mouth, hands frantically zipping his backpack. "My alarm musta not gone off. Am I in trouble?"

Teri could feel her irritation melt as it often did with Jimmy. There was rarely a need to reprimand this child who was his own harshest critic. Still, she pitched her voice sterner than she felt. "You're not in trouble this time. But I can't drive you every time you miss our carpool."

He immediately offered, "What if I come straight home after school and help get ready for Thanksgiving?"

"That works. You can set the table. We're going to use our good china."

"What's in China?" Carly asked, coming into the kitchen with an emerging smirk on her face. "Hmm?" she shoved a granola bar into her mouth and another one into her coat pocket.

"Nothing," Jimmy muttered.

"Jimmy, you're still *home*?" Carly pointedly looked at her watch and then at her mother. "Did he oversleep *again*? What is that, about the eightieth time this week?"

"Carly, just worry about yourself, please," Teri said. She turned her back but not soon enough to miss the "creep" mouthed by Jimmy and the churlish dismissive laugh by Carly.

"Hey, Mom, can I take the car?" At Teri's pause, Carly added, "You don't work today. And I could take Jimmy to school for you right now."

Teri hesitated, tempted by the allure of a quiet day at home. Then she remembered. "Can't. I'm meeting Tom this morning to pick out the new countertop."

"Oh, just so it's something important. I sure would hate to have the wrong countertop."

"Actually," Teri said, keeping her voice even, "so would I. But you can have the car tonight."

Carly shrugged, "Whatever ... thanks." She headed to the door without saying goodbye, but Teri ignored the bait, reminding herself in what had become a daily mantra: *Carly won't stay seventeen forever.*

As she reached for her keys, Jimmy opened the newspaper and began reading the comics. "Jimmy! Quit dawdling. You're going to get a 'tardy.'"

"Running late again, champ?" Len asked entering the kitchen, shoes and socks in hand. He followed Teri to the door and placed a hand on her shoulder, which she shook off.

"I've got to go."

"Are you upset with me?"

Teri managed a weak smile. "Not *yet*." She was rewarded with an appreciative grin. He turned and in the next moment shouted out, "God damn it." Leaning over, he rubbed his bare foot. "Teri, you've got to tell the workmen not to leave chunks of plaster all over."

"Don't blame me," she said, closing the door a touch harder than necessary as Len muttered, "Well, who wanted the kitchen redone?"

After dropping Jimmy at school, Teri decided on a detour to the Saint Louis Bread Company. Briefly, she considered a plain bagel but chose an elephant's ear instead. There was no sense in trying to eat healthy the day before a holiday. As she bit into the crunchy caramel and flaky dough, she thought about how much she hated sending everyone into the day grumpy with one another. It didn't bode well for the four-day weekend. She glanced across the coffee shop at the pastry offerings; on the other hand, a triple-chocolate mousse pie might go a long way in restoring good humor. She could cut the leftovers and place them alongside the pumpkin and pecan pies she'd ordered for tomorrow. Which reminded her, she needed to double-check what time the turkey could be picked up from The Rotisserie.

She'd never been much of a cook, and saw it mostly as a means to an end, but this year she had a legitimate excuse to order out the entire holiday meal. Nine people for Thanksgiving dinner and her kitchen under renovation: cabinets only partially in, dishes in boxes on the floor, a gaping hole where her dishwasher was supposed to have already been installed, and the countertop cracked for removal. When they began the project in September, it was with the understanding that everything would be finished by Halloween—and for certain by Thanksgiving. Then the foreman caught pneumonia and everything ground to a halt with the promise of resuming work the following week. At least once finished it would be "fabulous," as Tom the decorator was fond of saying—usually as he hit her with another inflated invoice.

"Teri?"

She glanced up into the earnest face of Stacy Rubin.

"We were worried when Jimmy didn't come to the car today. We honked for quite a while."

Teri felt herself bristle. Although she liked Stacy's son, Alan, who was not only a neighbor but also Jimmy's best friend, the perfection of the Rubin family was nails against her chalkboard. Just once she wished Alan would oversleep, forget to say thanks, fart or burp in the middle of a meal, or not remember to move his dishes from table to sink. Three Rubin kids, each one more remarkable than the next.

"Everything is great, just a little rough in the mornings." Teri's laugh fell flat in her own ears.

"Well, you know how we adore Jimmy. And we were hoping it wasn't anything—"

Teri stood to leave. At five foot six, she towered moose-like over the five foot two, size two and well-groomed Stacy. She sucked in her stomach and forced her lips into a smile. Mothers of best friends, wives of running partners, their seventeen-year-olds in a variety of shared car pools. Interwoven lives predicated on the minutia of schedules. In a moment of weakness, Teri had even invited the Rubins to their house for Thanksgiving. It had seemed the right decision for the five beats between the asking and Stacy's acceptance. Then Teri was stuck.

"Are you sure I can't bring anything tomorrow night?"

"Just yourselves," Teri trilled. "And I warned you about the state of our kitchen, right?"

"You did. I wish you would let me cook something. Or we could still move the meal to our house."

Teri flicked her hand as if to say the effort was no big deal, certainly nothing she couldn't handle. "We'll see you at six."

Driving to meet Tom, she smiled at the prospect of throwing the pre-cooked turkey and sweet potato casserole into a warming oven in time to create the aroma of a homemade meal for their neighborhood Martha Stewart. "I don't understand why you invited them if you're going to feel this much pressure," Len had said when she told him her dinner plan. But Thanksgiving was supposed to be about crowds. With Len's parents and Teri's dad long deceased, other than her own mother, they had virtually no family. The Rubins, too, appeared to be a bit of an island.

Teri pulled into the Create-A-Kitchen lot and sat for several moments with the car running, absently staring out the windshield, trying not to miss her mom. She picked up her cell phone, tempted to call Selia and tell her enough was enough, to let bygones be bygones. After which she'd confide in her mom that she was at loose ends, bored at work, her kids needing her less, the spark with Len just barely sputtering—confide and ask advice. What next? She pressed her finger to the first three numbers, and stopped. No. Holiday or not, Teri wasn't ready to forgive her mother and she was even less ready for Selia's rebuking of *her*. Ten months without a word, ten long, lonely, peaceful months. She tossed the phone into her purse, switching her attention to countertops and wall tile.

Several hours later, she stood in the center of her kitchen, squinting as she envisioned the sage and taupe samples covering entire surfaces. It would be a relief to replace all those dark tones and dated appliances. In the years since Len's therapy practice had taken root, she'd redecorated the dining room, master bedroom, and den, and found the process immensely satisfying. It was time for the kitchen, which, as Tom said, was the heart of every home. "Finally, Mrs. Berger, your kitchen will flow with the rest of the house," to which Len had raised an eyebrow and quipped, "Please tell me he's not talking about a burst pipe."

Humming, Teri opened the refrigerator, retrieved, and browned the half-pound of ground beef. Into the pot went the sautéed onions, tomato sauce, canned beans, chili powder, and oregano. She stirred and tasted; it needed more meat. She glanced at the clock, almost four. There was time to dash up to the grocery. Or she could punt. Take a bath, and relax for what would be her last few minutes of solitude. She stirred the chili again. Nope, it was way too soupy, and there wasn't enough to have leftovers for the weekend.

Teri grabbed her keys and went out to the driveway. It was raining. She considered going back into the house for an umbrella, but rushed to the car. She drove a slightly different route, turning left at Olive Boulevard to avoid the winding neighborhood streets she customarily took. Traffic was surprisingly light given the usual last-minute grocery shoppers. Perhaps, like her, more people were faking the home-cooked meal. The thought made her chuckle as she again heard her shameful trill to Stacy Rubin.

She flipped on the radio and began switching stations, trying to find a song she liked. The gravelly voice of Bruce Springsteen spilled into the car. She pushed up the volume and hummed along. Her foot tapped the beat against the accelerator. She pressed the brake and lightly skidded, surprised by the slickness of the damp road. Ahead, Teri noticed a car pulled over to the shoulder, hood up. The rain had increased to a downpour. A young woman stood beside the car, waving, drenched. On impulse, Teri switched to the right lane, intending to offer help, just as her purse began to ring. With her free hand, she dug past the wallet, checkbook, hairbrush, candy wrappers, searching to the bottom for her cell phone.

"Honey?" It was Len.

She cradled the phone against her neck and reached to turn down the radio. The stranded woman glanced her way as Teri veered closer. They locked eyes and for one suspended moment, Teri sensed something familiar in her face.

"Teri, you there?" Len asked, as a bolt of lightning ripped apart the sky and a cloudburst erupted. "Teri?"

2

ELISE

"WHAT THE HELL IS THIS?"

How to respond? Offense or defense, denial or remorse? She looked more closely at her mom and burst into laughter. She didn't mean to laugh, knew it would piss Rozlynn off even more. It was just the incongruity of the image: her mom dressed in her "I'm only a boring secretary" outfit—cardigan sweater, pencil skirt, one-inch pumps—and holding out a bagful of cocaine.

"Elise, what the hell is this?" Rozlynn repeated, her voice rising higher, just shy of her worst screech level.

"Why? You want some?"

In response, Rozlynn sank onto a kitchen chair and placed the baggie on the tabletop. It was so tempting to reach across and grab it, but Elise was hoping to avoid a showdown. This bag was all she had left; she'd need to stay cool until she could get it back.

"I thought you were through with all this nonsense." Rozlynn's voice choked on the last word and Elise felt an unexpected lump in her own throat. What neither of her parents recognized was that she didn't actually want to hurt them. She just wanted to be able to do her own thing and have them leave her alone.

She sat in the chair next to her mom and bowed her head. "Sorry," she whispered, not sure if Rozlynn heard and not sure if it mattered.

"What are we going to do, Elise?"

We?

"You've worn me out. I don't know what I did to deserve this."

There was no answer she could give that would make a difference. They'd been through this scene, had this same conversation, so many times before it might as well have been role-playing.

"When did it start up again? And please don't lie to me. You promised … " Rozlynn was now slumped fully against the chair, which made her look about ten years older than usual. For the first time, Elise realized her parents were starting to get almost old. Her mind recoiled at the thought of losing them—of being alone. She sat up straighter as if to overpower her mom and with as much nonchalance as she could muster, she shrugged, smirked, shrugged again. "Mom, why must you make such a big deal out of everything?"

Sure enough, the button was pushed. Rozlynn leaped up and leaned in close to Elise, undisguised disgust twisting her whole face. "You know what, you little brat? You want to snort away your life? Go ahead. I am done trying to help. In fact, I'm done, period."

"Are you serious? Every college kid I know does a little blow once in a while."

"*Every* college kid is *not* my daughter. And every college kid has not been abusing drugs for years."

Again, Elise laughed, not on purpose, it just escaped out of her mouth. Her mom was so friggin' straight, every strand of hair in place, her makeup caking her face too beige.

"You think this is funny? You sicken me." Rozlynn paused for a long silence that Elise refused to fill. Then in a low, flat voice said, "I don't know if I even love you anymore."

Whoa! She'd never said that before. Elise gripped the arms of the chair, squeezing so tight she could feel a sliver of wood splinter her index finger. "Fuck you!" she yelped as she and her mom lunged for the baggie at the exact same moment.

Rozlynn was quicker. She grasped the bag, stood, and in slow motion turned it upside down and scattered the contents across the table, the chair, and the floor, a snowstorm of talc-like mind-numbing powder.

Elise watched for a long moment, unable to react, her head screaming, *what the fuck*. She gripped her mom by the shoulders, and began to shake her, back and forth. Rozlynn's eyes rolled up and her mouth drooped open. Then she was fighting back, shoving Elise, kicking her in the shins, punching her in the stomach. Elise's cell phone clanked to the floor and as Rozlynn bent to grab it, Elise shoved with her full weight and her mother stumbled back, falling to the floor.

There was complete silence in the room. Rozlynn sprawled across the tile, her dark skirt dotted with flecks of white powder. Elise loomed over her mom, hands fisted. Suddenly, Rozlynn's eyes grew wet and tears started to trickle down her cheeks.

"Mom, I'm so sor—"

"Get out! Get the hell out of my house. I never want to see you again."

Elise reeled back, as Rozlynn repeated, "Get the hell out of my house."

Casting her eyes away from her mother, Elise took two steps to the table, licked her finger, and rubbed it against the white surface. The moment the tingling hit her lips and gums, she felt the fury begin to float away. With a calm which could only be bought and tasted, she turned to Rozlynn, "You're going to be sorry you ever said that."

"You little bitch," Rozlynn sneered, continuing to lay on the floor as Elise grabbed the car keys off the hook and stomped out, slamming the door so hard Elise could almost imagine it splintering into tiny pieces.

She waited until she was out of the driveway to burn rubber, suddenly raging with all the things she meant to say, everything she'd wanted to say her entire life. *Just once, Mom, just one goddamned time, can't you accept me for who I am? Why must you always make me feel like a loser? And what the fuck were you doing looking through my things? That coke was hidden in my drawers where you do not belong. I don't go through your crap.*

It had started to rain and as Elise turned on the wipers, she slowed down and began to think. She had about two hundred dollars saved in her account and about forty dollars in her wallet. Maybe she could drive back to Mizzou, sneak into the dorms, and lay low during the Thanksgiving holiday. That would give her time to plan what to do next.

I don't know if I even love you anymore. Jesus, that was about the world's worst thing a mother could say to her daughter. Impatiently, she swiped the back of her hand across her face, wiping away stupid ass tears. "Well, guess what, Rozlynn Horowitz, I'm not sure

I love you anymore either." The words seemed to echo in the car, meaningless with no hurting ears to hear them. "Fuck you!" she shouted, pounding the steering wheel.

The all-time irony was that she had come home excited to share good news for once. Two days before, she'd interviewed with the Stray Rescue of St. Louis for a paid summer internship. They told her they were considering several others and would get back to her in a couple of weeks. Instead, they'd called this morning saying she was their most outstanding candidate and the job was hers if she wanted it. They'd even suggested she work for a couple weeks during winter break.

Traffic was light, but the rain was picking up and the wipers squeaked without wiping. She sat closer to the windshield trying to see past the slants of rain and flipped on the radio. Bruce Springsteen was wailing in his deadbeat voice as if anyone would want to listen. Was that old geezer still around? She switched off the radio and that's when the car jerked, lurched, and went dead. The gas tank was on empty. "Are you shitting me?" Quickly steering to the right, she coasted onto the shoulder of Olive Boulevard, and barely missed getting side-swiped by the car next to her.

She reached into her back pocket and then remembered, her mother had her phone. There was no other choice; she got out of the car, opened the hood, and stepped to the front, waving for help. As she stood there getting more and more drenched, she imagined going home, telling Roz she'd go back into rehab, begging her mom for help or at least a hug. *I don't know if I even love you anymore.* No! There was no way Rozlynn meant to say that.

Suddenly a car crossed the lane, veering closer. The driver locked eyes with Elise and for one suspended moment Elise sensed something familiar in her face as a bolt of lightning ripped apart the sky and a cloudburst erupted.

3

TERI

THE SERVICE WAS GRAVESIDE. Teri's heels sunk into the damp, partially frozen earth, binding her to the spot. A bitter wind had caused the temperature to drop. She was dressed in the only black, non-cocktail-party dress she owned, thin cotton, and she could not stop her body's shivering. She felt Len's arm around her but shrugged him off.

They were standing directly behind the seated rows reserved for family. There was a large crowd, more, Teri suspected, because of the age of the deceased than the number of friends of the family.

El maleh rachamim, shochayn bam'romim, ham-tzay m'nucha n'chonah al kanfay Hash'china, b'ma-alot k'doshim ut-horim k'zo-har haraki-a mazhirim…

Teri heard the words as wind in a tunnel. The *El Maleh Rachamim*, a remembrance prayer for the soul of the departed, recited at a Jewish funeral before the casket is lowered.

The rabbi cut an imposing figure, tall, broad shouldered, and overweight. He spoke with a deep sonorous voice that appeared to be genuine in its grief. "It is a Jewish tradition to bury our own dead, and so I now invite you to place three shovelfuls of dirt onto the casket. There are many interpretations, but the one I prefer considers this the last act of caretaking you can do for the deceased." He paused, pulled on his silvery gray beard, and in a softer voice continued. "As a parent covers a sleeping child with a blanket, so you now cover your beloved. I ask that first the parents and family members come forward; afterward, anyone who wishes to participate may do so."

The mother and father walked to the casket together, his hand on her elbow. Her expression was dulled in the flattening effect of someone drugged; her movements as she reached for the shovel were jerky and stiff. The clumps of damp earth resonated as they fell six feet, thudding onto the plain pine box. The father's face was streaked with tears, and after his first shovelful he collapsed to his knees, picked up a handful of dirt and wailed, his voice only slightly louder than the wind, "No. No. No."

Teri stood frozen in place as mourners shoveled dirt onto the casket until it was nearly covered. Again, Len tried to draw her close and again she shook him off. Comfort was the last thing she wanted—or deserved.

Yit-ga-dal ve-yit-ka-dash she-mei ra-ba …

And now the Mourner's Kaddish, the Hebrew prayer recited moments after the casket is lowered into the ground and covered. It was actually a prayer of hope, about life, never mentioning the word death. But to anyone Jewish it was the familiar refrain of sorrow.

. . . b-a-ga-la u-vi-ze-man ka-riv, ve-i-me-ru: a-mein.

Teri turned away and shouldered through the crowd. She heard murmured whispers, but hurried, head bent, beyond the throng of bodies. She waited in the car for Len as the mourners slowly filed past, averting their eyes when they saw her. A blast of cold air hit Teri when Len slid into the driver's seat.

He turned to her. "Let's go home."

"We have to go to the *shiva*."

Len's mouth tightened into a thin line, but he didn't argue. He stopped along the way to fill the gas tank, so by the time they got to the *shiva* house, they had to circle the street and park two blocks away.

Teri squeezed back when Len took hold of her hand, but she held herself upright so no other part of her body touched his. She knew if she let herself feel anything at all, she would lose the control she needed to get through this day.

"We don't have to do this, you know," Len said at the front door.

Yes I do, she might have answered, but instead, leaned down and poured water from a pitcher onto her hands and into the large bowl set on a porch table, the washing away of death's spirits before entering a Jewish house of mourning. She opened the door—one never knocked at a shiva house—noted the dining room table filled with platters of food, the flickering, blue, memorial candle on the mantle, the hall mirror covered by a sheet, the small stools reserved for immediate family. She noted with surprise the traditional observances seldom seen anymore and surmised the family was clinging to the ages-old rituals in the face of this shocking death.

"I can't." She shoved past Len, stumbled down the porch steps, and raced away from the house.

"Teri, wait," she heard Len from behind, but she kept going until, panting, she collapsed against the hood of their car. "Oh, Lenny, what am I going to do?"

He gathered her close to his chest and for several moments she allowed herself to go still, to be enveloped in the warmth of his arms, until her knees buckled and she slid to the frozen ground, pulling him down with her.

❦

IN THE DIM LIGHT, Teri glanced over at the liquor cabinet then studiously looked away. Having woken again yesterday to a cottony tongue and parched throat, Teri had promised herself no matter how long the sleepless night, no matter how much her mind was racing and her heart pounding, she would not succumb to the numbing escape of a two a.m. drink.

Len kept telling her it was an *accident*, not her fault, could have happened to anyone, she should not be feeling such paralyzing guilt… as though any of that was remotely relevant. As if the word, *accident*, could have the power to change the outcome. Didn't he realize his labeling of the event only exacerbated her torment as she lay awake nightly, replaying over and over the trivialities of that day. Was it really only a week ago? Didn't he understand how even the tiniest decision here or there could have, *should have*, altered everything?

If only. . .

In tonight's episode, she still doesn't let Carly take the car to school. She still runs out of burger and decides to go to the store for more. She doesn't go back in for an umbrella or drive her usual route. It's pouring rain, so she still skids as she tries to pull over. But, as *should* have been the case, she manages to stop several inches shy of the stalled car. She gets out, trembling at the near miss. The stranded woman borrows the cell phone, calls for a tow truck and Teri drives on to buy the hamburger meat. That night over chili dinner she mentions she almost had an accident. Carly and Jimmy are bickering over the last piece of cheese garlic bread and don't seem to hear her. Len casually says, "Oh, you're kidding," and goes on to talk about his late "emergency" appointment who never showed up and the interesting new client he saw earlier in the day, an intensely driven woman with aspirations for a six-figure salary and two-figure weight. Teri is briefly annoyed at her family's indifference but she rationalizes it's not as if anything did happen. She feels again a moment of relief and the incident is forgotten.

Or...she decides to go to the store, but she does go back into the house for an umbrella, which is upstairs in Carly's bedroom and takes several minutes to find. Subsequently, when Len calls, he catches her at home. She is annoyed to find out he has an unexpected late appointment and he will be working late. So his playful *wanna be my little Thanksgiving turkey* was a seductive hoax. As she drives a different route than usual, she broods about the lack of romance in their day to day and wonders if there isn't more to a decades-old marriage than just being at ease with one another in a predictable routine. She chides herself; she's just in a funk at the prospect of the holidays without her mother. She passes the Olive and Highway 270 intersection and scarcely notices an abandoned car, the driver having gotten help from someone else minutes before.

Or...Teri, who *never* stops for strangers, drives past. Or she takes her usual route and never even sees a stalled car. Or she serves soupy chili. Or...or...or...

"Stop!" She jolted upright. "Just stop," she screamed. Then softly, "Stop." She listened in the dim silence to her quick breaths. The liquor cabinet beckoned. Willfully, Teri sank deeper into the couch, pulling her knees to her chest. She rubbed her wrists, recalling the cutting heaviness of the handcuffs.

The young police officer ... My God! He was barely older than Carly. He had looked at her with apology. A first death for him, he'd confided. Yeah, for her too, though she couldn't remember if she actually said the words or if they had just reverberated in her head as the police radioed in for her records, analyzed her breath, questioned her and questioned her, and finally unlocked the cuffs and told her they would decide whether to arrest pending investigation.

Across the room the *St. Louis Post Dispatch* lay face up, daring Teri to reread the three paragraphs she'd worn thin from rubbing her thumb across its newsprint so many times. There was no reason to read what she'd already memorized, yet she rose, stepped past the recliner, opened the week-old paper to the obit page and sank back onto the couch.

ELISE HOROWITZ, November 26, 2003, age 20. Beloved daughter of George and Rozlynn Horowitz, loving granddaughter of the late David and Thelma Horowitz and the late Norman and June Goldberg.

Miss Horowitz was enrolled as a sophomore at the University of Missouri-Columbia, studying to become a veterinarian assistant. During school breaks, she volunteered at the Stray Rescue of St. Louis.

Funeral services to be held Sunday, November 30, at Temple B'nai El with graveside services to follow. Shiva will be observed at the home of George and Rozlynn Horowitz. Memorial contributions preferred to the Stray Rescue of St. Louis.

If only ... Maybe Len doesn't call at that exact minute. Or he calls and she doesn't answer because she knows ... yes, she knows the pavement is slick and she has a hard time talking on the cell phone and concentrating on the road. And because she's driving in the rain, she's purposefully not playing with the radio. She's not changing lanes with half-attention. In this episode, there's not even a near-miss as she pulls onto the shoulder ahead of the stalled car and offers the young woman, Elise Horowitz, a ride to safety. In this episode, she really isn't at fault.

She chewed at a fingernail already gnawed to the quick and wished she could cry. But tears belonged to the innocent. Forcing her hands from her mouth, she rubbed her wrists again and began to count backward from fifty. When she reached thirty, she pounded a fist against the cushion. "Screw it." Her frustration echoed in the empty room as she bolted up and headed directly to the liquor cabinet.

4

TERI

"TERI WILL YOU PLEASE STOP PACING? You're making me crazy."

She stared across the conference table at Len, stood frozen for several pointed moments then resumed. She didn't want to pace. She didn't want to piss off her husband, but she just couldn't stop her body from shaking. What he didn't understand was that even when sitting, she was still pacing, as if a train was racing through her brain and to every part of her body.

"Five more troops died in Iraq this morning," she said.

When Len didn't respond she shook her head back and forth. "I don't know why this doesn't make you want to scream. More than two thousand wasted deaths, not counting the injured, or all those Iraqis, which no one considers. And don't even get me started on Afghanistan." Her voice had risen to a fevered pitch, loud enough for the receptionist on the other side of the glass wall to glance their way then quickly avert her eyes.

"I don't like these wars any more than you do, Teri. But I don't think you should be keeping count of the dead at this point."

Her mouth gaped open. "Are you actually telling me what I should and shouldn't *keep count of*?" She knew him well enough to recognize he was weighing a number of responses and she waited, curious to see who would reply: the implacable, ever-reasonable Dr. Berger, the exasperated husband, or the sensitive partner who was continuing to give her free reign to act out her grief and confusion.

When he did speak, his voice was unnaturally calm, his words surprisingly belonging to none of the above.

"Do not confuse me with your mother."

Selia. As always her presence electrified the tension in the air, even when a thousand miles away. Teri was still struggling to come up with a retort when the door opened and a middle-aged man practically fell into the room.

"Rex Martin. I hope you haven't been waiting long," he panted, sticking out his hand but withdrawing it and settling into a chair before either she or Len could react.

Teri tried to hide her alarm. His name had been mentioned by several sources as "the best," a name that conjured an image of a three-piece, pinstriped suit, heavily starched dress shirt, and innocuous tie. That described the person who was supposed to restore her life, not this disheveled man who slumped before her in a wrinkled, blue shirt and bright orange tie that hung loosely around his neck like an unformed afterthought to professionalism. Beads of perspiration dotted his forehead and half-moon sweat stains purpled his shirt when he raised his arms to push back hair weeks in need of a haircut.

Teri felt a tremor of fear. She walked around to the other side of the table and moved a chair close enough to Len so her upper arm brushed his when she sat, and she could easily grasp his hand.

Without preamble Rex Martin launched into legalese, presenting so many nuanced scenarios Teri ceased to be able to absorb anything beyond the repeated references to the twenty-year-old victim, Elise Horowitz.

"Tell me again, you actually *knew* her?" Rex asked.

When she didn't answer, Len said, "We didn't exactly know her. She went to the same school as our daughter but was three years older. Right, Ter?"

She stared straight ahead, picturing Elise outside the high school, standing on the top step alone, shoulders hunched, as Teri honked for Carly who was surrounded by a group of laughing friends.

"Mrs. Berger?"

She startled back to the moment.

"The citation?" Rex said.

"Oh, sorry." With a hand that wouldn't stop trembling, she retrieved from her purse a mustard yellow sheet of paper and flattened it against the table. At the top, in large capital letters was the word CITATION. Immediately under the heading was CRIMINAL INVESTIGATION and two lines down her full name, TERIANNA MEYER BERGER.

Rex perused the paper and dipped his chin in satisfaction. Yes, he said, it was clearly an accident according to the police report. The question now would be was Teri guilty of criminal negligence or simple negligence? Was talking on the phone, switching lanes too fast, and not showing prudent judgment during a rainstorm merely an absence of ordinary, reasonable care or was it gross negligence? Would she be prosecuted for involuntary manslaughter? Or would the police and courts decide that, but for the circumstances, the accident would not have happened? In which case the criminal charge would be dropped.

"We should know within a couple of months." Rex's voice became gentle as his brow knitted in a pained expression. "Unfortunately, there will probably be an article in the newspaper no matter what's decided. But I'll call you first as soon as we hear anything."

Next there was the issue of the civil law wrongful death suit. He would refer that case to another attorney in his office, who handled such matters. But he was confident a settlement between the Bergers' insurance company and the "surviving party of the deceased" could be reached. It was a matter of determining the "value of the life" of the girl, which would be considered less since she was still a dependent and not yet earning an income. So long as her "value" didn't exceed the half-million dollar maximum coverage of the Berger policy, a settlement should be forthcoming.

"We'll for sure pay. More if you think we should." Teri ignored Len's shaking head and Rex's upraised hand as she bolted from her chair and began pacing. "We could sell our house, sell our stocks. Even that's not enough, though, is it? Should I just plead guilty up front? We all know I *killed* her."

"Mrs. Berger. Please! I appreciate what you're saying. But let our firm handle this." Rex exchanged a glance with Len she couldn't read. Did they think her hysterical? Noble? As if either of them could begin to understand. She glared at Len until he turned away, then she flopped into the nearest chair and put her head in her hands, struggling to catch her breath.

An awkward silence stretched for long moments until Rex cleared his throat, rose, and pushed his chair away from the table. "Any other questions?"

"You're pretty confident, though, right, Mr. Martin?" Len asked.

"Dr. and Mrs. Berger, I am reasonably certain the chances of Mrs. Berger being charged with criminal negligence are minimal." He stuck out his hand and this time waited for Teri to grasp the sticky, clammy palm before pulling his arm away to tuck the tail of his shirt into his pants.

Teri couldn't resist, "Well, okay. I mean, orange is so not my color."

The look Len shot her was withering, but Rex gave a surprised laugh. "My advice? Resume your life, and try not to blame yourself. This wasn't murder; it was, at worst, a brief lapse in judgment resulting in a tragic consequence. In simplest terms, this was a car accident."

IN THEIR CAR, Len immediately said, "All things considered that went rather well, don't you think?"

"Yeah, if you're not Elise Horowitz."

"Teri …"

She watched out the car window at the passing blur of office buildings. She rarely ventured downtown and was continually surprised by the St. Louis cityscape. The buildings were impressive from the outside, and well-kept despite their growing vacancy rates. The Gateway Arch gleamed against the skyline, magnificent in its engineering and structural genius.

"You know, not one person died by accident during the entire building process. But the two ends almost didn't align at the top."

"What are you talking about?" Len asked.

"Nothing," she sighed, lapsing into silence as Len pulled onto Highway 40 and began the fifteen mile drive back to their home in a suburban west county.

Len placed his hand on hers. "Sweetie, you really shouldn't have offered our house and stocks."

Feeling as peevish as she'd acted, Teri jerked her arm out of his range. "You don't remember, do you?"

"What?" His voice was carefully modulated, as if holding his breath before a bombshell.

"Nothing," she said. "It doesn't matter. Just take me home." She pushed her seat to recline, and closed her eyes. At one point, she glanced over at Len through slitted eyes and was startled to see a slow trickle of tears slipping down his face. How she wished she could fold herself against him, comfort them both—as she remained frozen in place.

When he pulled into their driveway, he turned to her and in a voice so quiet she had to lean closer to hear, he asked, "Teri, why are you angry with *me*?"

It blurted out of her. "Why did you call me at that moment?"

He reeled back as if slapped and she nearly relented, nearly asked him to cancel his afternoon clients and spend the time fixing her problems instead of those belonging to paying strangers. Instead, she deliberately opened the car door and stepped out.

"Oh, Lenny, I am so sorry. Can you forgive me?" she mouthed into the vacuum left by his disappearing red taillights, then thrust out her arms and shouted out to the sky, "I ... don't ... deserve ... forgiveness."

5

JIMMY

"JIMMY, BETTER HURRY. It's five til." His mother's voice carried upstairs from the kitchen, sounding impatient and tired.

He touched his p.j. bottoms. Damp. Hurrying out of bed, he pulled the blanket all the way up past the pillows and tucked everything in so no one could tell. He threw on the same outfit he'd worn yesterday and closed his door. His mom barely glanced up when he slid into the kitchen. There was just enough time to pack a lunch and grab some cereal. He reached into a box on the floor for a bowl.

"Is your shirt clean?" she asked.

"Uh, kinda, I guess." A mouthful of Cheerios flew onto the table, one soggy circle landing squarely on his mom's arm. Jimmy waited for her to brush it aside or fuss at him for talking with food in his mouth. Nothing. Her eyes were red and puffy like she'd been up all night crying.

Outside, Mrs. Rubin honked. Jimmy leaned over and kissed his mom's cheek. She smelled bad, like his gym clothes. "I love you, Mom," he whispered and left without turning to see if she noticed.

He hopped up into the van, scooting across Alan's outstretched legs and around the booster seat where four-year-old Becky sat.

"Seat belt on?" Mrs. Rubin glanced at him from the rear view mirror. Her eyes were clear and sharp, her smile huge. Jimmy nodded and slouched against the bench seat. Alan had the coolest mom in the world. She listened to pop radio every morning and knew more lyrics than he did. She watched *Power Rangers Ninja Storm* with them, and was sworn to secrecy not to tell their other friends that they still liked cartoons. She went to all the soccer games, baked cookies from scratch, drove every car pool, and hung around in case any kids wanted to go somewhere afterwards. He knew his mom didn't like Mrs. Rubin and he couldn't figure out why.

Absently, he scratched a scab on his arm and felt something sticky, a drop of blood on his fingertip. He looked around for a tissue and not seeing one opened his backpack for a napkin. Aw, man, he'd forgotten to put his lunch in his pack. Probably left it by the box of dishes. He wondered if his mom was ever going to let those workmen return to put in the kitchen cabinets, but he was afraid if he asked she'd just start crying.

"You playing in the soccer tourney this weekend, honey?" At his nod, Mrs. Rubin continued, "Want a ride? Mr. Rubin or I can drive both ways. Tell your parents not to worry about it."

"My mom can drive. It's probably her turn."

The silence was immediate. Jimmy caught the glance between Mrs. Rubin and Alan. Suddenly, he realized his mom hadn't driven his friends anywhere since the accident—not even once. They didn't trust her to drive.

He stared at the back of Mrs. Rubin's head. Unlike his mom, whose hair was reddish-brown, shoulder length, and curly, Mrs. Rubin's hair was pitch black, almost as short as a man's, and never messy, even in the morning. For that second he wanted to grab one of those perfect layers and pull until she screamed, until she knew how bad it felt to hurt. Then she winked and gave a look so sweet and loving, he blinked a bunch of times so she couldn't tell what he'd been thinking. "Sure," he said. "That'd be great."

"Hey, Cheese Berger, you wanna play some ball after school?" Alan asked.

Jimmy looked at the inch of yesterday's snow on the ground. "Yeah, whatever."

"But at my house, ok?" Alan asked so quickly Jimmy couldn't suggest otherwise.

❧

The day turned even worse. Twice he got yelled at for not paying attention in class. In current events, they talked about the death penalty and all Jimmy could think about was his mom in an ugly orange uniform walking up to a chair where they would plug her into a wall and turn her into toast. He almost wet his pants, but luckily the bell for recess rang just in time. He ran into the bathroom and shut the stall door, trying not to cry. He heard the bathroom door open and some kids come in.

"You moron. I can't believe you brought in that article about prisoners. How do you think it made Berger feel?"

Alan was defending him! But his supposed best friend went on, "You know she's probably gonna go to prison."

"You kidding? I thought it wasn't her fault. That's what my mom heard."

Alan's voice answered, "Well, it may not have been her fault but she killed someone. My dad's a lawyer and he says she'll go free except I bet she won't. I mean the girl she hit died."

He flung open the stall door.

"Cheese!" Alan jumped back, his face all red, like he'd been caught cheating. "I, uh …"

Jimmy stomped as hard as he could on Alan's foot as he walked past, just barely keeping himself from shoving Alan against the wall or sink, but only because he didn't want to be sent to the principal.

He ignored his new worst enemy the rest of the day, making sure Alan knew they would not be playing ball together after school, or ever again for the rest of their lives. And he refused his usual ride home with the Rubins. He had thought Alan understood, but maybe nobody outside his family could know what it was like. Maybe he just wouldn't have any other friends ever again. Sitting alone on the bus, Jimmy heard a couple of the guys whispering, probably about him, but he couldn't tell for sure.

He entered from the back porch, hoping to sneak into the house and tip-toe unnoticed up the stairs—no luck. His mom sat in the kitchen in the same chair as this morning, still wearing her pajamas and slippers.

"Jimmy, you home already?" She picked up a spoon and absently stirred inside an oversized mug.

"I thought you don't drink coffee in the afternoon. You said it keeps you up."

"Well, seems I'm awake all night no matter what I do. So I may as well try to wake myself up in the afternoon." She smiled her new fake smile, the one where her face twisted like she was in pain. Her hands shook as she raised the cup to her lips. "It's cold in here, don't you think?"

"Uh, no. Not if you're *dressed*." He didn't even try to hide how mad he felt. It was four in the afternoon. Mrs. Rubin had probably been to a gazillion places by now.

The ring of the phone seemed to startle them both. His mom slumped into her chair as if to hide in case someone was calling to give them more bad news.

"You going to get it?" he asked.

"I don't think so. I don't really feel like talking to anyone right now. You?"

He shook his head so hard it seemed to rattle. "It's probably just Alan—wanting to play ball. Like who would want to play with that loser anyway?" As he walked out of the kitchen he heard his mom say, "What's wrong, Jimmy?" He ignored her the way she always ignored him.

Upstairs, he plopped onto his bed then immediately sat up to avoid the gross smell of dried piss on his sheets. He opened his backpack and pulled out his binder. Inside was the note from Katie, the red-haired girl who sat in front of him. She had folded the paper into a triangle and tossed it over her shoulder when the teacher wasn't looking. "Open it at home," she'd whispered just as the teacher turned back around.

Dear Cheese,

Wuzup? Amanda says I like u, but really it's Amanda who wants to go out with u. Let me know if you wanna go out with her.

UR2Qt2B#2UR#1.

Yur friend, K.

He brought the crinkled paper to his nose and sniffed. It smelled flowery—girly, like Carly's shampoo. He hugged the note close. Amanda liked him! Amanda, only the prettiest girl in the entire fifth grade. She liked *him*!

He got up, locked the door, pulled a pile of sweaters down from the top closet shelf and reached to the back for the old tackle box his dad had thrown out last summer. Jimmy had saved it from the trash, washed out the blood and cruddy fish hooks, and now hid all his secret treasures inside. Only Alan knew about the box. That way, if Jimmy ever died, like in a car accident, Alan could destroy everything. Now, he'd have to tell someone else since he planned on never talking to Alan again.

He unlatched the rusting hook and put Katie's note under the letter he'd written to his Grandma Selia, but had never mailed. He probably could have mailed it, except he'd have to ask for her address and his mom and dad would get that awful scrunched up expression they always got if his grandma's name was mentioned. So he just kept rereading the letter and hiding it in the box next to the condom package he'd found in Carly's underwear drawer.

Dear Grandma Selia,

I wish I could talk to you. I don't know why you don't ever call or visit anymore. No one will tell me. But I bet if you knew what was going on here—"

"Jimmmeeee, where's my brush? Did you take it?" Carly was clomping up the stairs. She must be wearing those stupid, thick-soled Doc Martins she thought made her look cool but only made her sound like an elephant.

He shoved the letter into the box and snapped it shut as his sister banged on his door.

"Hey, open up, weirdo. Mom! Jimmy locked his door again!"

He pushed back the box until it clunked against the wall, threw the sweaters on top and rushed to the door then turned around, got the box down and pulled out the condom.

"Mom, tell Jimmy to open the door."

No response from their mom, who was obviously ignoring Carly.

He opened the door and held up the condom. "Want to tattle about this too?"

"You little shit. Where'd you get that? I'll tell Mom on you."

He laughed. "Yeah, right. As though you don't know where it came from." He shoved the condom into his front jeans pocket.

She leaned close to his face and hissed against his nose. He could actually feel the air her anger blew out. "If anyone finds out about this, you'll wish you were never born."

She slammed his door shut. He jumped back, barely saving his face. "And you better not have taken my hairbrush," she shouted as she stomped down the hall.

He pulled the condom packet out of his pocket. It felt weird, like a hard ring with something gushy in the middle. Last year, before they'd even had a sex-ed class, Mrs. Rubin had showed them how to unroll a condom on a banana. He'd almost puked and the idea of Carly and Jason using it was even worse.

Jimmy sank down onto his bed and took out his assignment book. He started thinking about the fight with Alan and the girl his mom killed, and stared at the page so long it blurred. Carly said he should remember Elise, but even when he squeezed his eyes shut he couldn't picture her face. The image that popped up instead was of a girl smushed between two cars. Jimmy sucked his chest in, trying to make his body go pancake flat. He rolled over onto his stomach. He needed to go put his sheets in the washing machine since his mom probably wouldn't do that. Or, maybe he'd just lie here a while and think about Amanda. Yeah, that's what he'd do. Too bad Alan would never know the biggest news of the century.

6

TERI

TERI GLANCED AT THE CLOCK and sighed; another day had passed. The kids would soon be home from school. Time to get dressed. She slid out of bed and shuffled across the room to the closet. Her eyes glazed over as she tried to assemble an outfit, which would make it look as though she'd gone to work. For the past three Mondays and Thursdays she'd awoken determined to resume her two-day-a-week job, and for the past three Mondays and Thursdays she'd called the nursing home asking for one more week's leave of absence. It wasn't as if anyone's health or safety depended on Teri showing up at Delmar Gardens with a stack of carefully selected library books. But the residents looked forward to the distraction of her visits and the promise of traveling beyond their wheelchairs into the worlds of wonderful fiction. She knew she was letting them down.

The one time Teri had gone in after the accident, no one had seemed critical or even particularly impressed. "By our age, we've all had some sort of disaster. You just keep going," ninety-two-year-old Esther Fishgolde had said as a silent chorus of nods traveled the room. "Now, tell me, honey, did you bring me the new Jacquelyn Mitchard novel like you promised?"

But driving home that day on hyper-alert, her eyes darting in every direction for a potential catastrophe—one of the few times she'd forced herself to go out at all—she had felt challenged beyond her limited reserve. This morning when the assistant director called, she had promised to come in, just as she'd assured Len she would.

Then she laid back down for a short power nap and woke up three hours later.

She pulled a pair of black wool pants off a hanger; they felt scratchy in her hand. She dropped the pants to the floor. What was the point in pretending? She reached into the hamper to retrieve a pair of loose gray sweats and hooded sweatshirt, shook out the dust and sniffed. Not too bad.

Walking toward the stairs, she caught an overpowering whiff of urine. She opened Jimmy's door and nearly gagged. "Oh, sweetie," she moaned. Closing her mouth and pinching her nose, she stripped the bed, clutching the damp sheets, blanket, and stuffed dog to her chest. She took several shallow breaths and hurried down two flights of stairs to the basement laundry area. Inside the washer, a mass of forgotten towels was flattened against the sides of the machine. She shoved the towels into the dryer, the bedding and Dawg into the washer, and made it back to the kitchen just as Jimmy came in. He immediately averted his face but not quickly enough.

"Honey, are you crying? What's going on?"

"Nothing," he mumbled.

"Jimmy—"

He grabbed a bag of potato chips from the pantry and scurried out. Her eyes followed his backside as he climbed the stairs to his room. A good mother would yank him back and demand to know what sorrows caused a fifth-grade boy to cry in the middle of the afternoon. She wanted to believe that a month ago she would have been that mother. But now?

Without looking at her watch, she knew it was four o'clock. The exact time, twenty-nine days ago, when she made that decision to go out for more hamburger. The Botched Berger Burger, she'd quipped to Len. He'd tried to laugh, she had to give him that, but Len never could abide false humor. Occupational hazard, he said.

The kitchen had grown darker as a blanket of light gray clouds moved across the sky. Just what she needed—a white Christmas to rile up the weathermen. Lately, she'd begun binge watching local television news, fascinated by the way the anchormen covered accidents and tragedies. No matter how objective they claimed to be, overtones of blame and guilt always seeped through.

"Uh, Mom?" Jimmy stood in the far corner of the room as if to hide in plain sight.

She stretched her lips into what she hoped was a smile. "Come in, sweetie."

Streaks of dirt covered his face where he'd wiped away his tears. Teri peered closer then drew back in alarm. "Jimmy, is that blood?"

"It's what I have to talk to you about." He withdrew from his jeans pocket a folded piece of paper. "I need you to sign this."

A myriad of responses went through Teri's head as she read the principal's report, from concern to anger to exasperation. "You better tell me what happened."

As Jimmy talked, haltingly and with sparse details, Teri looked around the kitchen at the unhinged cabinets, the partially peeled wallpaper, the hole between the sink and the counter where the new dishwasher was supposed to go. Tom the decorator had grown so frustrated with her unreturned calls he had canceled the workmen. Yesterday his invoice arrived in the mail, with a terse note that he expected full payment whether the Bergers finished the project or not.

"So, am I in trouble?"

Teri sighed. "Tell me once more, what happened?"

A worried expression creased his brow and Teri vowed to listen closely. Her absentmindedness scared her children, but she couldn't seem to focus on anything anymore. Stop! She was still doing it.

"… and so when Alan said it *again*, I got really mad and shoved him, and he punched me in the face, and my nose started bleeding."

"But, Jimmy, what did Alan say?"

"Mom! I've told you a hundred times. Forget it. Can you just sign the paper? Or they won't let me back in class."

For a few moments, Teri resisted. Through the fog, she sensed something important had occurred. But, really, how important could it be? Jimmy was alive, wasn't he? She scribbled her signature across the line.

"Oh, and my teacher said don't forget about the party tomorrow."

She waited until he went upstairs before she allowed her head to sink onto the table. She didn't deserve such a sweet sensitive boy. He'd always been so good. And Carly too. Yep, Teri was lucky. So goddamned fucking lucky, in fact, she'd walked away from the accident with barely a scratch. Except in her sleep. There her face gushed with blood, sometimes from windshield shards, sometimes from the brutal fists of fellow inmates. She'd awaken from those dreams stunned, covered in sweat, the horror of possibility flattening her to the sheets.

Just once, she'd confessed to Len that she was having recurring nightmares. In each she was imprisoned and shackled by chains too heavy to lift her feet.

"It was an *accident*, Teri," he'd repeated *ad nauseam*.

"But, Len, what if ... ?"

"You heard Rex. It's all going to be okay." He'd pulled her close, hugging her too long, waiting, she knew, to see if she'd respond. She had stood there, arms drooping against her sides, unable to hug him back. Teri was just superstitious enough she dared not admit aloud her two deepest fears: That she would be found guilty. Or that she would not.

⁓

THE CUPCAKES WERE DIVIDED into two groups, one group with blue and white swirled frosting, apparently to represent the colors of Chanukah, the other with green and red for Christmas.

"You like the cupcakes?" Stacy Rubin asked. When Teri didn't answer, she added, "I thought it would be nice for the kids to pick their own holiday colors." Her voice dropped conspiratorially and she actually leaned in so close her tight, bony chest banged against Teri's arm. "I hate the whole idea of bringing religion into the school; however, if we must, it's up to us to take care of our own. Don't you agree?"

Teri couldn't imagine disagreeing more, but it was easier to nod yes than to engage in a conversation.

"Okay, boys and girls, I need everyone to come up and take three styrofoam balls, several toothpicks, and your choice of eight small decorations. We're going to build the best snowmen ever! And guess what? They won't ever melt!" Stacy's voice was pitched high, the cheerleader straining to re-emerge from a forty-year-old throat.

Teri shuffled back to a corner, hoping that in the confusion of creating a classroom of non-melting, non-biodegradable snowmen, no one would notice her. When she'd signed on to be a room mom, back in September, she'd known she would be coupled with Stacy Rubin and would dread finding herself in a role that didn't fit. By nature a private person who struggled with social small talk, Teri had never felt comfortable joining the gaggle of mothers whose conversations evolved from poopy diapers to little league MVPs. But Jimmy had requested it for this, his last year in elementary school. Carly had never asked.

Leaning against the wall, Teri was able to observe Jimmy as he maneuvered among his classmates. Though he was acting the part of a carefree child, she knew he was acutely self-conscious about her presence, continually casting wary glances as if waiting for her to be recognized.

As though reading her mind, Stacy yoo-hooed from the middle of the room. "Mrs. Berger, don't you go hiding. Come party with us!" In a voice spirited by deliberate innocence, Stacy added, "Kids, does everyone remember Mrs. Berger? Jimmy's mom."

Suddenly all eyes were on her as Jimmy's face flushed red.

"Is she the one?" a pudgy dark-haired girl whispered to a blond boy Teri didn't know. The boy whispered something into her ear and the girl's hand flew to her mouth. "Omigod," she squealed as the boy burst into laughter. He turned and stage-whispered something to a group of others standing nearby. The word *killed* detonated in low voices across the room. Within moments, everyone was staring at Teri with expressions of curiosity and alarm.

Jimmy clenched his fists as he took three steps toward the blond. "Fight!" someone shouted and immediately the kids formed a circle around the two boys. Without hesitation, the classroom teacher clapped her hands together and strode into the space between Jimmy and the other students. "Snowmen, children. Let's not forget about our snowmen." With jutting elbows, she jabbed the air around her in a no-nonsense motion that sent the kids scurrying back to their tables—toothpicks and decorations in hand. The near fight appeared to be forgotten, though the gaiety of high-pitched voices sounded desperate and fake in Teri's ears.

For her son's sake, Teri chose to ignore the way several of the girls tensed in visible fear as she moved among the children, though she did *accidentally* bang against the blond boy, not even bothering to bite back a menacing smile. When treat time came, she selected the box of green and red frosted cupcakes and placed them one at a time on every child's desk, even those she knew to be Jewish. From the corner of her eye, she could see how Stacy had stiffened, how she nearly had to clasp her hands together to keep from swapping out her precious icing colors for the correct children. For the first time in a month, Teri felt a laugh rise up inside her as she imagined sharing the story tonight with Len. It wasn't like she was proud of her churlishness, but sometimes gratification needed to be grabbed where it could.

Finally, the holiday party was winding down. Teri's rancor had faded along with her energy. The tension in her shoulders and spine was just relaxing when the same blond boy blurted, "Anyone wanna play hangman? You know, *hang man*." He walked to the chalkboard and drew six underscore lines across the top of a scaffold.

The six-letter word could have been anything, but the moment Teri saw Jimmy's pale face she knew a disaster was in the making.

"B?" shouted the girl in whose ear he had whispered. Grinning with the zeal of a child who finds himself in the throes of the power of cruelty, the boy quickly scribbled a large cap B on the first letter space.

Jimmy cast a pleading glance at Teri, his eyes reddened by held-back tears. Still, she did nothing, frozen by an inability to prevent or protect.

"E," said a familiar-looking girl in the front row, breaking into laughter as the boy placed, with flourish, a lowercase "e" on the second and fifth spaces and a "g" before the second "e."

Waving her arms, the teacher stomped out from behind the desk, reinforcing a classroom obedience no room mother could command. "Enough! Back to your desks. Now." The boy hurried to sit as the bell rang, marking the end of the party, the day, and the semester. Within minutes, the room emptied of nearly everyone but Jimmy, who seemed glued to his seat as he continued to search Teri's face.

She ducked her head in shame, and went over to her son, placed both hands on his shoulders and tried to squeeze apology and love and support onto him without saying a word. As Jimmy stood, she moved to hug him but he shook her off and whispered, "Mom! Not here!"

Stacy motioned for Teri to wait. They walked out together, the boys following several feet in back, though not talking to one another.

"I hope this wasn't too difficult for you," Stacy said.

"It was fine," Teri said briskly.

Stacy probed for several moments, inviting more.

"Really, it was fine."

"Well, okay. We'll get together sometime after the holidays to plan the Valentine's party for the class. And, Teri, you know you can call me or come over anytime you need to talk. Just because we, uh, couldn't get together for Thanksgiving dinner doesn't mean we can't plan another family dinner. In fact, we'll have you over New Year's day. And this time, I'll make the entire meal. Sound good?" She actually clapped her hands, but visibly deflated as Teri pointedly ignored the invitation and instead headed with Jimmy to their Honda Accord while Alan and six others followed Stacy to her large, kid-friendly van. According to Jimmy, the Rubins' van had a DVD player with a flat screen visible to all middle and back seat passengers. As he'd relayed this latest marvel of the Rubin family, he'd stared at his shoes in order not to see Teri's critical judgment.

At the car, Teri asked, "You want to invite someone to our house?"

"Naw, not today," Jimmy shoved his chin down so the barely discernible words were muffled against his coat. But the tone was unmistakable: Don't ask me to tell you what I can't bear to say.

She drove slowly home, taking side streets whenever possible to avoid traffic, continually glancing in her rear and side mirrors, shifting in her seat to compensate for blind spots. Jimmy was panting softly next to her, unnerved by her anxious driving. But he didn't comment until they were almost home. "Mom, you didn't even do anything wrong. Dad said that's why you're not gonna go to jail. Right?"

Teri's hands were shaking as she grasped the steering wheel, but she kept her voice steady. "Jimmy, sweetheart, listen carefully. Your dad is right. Everything is going to be fine. And I'm not going anywhere."

As soon as they pulled into the garage Jimmy mumbled, "Thanks for coming," and darted out of the car, leaving his half-finished snowman and red and green cupcake on the floor, where they would invariably be smashed the next time someone rode with Teri.

7

LEN

"DR. BERGER? So what *do* you think?"

Len glanced at the imploring face in front of him. The last thing he'd heard was something about how much her boss was making her uncomfortable. She looked anxious, a young woman who was intelligent, ambitious, attractive, and who couldn't seem to stop herself from regularly vomiting up breakfast, lunch, and dinner.

"More importantly, Gretchen, why don't you tell me what *you* think?"

She squinted as though deciding whether or not to call his bluff. Then she leaned back and covered her eyes with her palms, a gesture which often ushered a revelation.

Len relaxed. He felt cheapened, but at least he'd spared the client his own indiscretion. For the rest of the fifty-minute hour he forced himself to listen, even managed a reasonably illuminating insight that seemed to comfort her.

After Gretchen left, Len sank into his overstuffed chair and stared at the ceiling. He'd killed a spider with a rolled up magazine several days ago and had not wiped away the residual body parts or gook. He found himself studying it more and more, a Rorschach test. Today the black smear looked like the accordion-smashed hood of a car. Some days it resembled crushed limbs.

It was only human, inevitable really, to drift while a client spoke. But to totally "zone out," as Carly would call it, was unforgivable. Lately though, it was tough to give credence to his clients' despair. He'd seen it too often–the slow, inexorable burn-out until one day the therapist found himself sprawled across another therapist's couch whimpering, *"I don't give a shit."*

He'd vowed if that ever happened to him he would get out—immediately. When he started needing his clients to help *him*, or when he inadvertently measured their problems against his own, it was time, that session, that moment, to walk. But Len wasn't about to walk. Not while his work provided what he'd always promised himself he'd never settle for, an escape.

Settle. Now that was an interesting word. He thought about the way a foundation *settled*. The way his lawyer friend would call and, with thick disappointment, tell Len the case he'd been gearing up to take to trial had *settled*. How so many of his clients finally reconciled their internal angst by *settling*.

And now, he and his family waited for their lawyer to call, waited for Rex to inform them a settlement had been reached, or they would be going to trial. Rex had said it might be as early as mid-January. The closer they got, the more anxious Teri grew. At night she'd toss and turn, kicking off then pulling on the blankets, until finally, heaving a sigh, she'd get out of bed and stumble across the carpeting and out of the room. More often than not, Len found her the next morning sprawled across the den couch. Even in sleep, her face was twisted and her eyes seemed to twitch under the lids in restless fear.

"Knock, knock."

Len quickly moved his legs off his desk and sat up straight, struggling to re-adjust his face. "Marilyn."

"Your five-thirty is here. I'm leaving for the day, so I'll lock the outside door if it's your last client."

He nodded.

"You okay?" she asked with the intuition they'd developed through ten years of partnership and friendship.

He smiled as convincingly as he could.

Marilyn frowned. "You look beat, Len. Why don't you take a little time off?"

He flashed to the suffocating silence when he found himself alone with his wife. "No, I'm okay."

"You're great, I can tell. And what about the kids?" she asked in the same tone her clients found soothing. "Did you ever find out why Jimmy has been getting into fights at school?"

Len hesitated, not wanting to bring his children into this office where the problems so often seemed hopeless. "Apparently kids have been saying Teri should go to prison for killing someone. Even his best friend, Alan, or should I say *former* best friend," he said as they exchanged the indulgent smile of adults discussing children.

"Poor Jimmy," she said.

"Yeah."

Marilyn was a wonderful therapist and friend. Still, Len resisted telling her the rest. Teri had discovered Stacy Rubin wouldn't allow her to drive Alan anywhere, which pissed Teri off so much she insisted Jimmy not go over to the Rubins' for a while. And since no one had even broached the idea of taking their annual winter vacation trip to Chicago, Jimmy had spent most of the Christmas break watching television at home while Teri sat at the kitchen table staring off into space, and Carly either disappeared with friends or stomped around their house in perpetual irritation. "I think once we hear from the lawyer—I mean assuming …"

"Of course she'll win. But you know, Len, sometimes even therapists need to talk to someone."

"Thanks, Doc. I'll keep it in mind." He brought his finger to his brow and tipped an imaginary hat.

Her eyes locked with his. "Well, I'll see you tomorrow."

The door closed softly and he slouched deeper into his chair, studying the splattered bug once more. This time it looked like a body outline, chalked to mark a slain victim, limbs askew.

The ambulance had already removed the body by the time Len arrived at the accident scene. Police cars, at least a half dozen with their lights flashing red and blue bursts against the pouring rain, blocked off the area. There was glass everywhere, more than he could have imagined. He had to keep stepping around it as he stumbled past the stiff arms of police. "She's my wife. She's my wife," he kept mumbling. When he saw the two cars, both crushed in accordion folds, Teri's more than the other, his entire body began to tremble and he thought he might actually fall to the ground. Then he spotted Teri and adrenaline propelled him to her side. She didn't seem to notice his presence, so he stepped back. That's when he saw the blood. It was a large, deep-red puddle, spreading rapidly in the rain, staining the glass shards to shades of pink. He'd watched in numbed fascination as a rivulet drained onto the toes of his brown leather shoes. Later, he'd shoved the shoes into the back of the closet and had not worn them since.

The door opened and closed in the waiting area just outside his office. Len glanced at his appointment book and perused the patient's file—a fifty-year-old man whose marriage was falling apart because his wife seemed unrecognizable to him. Great. Len closed his eyes, imagined the inside of a completely lightless box to clear his head, stood and answered the door to the next client.

8

TERI

TERI STARED AT THE UNOPENED envelope for several moments before tossing it onto a pile of mail that she'd been ignoring for days. She didn't have the energy or interest to be concerned with bills, but this envelope filled her with a sense of dread. It was from Farmer's Insurance and would contain notification of her increased rates.

As she poured herself a glass of Merlot, she thought about the only other car accident she'd had. It was on her sixteenth birthday, the day she got her driver's license. She was pulling out of the Steak 'n Shake parking lot, laughing with friends, when she had banged hard into the rear of a parked Oldsmobile Cutlass. The owner was a surly, older woman who happened to witness the incident. She was so indignant Teri was defensive and angry rather than frightened. Until she got home and had to face her parents. Selia's response had been typical: she'd calmly told Teri everything she did wrong, how she should have reversed, what a good driver she herself was.

Teri's dad had put his arm around her shoulder. "Well, sweetheart, at least no one was hurt and you got your first accident out of the way. Now you won't have to have another."

She shook her head as if to shake away the memory, gulped down a glass of wine, and was pouring another just as Len walked in.

"Smells good in here. You cooked?"

"Veal cutlets. I've got cheese lasagna too."

Len peered into her glass.

"You want some?"

He assumed his Dr. Berger look, where his face took on the blank expression of a sponge. Then as quickly, he frowned, the face of the husband. "No, not now." He sized her up, taking in the unwashed hair, the wrinkled jeans. "You didn't go to work *again*?"

She wanted to explain that just cooking had taken everything out of her. How she was trying. How when she'd slipped on the dirty jeans today and found a months-old, pre-accident ad for a mentoring job she'd been considering, she'd stuffed the paper back into her pocket instead of throwing it into the trash. "Maybe next week. Or … you know. Once we hear from the lawyer."

"Teri …" His voice faltered, then dropped off as Carly and Jimmy burst through the front door with noise and energy.

"Hey, something smells great." Jimmy's nose seemed to wiggle as he approached the stove and opened the oven door. When he was younger, they used to call him "Bunny." That was before he became "Cheese" Berger, a name bestowed on the baseball field, which in the past year had stuck to him.

Carly glanced at the frying pan and said nothing. Her sullen silence lasted until the family was seated and Teri offered a serving of the veal.

"You're kidding, right? Do you *know* how they make veal?"

Teri caught Len's eye.

Carly continued, her voice haughty. "They breed these sweet little calves in the most horrible way, forcing them to live in nets, which hang above the ground. And they only feed them to get them fat enough to kill."

Jimmy's mouth dropped open.

"While dripping with blood they—"

"Enough," Len said. "Go fix a peanut butter and jelly sandwich. No one is going to make you eat the veal."

"Don't tell me *you're* going to eat it. After what I've *told* you."

Like his daughter, the surest way to get Len to do the opposite of what one desired was to push him against a wall. With flourish, he lifted the largest piece from the platter, cut off a hunk the size of a silver dollar, and stuffed it into his mouth. "Mmm, it's great, Teri."

"Daddy, that's so gross."

Teri sighed. "The conditions for cows and chickens aren't much better."

"Well, I guess I won't eat *any* meat ever again."

Teri looked at the veal, and recalled its fresh pink state of an hour before. What difference could it possibly make? The animals were already dead and whether or not the Bergers ate them, they would not be coming back to life.

As though reading her thoughts, Carly sneered. "You know, Mom, maybe none of us should eat meat."

The soupy chili, stirring, deciding whether or not to add more burger. She had shoved the meal down the disposal hours after the accident, the meat dried to clumps and the sauce thick and gluey.

"You're not answering. You get mad when I don't answer."

"Carly, enough," Len warned.

"I'll take some." Jimmy pushed his plate toward the platter, and began shoveling large pieces into his mouth.

They ate in charged silence, punctuated by an occasional knife scraping the plate. Teri cut a bite of cutlet for herself. It was overcooked. She watched Len slide the veal to the side of his plate while he made room for a larger slice of lasagna. Carly, ever the family eagle, shot her mother a look of smug satisfaction. Teri was too tired to engage.

Len looked tired too, the kind of bone-weary pallor that dulled his skin. He turned to Carly. "You were at the library with Jason?"

"So?"

"Working on homework?"

"No, Dad, I was reading *Popular Mechanics*."

"Carly—"

"I've gotta go," Carly said, pushing her chair back from the table. "Becca's picking me up. We're going back to the library."

"Liar." Jimmy's taunt was just audible enough for everyone to hear. Second child, he'd fine-tuned tattling to a science.

Len persisted, "You didn't answer me. Are you and Becca working on homework? It's a school night, you know."

In the beam of his attention, Carly dropped her haughty stance. She mumbled, "Yes, Dad. Can I leave now? She'll be honking soon."

"Fine," Teri answered, circumventing Len. "The library closes at nine; be back by nine-thirty."

Carly rolled her eyes and pointedly stepped over a box of dishes on the floor. "Don't forget, Mom, no more meat for me from now on."

Jimmy took his plate to the sink. "I have to finish my math." He pecked dry lips against both of his parents' cheeks and left the room.

The silence was immediate. Len seemed uncertain whether to get up or stay.

"You want some coffee?" Teri asked. "I'll make real."

"Naw. Don't bother." He looked straight at her. "Thanks, though."

She loved his eyes, the color of bronze. He was destined to become a therapist. It was nearly impossible to remain hidden in front of those eyes.

"You seem tired."

He glanced away. "Yeah, I guess so."

"Bad day?"

He began twisting his wedding ring. They had both lost weight since Thanksgiving. Neither of their wedding bands seemed to fit anymore. "I don't know, Teri. Sometimes …" He winced. "Sometimes I just can't hear it anymore."

She waited patiently. To interrupt Len often meant to abruptly end his conversations. He needed to think through whole paragraphs before he could speak sentences.

"Everyone's troubles. They go on and on and on."

"Why don't you go to the beach or somewhere for a week?"

He asked quietly, "Do you want me to go?"

They had never taken separate vacations, though the idea suddenly seemed appealing. She had the sense if she pushed, he might even consider it. But when she opened her mouth, she said instead, "This week would have been Elise's birthday."

He was silent so long she wasn't sure he'd heard. Then he put his hands on the table, palms up. "Honey …"

"I keep thinking about her, Len, about how she looked—at *that* moment. And also when she was younger."

"You mean in high school?"

"Did you know Elise was in a juvenile detox unit?"

He started, "Wow. I hadn't heard," and then as quickly, visibly recomposed, forcing his expression into the neutral, attentive face he showed his clients. "But, Teri—"

She held up her hand for quiet. He couldn't help himself, and she didn't want to hear what the therapist had to say. "I thought you should know because …" She stalled, trying to decide. Clearly, he didn't remember. Her heart hammered, her ears clouded with a whooshing noise and for a moment she worried she might actually pass out. *Tell him.*

The phone rang. Len and Teri looked at each other. Carly pushed the kitchen door open. "Phone for you, Mom, and Becca's here." The door swung behind her then immediately re-opened as she stuck her head back in. "By the way, I think Grandma Selia called earlier."

Teri gulped. "Grandma Selia? You sure?"

"Well, it sounded long distance, but she seemed to be trying to disguise her voice. She wouldn't leave a name or say hi to me or anything." Carly shook her head. "She's really weird."

Her mother? Calling after all this time? Teri felt a rush of anxiety and pleasure as she picked up the kitchen receiver. "Hello," she said breathlessly.

"Teri? It's Rex Martin. I've got great news for you."

Teri slumped against the wall. She held the phone away from her ear by an inch and motioned for Len to come listen. She could feel his body heat as he cleaved to her side.

"It's over, Teri. I was successful in getting the criminal case dropped and the matter is closed."

"Over? Really over?" She went limp and handed the phone to Len, too shaky to hold it. His face flushed with something that should have been pleasure but appeared as complex as what she herself was feeling. She felt the resonance in his chest as he boomed his hearty thanks and hung up the phone. Then they were hugging and crying, clinging together so tightly she almost couldn't catch a breath.

Teri let Len lead her toward a chair. "What—what did Rex say?"

"Not much else. Even the civil case is just waiting on a minor technicality. Apparently the Horowitz lawyer said they plan to accept a settlement offer without any further negotiations."

"For how much?"

"Rex didn't say. We'll find out more when we meet with him."

She'd never even selected an insurance policy. Len had always handled all that. She stood and wrapped her arms around him and nestled her face against his neck, breathing in his familiar scent, the hint of sweat, the spice of his after shave.

"Now I have to go there," she whispered against his ear.

He pulled back. "Go where?"

"To see Rozlynn Horowitz."

"Rozlynn Horowitz? Why on earth would you go there?"

"I have to tell her—"

"What?"

She shrugged. "That I'm sorry."

"Surely you're kidding." He stepped away, struggling to remain calm. "It would be a *huge* mistake to go. It will just cause both of you more pain."

"Len, I killed her only child. Imagine it—you and I are both only children."

"No, Teri, that makes no sense. You heard Rex. It's over."

She felt the tears well up and impatiently wiped her eyes. She needed to be strong. She needed Lenny to understand. "To bury your child is the worst possible nightmare. I caused this, Len. I *have* to go see her."

His face flushed red, his whole body suddenly stiffened. "So you're not asking my opinion? You're telling me. Well, do me a favor and don't tell me." He turned and stomped out of the room, shoes clomping hard against the floor, stomping like both of their children did when mad.

Teri sank onto a chair and pulled her knees to her chest, digging her heels against the cushion. She surveyed the table full of dishes she would have to wash by hand because there was a hole in the middle of her kitchen where a dishwasher was supposed to be. On the greasiest platter was the veal, uneaten and dry.

9

TERI

TERI STOOD TO THE FAR SIDE of the front door so Rozlynn Horowitz couldn't see her through the peephole. She heard the unlocking of the chain, the double bolt, the key lock, and felt a tightening in her chest. There was still time to leave.

The door opened an inch and Rozlynn instantly moved to block the entry.

Teri tried unsuccessfully not to gasp. Rozlynn looked terrible. She was at least fifteen pounds heavier than at the funeral, pale and bloated. Her chestnut hair, which Teri remembered as her outstanding feature, hung limp and lusterless.

They stood on opposite sides of the screen. "I'm Teri Berger."

"I know who you are."

"Is it okay if I come in?"

"Why?" Rozlynn's retort was immediate.

"So we can talk?"

Rozlynn glanced outward for several moments then stepped away from the door.

Teri followed her through the den and into the kitchen. Rozlynn motioned toward a chair filled with stacks of newspapers. "Just throw them on the floor next to the other pile."

The top page was dated January sixteenth, several weeks old. She placed the papers down and sat. Rozlynn was still standing, her breasts cumbersome and loose beneath her sweatshirt. Her eyes seemed to follow Teri's. She stiffened and wrapped her arms across her chest.

"I know from, you know, the paperwork, today is—was, Elise's birthday. I guess I thought maybe it would be even harder today than usual. I just wanted to come by."

Rozlynn was staring as though Teri were speaking in a language in which only an occasional word could be recognized. "Today just means Elise still stays twenty." Her voice was flat. "Why do you care?"

"Of course I care."

Rozlynn continued to stare, her face expressionless, but something hard in her eyes made Teri look around the kitchen. It was a shrine to Elise. There were photographs of her covering the refrigerator, hung on all the walls, even perched in the windowsill over the sink. Opening her purse, Teri dug around for her glasses. She shoved the newspapers aside with her foot and walked to the refrigerator. "Do you mind if I look?"

Rozlynn didn't respond.

Top row, freezer door: Elise as a baby, chunky and bald. The toddler, her face beaming as a child who knows the camera is upon her—again—because she is the center of the universe. Elise stepping onto a school bus bearing a conflicted look of terror and pride. In her Brownies uniform. At a dance recital. She had the kind of face that grew older without altering.

Moving down the refrigerator, things changed. There was one of Elise on what seemed to be a homecoming date, standing next to a boy several years older and as many inches shorter. She looked wary, her body rigid. Elise standing in front of a row of kenneled cats at an animal shelter, dressed shabbily, forlorn, as if a stray herself. The next picture must have been taken at her high school graduation. Here her face had grown angular and pinched. In a flowing graduation robe, she was obviously rail thin. Her wrist bones stuck out like knobs, her brown hair hung limply over drooped shoulders. One more photo, of twenty-year-old Elise. She was fuller, no longer gaunt, her hair dyed blonde and permed curly.

"Pretty girl, uh, young woman."

Rozlynn frowned. "She died pretty."

Teri saw again Elise's look of horror, the bugged eyes, outstretched arms, wide-mouthed shriek. But the photo of Elise with the high cheekbones and tentative smile, that photo, positioned on page one the day after the accident, that picture was pretty. She did die pretty.

Teri moved back to the kitchen table and sat. "Now that the lawsuits are over, I—"

"Do you understand what happens when you bury a child?" Rozlynn's voice was low, coming from some place deep inside her throat. "You bury the past, the present, and the future." Rozlynn ran her fingers through uncombed hair. "I still get mail for her. Catalogues, charge card offers, *Spin*. My husband says I need to cancel everything."

Teri felt like she should say something, anything, but her tongue was too dry to speak.

"I'm glad we get her mail," Rozlynn continued, her voice listless. "It's like having her in the house. Crazy, but I still listen for the door to open and for her to walk in. I'm waiting to finish our last conversation."

"I know," Teri said softly. "I mean, I think I can imagine."

"I want to ask you something," Rozlynn said. "How do you sleep at night?"

"I don't."

Rozlynn inhaled sharply then slowly let out a breath. "I just wondered if you did."

Teri could feel her spine straighten, could feel something bubbling up inside her like a blast of heat. *It's not my fault!* She wanted to scream. *I put my fucking foot on the fucking brakes and tried to stop. I am not a criminal.* But the raw anguish on Rozlynn's face silenced Teri.

"Wanna hear the best goddamned part? The reason she was stranded that day is she didn't have her cell phone. I took it from her. Felt like she wasn't responsible enough, didn't deserve it."

"Well, it's good to try to teach the value of—"

"Oh, don't be an ass," Rozlynn snapped.

Teri slumped forward and put her head in her hands. She could hear the wind rustling against the window. A massive snowstorm was predicted for tomorrow, up to eight inches or more. The newscasters were urging people to buy their essentials today—to avoid unnecessary driving on slick streets.

"You have children." It wasn't a question.

Teri looked up. "Two. A son and a daughter."

"Right, Elise babysat for them, if I recall."

Teri struggled to answer calmly but it came out more of a stutter, "Uhh. Just a few times. I mean, my husband didn't even—"

Rozlynn interrupted, "That must have been before—" She sliced the air with her hand as though to wave away a memory. In a husky voice, "So you love them? Your kids?"

"Of course I love them. I'm their mother."

"You ever tell them you hate them?" Rozlynn was biting her right thumb cuticle. A tiny pool of blood welled at the base of the thumbnail. Rozlynn pressed, "You ever say anything like that to them?"

"We've all had our moments when we've felt it, if not said it."

A drop of blood fell to the table. Rozlynn put her elbow squarely against it, smearing the red to a pale stain. She leaned in and studied Teri's features the way a mother might scrutinize a bus driver about to ride off with her kindergartner. "What made you think you'd find me at home?"

Teri paused, weighing her answer. Truth she never considered Rozlynn might be somewhere else. "I don't know. Do you work? I thought you didn't."

"Actually, you thought wrong. I did work, full time in fact. I was working for a marketing firm, secretarial stuff." She smiled wryly. "Money for college tuition. My husband too, picking up extra hours when he could."

"Oh." Teri's mouth felt like cotton and the back of her eyes ached. She flashed to Len's angry reproach about this visit. What *had* she expected? Forgiveness? Understanding? Her jaw unhinged and she began to babble, knew she was babbling, couldn't stop herself. "I haven't worked much in years, not since, well, since Jimmy was born. It was just so hard, juggling two kids, a job, a husband. But now, I've been thinking I need to do something. Though I can't quite imagine trying to enter the workforce after all this time. I've been restless for a while, but I don't know what I want to do." She stopped, suddenly aware of the sharp silence. Rozlynn was eying her with an expression that reminded Teri of one of Jimmy's comic heroes whose glare could burn holes in objects. She needed to get the hell out of here.

"I better go. I just wanted to—I guess I needed to—stop by. To see you." She stood and pushed the chair back, taking care not to topple the heap of newspapers. "Rozlynn, I am really, really sorry."

Rozlynn cocked her head. "Sorry?"

Teri clasped her hands and, head down, whispered, "This accident changed my life too. I can't sleep or eat. I keep thinking if only—"

Rozlynn slammed her palms against the table and hissed, "Surely you're not looking for pity from *me*?" She bolted over to Teri, gripped her shoulders and squeezed with the same frustrated gruffness a mother might show her errant teen. She leaned in so close Teri could smell stale coffee and unbrushed teeth.

"The last word I ever said to my daughter was 'bitch.'"

Teri stumbled back. "Oh, Rozlynn, I'm—"

"No." She held up her hands.

"But every mother at some time—" Again Teri stopped.

"Every mother, what? Calls her daughter a bitch and has it be the last word spoken between them? Forever? Maybe every mother thinks it, but that *was* my last word. Something I have to live with for the rest of my life." Rozlynn's face had grown pale and a small glob of white spittle stretched between her top and lower lips as she spoke. "You make it sound so simple." Her voice rose to a squeaky pitch and her face twisted to a sneer as she mimicked, "'Of course I love them. I'm their mother.' Well, do you know how complicated a mother's love can be?"

Teri flashed to an image of her own mother, the rage and disbelief on Selia's face when Len had kicked her out of their house. The hole in Teri's life since. Yes, Teri knew all about complicated love.

She locked eyes with Rozlynn, neither woman looking away. Only when Teri realized her fists were clenched and her neck taut did she will herself to let it go. She closed her eyes, counted backwards from ten, then from twenty, by which point Rozlynn had moved away and was shuffling down a darkened hall toward the bedrooms.

Teri stood immobile, surrounded by the shrine to Elise. *Bitch* echoed in her head, the word as sinister as a skid.

Minutes later, she sat in her car trembling, seatbelt on, keys in hand. Glancing toward the house, she thought she saw a shadow move from behind a curtain. How many times had she herself stood surreptitiously looking out a window, waiting for a delayed school bus, a late carpool driver, or a date to bring her children safely home. She'd always thought of it as the mother's hallmark: the peering out and waiting, that pinch in the chest as minutes tick by, as you tell yourself nothing is wrong, it couldn't be, yet, in that moment, feeling the certainty of vulnerability.

Neither of the kids had liked Elise. Carly, especially, would beg Teri, "Please, Mommy, don't use her. She's creepy and spacey, and she smells funny." Elise certainly wasn't a first choice, but she lived so close, less than a ten-minute drive away. Len was traveling so much during that period, going every weekend to Kansas City when his mom was dying, and Teri just needed an occasional break, time away from full-time parenting. And Elise was always available. So when everyone else on the list had said no, and she did always try the others first, she would call and Elise would say yes.

Teri turned on the ignition, backed out of the driveway, and drove slowly home, retracing the route from when she would pick up Elise to babysit.

10

CARLY

THE ROOM WAS FILLED with the cloying smell of incense. They probably were smoking pot in the back, which was fine so long as the guy about to stick assorted needles into her hadn't touched the stuff. Carly looked into his eyes. The pupils, nearly the size of his iris, offered little reassurance.

"You pick a stencil?"

His t-shirt was frayed at the neckline and torn under his right armpit. Crumbs of food stuck to the front. A gold hoop ring connected one nostril to the other, contrasting with the silver hoop dangling from his left eyebrow and the silver ball piercing his tongue. Carly could feel the French fries she'd just eaten rising up her throat.

"I think I'm going to be sick," she said, covering her mouth with her hands.

"Hey, Dollbaby, you get sick on my station and you're outta here faster than the ink can dry." He laughed, actually cackled, like he'd said something funny.

Carly breathed deeply. "I'm better. Just nervous, I guess."

"There's nothin' to be nervous about. Some ink, couple needles, and you got yourself a tattoo gonna last your whole life."

She held her hands over her nose, inhaling the familiar scent of her perfumed lotion. Happiness, Jason's favorite. "This one." She pointed to a picture on the first page. It seemed simple. Less painful? "I want it on my ankle."

He glanced at the stencil. "Cool. You pick it, I paint it." He grinned. His teeth were surprisingly straight and white, of toothpaste ad perfection. "Anyone explain to you how this works?"

Carly shook her head no.

"We use a single needle for the thin outline, the threes for heavier outline, sevens for color and fourteens for full color."

"Fourteens?"

He held up a slim rounded disc that held a cluster of needles, all about an eighth of an inch long. "See. Fourteen needles on this spool. Gives us the deepest color, the one we use to make your boyfriend say, 'Oh baby.'"

Carly tasted the fries again. It was all she'd had to eat today, but she seemed to keep eating them over and over.

"Now's all I need is Mommy's John Hancock and we'll begin." He winked as Carly reached into her back pocket and retrieved a folded-up slip, penned minutes before as *Teri Berger*. He peered at the signature, winked again. "Look, I think the whole idea of needing Mommy to say yes is pretty stupid. This is art. Does Mommy tell you when you can go to the Art Museum? Know what I mean? Okay, you hang tight, I'll be right back."

The moment he left, Carly felt her resolve weakening. It might hurt or she could get an infection. Plus, her parents would be furious. It was a stupid, impulsive idea. She leaned forward to grab her backpack, then heard, "Carly?"

"Markieta. What are you—?"

"Don't tell me *you're* getting a tattoo." Her laugh was shrill and loud.

She and Markieta Banks had been in gym together last year, had showered at the same time three days a week, and had never exchanged more than a few words. "Uh, maybe not. You?"

Markieta flashed a wide smile. "Just another hole in my ear."

Carly heard approaching footsteps and inwardly groaned.

"Okay, Dollbaby, which ankle you want the tattoo on?" He paused, took in the sight of the extra girl. "Whoa. I've got four ankles to choose from? This is my lucky day." He reeked of smoke and it didn't smell like cigarettes.

"Hmm …" Markieta hummed the word as she sauntered away, her lean hips swaying, her back and head model-straight.

Carly's eyes followed Markieta. What if she told someone and it got around the school before Carly showed it to her parents? The principal might call home or the school nurse. She started to scoot down but stopped herself. Why would Markieta give a shit what she did? Carly sat back, heart hammering, and placed her foot onto the tabletop.

"See this?" He held in his palm a pistol-shaped tool. "It works like a sewing machine, punching needles about thirty-two-hundred times per minutes." He laughed. "Hey, no need to faint. Looky, you think I'd do this if it hurt?" He lifted up his shirt.

Carly gasped, uttered, "Whoa!" then unabashedly stared. His *entire* chest was covered with ink and no hair. A thick orange and brown spotted snake wound around the trunk of an elongated apple tree. Bright red apples covered the branches and encircled his nipples. Worms were crawling out of the fruit and intertwining with one another, circling back down to the snake. It was the largest and most elaborate tattoo Carly had ever seen.

He pulled his t-shirt down and grinned. "Like it?"

She gulped and nodded. She was afraid she'd spew fries if she spoke.

"You got yourself seven layers of skin. I'm going into two, well, maybe three. But no more." He smiled broadly, that ridiculously perfect smile. Then he leaned in close to her ankle, his forehead wrinkled in concentration, and inserted the single needle spool.

She had to admit, it didn't hurt much at first. It was irritating, like having one's hair pulled, and her ankle felt tingly as though it had fallen asleep. She kept her eyes closed the way she did at the dentist. She heard and felt when he changed spools to the denser needle clusters. Hot, piercing stabs began. She moaned, clenched her fists and tried not to cry. At one point, she almost asked him to stop, but at that moment the pain ceased and the tingling resumed. He had told her it would take about twenty minutes. It seemed much longer before finally he said, "Take a look."

Carly squinted. She could barely make out the dark green outline filled in with a rich shade of kelly green. She opened both eyes wide and pulled her ankle close. "It's perfect," she told him and was rewarded with a dazzling smile.

"Told ya."

"Yeah. You did." She gazed in amazement at the nickel-sized tattoo. It was placed above her outside ankle bone in the slight groove where the skin hollowed, giving the tattoo a three-dimensional look.

She watched as blood pooled and the skin began to redden and swell. Tentatively, she reached down and gently rubbed her fingers across the area. She glanced at her fingertips.

He laughed. "That ink ain't going nowhere."

"It, it's awesome."

He was beaming. She could almost imagine the snake expanding, the apples dropping off the branches as his chest puffed out with pride. "I apprenticed with Paul, ya know. I'm the best this studio's ever seen, they tell me." He smiled as if he were the only one in the room with thirty-two teeth. "You are officially tattooed forever."

She had a sudden image of her parents' faces when they saw it: her dad's disappointment, her mother's disapproval. Shit. Forever.

He pulled out a three-inch square bandage. "Gotta cover up 'til bedtime. No baths or swimming for a week. This baby will scab, then look glossy and feel kinda thick for a while, maybe even a month, 'til it's smooth as a baby's butt. Might hurt a bit and require a bandage to keep it from oozing, but that's normal. And don't scratch it."

As he unwrapped the bandage she stopped him. "Wait. Let me see again." A beautiful bright four-leaf clover.

"So since I gave you this lucky charm, I don't suppose you wanna be my lucky valentine?" he asked.

Carly tried to control her shudder, forced a smile, embarrassingly aware of the imperfection of her own slightly crooked teeth.

11

TERI

THE PREDICTED SNOWSTORM had passed them by with air currents from the south blowing in unseasonable warmth instead. Taking advantage of the mild winter evening, Teri and Len were sitting in the screened-in porch, legs outstretched, newspapers spread across their laps. For the first time in months, Teri could actually feel her spine relax. Then Len asked, "You see the follow-up article about the case dismissal?"

Damn! It never ended. "Well at least it's buried in the back section."

Len peered over his reading glasses. "Any new reaction from the kids?"

Jimmy had thrown his arms around her neck and clung to her. Carly had immediately teared up and asked, "Can we just forget about it now?"

Teri looked at her upturned palms, remembering a fortuneteller at a fair who had once told her she had an unusually long lifeline. "They haven't said much."

Len raised the paper and continued reading. Teri slumped further into her lounge chair and stared out from the porch. Their house was on a cul-de-sac with the backyard bordering a large, steep area of wooded common ground. They'd seen coyotes, a red fox, and deer in their yard over the years, heard the hoot of an owl, even sidestepped snakes. The trees would soon begin to thicken with leaves. What would it be like to step into their density and quietly disappear?

"I jogged with Michael Rubin this morning. He and Stacy want to get together with us for dinner."

"Give me a break."

"I thought you might say that. But, honey," he waited until Teri met his eyes. "We haven't seen any of our friends since the accident. When's the last time you went out for lunch?"

She shrugged. They both knew the answer.

"It's time." When Teri didn't respond, he picked the paper back up but continued to stare off into space. She was just about to get up and go into the house when he broke the silence. "By the way, Michael says Alan and Jimmy are in a fight again. You know anything about this?"

Teri shook her head. "You better talk to him."

"Talk to who?" Carly stepped onto the porch, backpack slung over her shoulder. She let it plop to the floor and sank onto a nearby chair.

"Where you been?"

"Daddy, why do you always ask me that the minute I get home? Can't you just say, 'Hi, Carly, how are you?'" She was smirking, a cross between playfulness and annoyance.

Len opted for the playful. "Hi, Carly, how are you?"

She rolled her eyes.

"What happened to your ankle?"

She yanked her jeans leg down. "Uh, from a nail. On a board. From play practice."

"You're not in the play." Teri could hear the accusation in her own voice and sure enough, Carly stiffened her shoulders.

"Well, Mom, you don't know everything after all. I've been asked to help with costumes." She flounced her hair over her shoulder. "Anyway, it's a miracle we haven't all broken our ankles on those stupid boxes all over the kitchen. Are we *ever* going to get the kitchen finished?"

Len held out his hand. "Let's just stick to the subject. Must be a nasty cut for a bandage that big."

"Daddy, I told you it's nothing. This was all they had in the first aid kit." She shot him a piercing glare and hobbled into the house.

They sat without speaking for a few moments. Len was tipping his chair, something they'd both fuss at their kids for doing. Teri spoke first. "You know she was lying, don't you?"

"Clearly. What do you suppose happened?"

"Who knows?"

"Teri, when *are* you going to do something about the kitchen?"

"Hey, you never even wanted me to redo it."

"Yeah, but now … it's been nearly three months. We can't keep living out of boxes." He leaned the chair back down on all four legs and cleared his throat. "You went to see Elise's mother, didn't you?"

She ran through myriad responses, but answered simply. "Yes."

They locked eyes, each aware the other was struggling with how far to push. Teri looked away first. She walked to the edge of the porch, placed her palms against the screen.

"I want you to start taking Prozac."

Keeping her back to him, she shook her head no.

"You don't have to feel this terrible."

Yes I do. I killed her.

Len had come up behind her. "Your own children are still alive. They need their mother." When she didn't respond, he squeezed her shoulders slightly firmer than loving, reminding Teri of Rozlynn's sticky tight grip. "Well," Len huffed, "I'll find out what's going on with Jimmy, but you better go talk to Carly." He grabbed the newspaper and walked back into the house.

She pressed her face hard against the scratchy metal of the screen. Coyotes were more afraid of humans than humans were of them. If she entered their den, would they run scared, ignore her, or attack?

HOURS LATER, Teri stood in Carly's doorway, watching her sleep. Defenseless, her daughter seemed the milk-sweet girl of years ago. Her body was longer and fuller, but Carly still slept as she had since moving out of a crib and into a bed: on her back, legs stretched out straight, and arms crossed against her chest. Her mouth gaped open; a sliver of drool rhythmically slithered up and down with her soft snores.

Teri inhaled as she entered the room, the mixed smells of female adolescence filling her nose. Perfume, athlete's sweat, muddy socks gone mildewed. Carly was a year from leaving for college, yet Teri could already imagine how she would miss the earthy scents of Carly.

She sat down on the side of the bed, reached out, and caressed Carly's brow, wiping a strand of hair up and away.

"Mom?" Carly's voice was thick.

"Yes."

"What's wrong?" Her eyes were closed, words warbled.

Teri continued to push the hair from her forehead. "Just wanted to talk to you."

"Hmmm," she smiled with closed lips and shifted her body against Teri's. The room was still. Then, abruptly, Carly yanked the sheets over her legs. "Mom. Move. You're sitting on my blanket."

Teri stood up and in a flash Carly covered herself to her chin. Even in the dim light Teri could see she'd turned ashen.

"Carly, what's going on?"

"Nothing! Go away. Let me sleep."

Teri shifted her weight from leg to leg, as Carly lay unnaturally still. She watched silently for several moments then scooted out and closed the door firmly, but quietly, in order not to wake Jimmy. She stood for a long time slumped against the doorframe and was about to leave when she heard crying. It was soft, so soft Teri almost missed it, but the muffled cries drifted beyond the space separating them. Teri went back in. This time when she sat near, Carly didn't move.

"What are you trying to hide?"

Carly placed her damp cheek again Teri's thigh. "Promise not to be mad?"

"I can't promise. But you may as well tell me anyway."

"No, you have to promise."

"Carly ..."

"Mom ..." They both smiled, but as quickly Carly's face changed. She seemed suddenly a scared and confused young girl.

"Okay. I promise."

Slowly, Carly pulled the sheet down. She uncrossed her ankles and gingerly removed the bandage.

"Oh." Teri stiffened. "A tattoo? Carly, how could you?"

"Mom, you promised."

She stared at her daughter's ankle. "But a tattoo? Why?"

"Why not? It's my ankle."

Without her glasses, Teri could just make out a fuzzy green shape. "What is it?" The ankle looked tender. Teri pressed lightly against the skin, then a little harder until Carly winced. Teri leaned in and through the swelling, in the dimple, discerned a four-leaf clover. She shook her head back and forth. "Jesus, Carly."

Carly's eyes flashed in angry challenge. "Give me a break. Everybody gets a tattoo these days. At least half the girls in *Cosmo* have one and they're all gorgeous."

"Yes, and how many of those gorgeous, tattooed girls live in St. Louis where—well, you know what kinds of kids get tattoos here. What's next? A motorcycle?"

"So what? It's not like you care about me anyway."

Teri ignored the defiant hurt in her daughter's voice. "Of course I care about you. What a stupid thing to say, and this tattoo was a stupid thing to do." She stared at her daughter's swollen ankle. Then it hit.

"Did you do this on purpose?"

"What?"

"Who do we both know with tattoos all over her body?"

At Carly's blank look, Teri exploded. "Don't play innocent with me. Are you going to tell me you didn't remember Elise had multiple tattoos?"

"Huh?"

Teri could see it as clearly as if she stood in the room, Elise with her straggly, straight, mousy-brown hair that always covered her face. She would twist her hair to one side and suck on the ends of a ropey strand, displaying a coiled snake on her pale neck, a small rose peeking out from the black, low-cut tops she regularly wore, a grinning rat dimpling at her knee, a jagged heart above her wrist.

Carly grabbed her ankle. "Mom, I didn't mean anything ..."

Behind Carly on the top bookshelf a raggedly Oscar the Grouch sat perched next to an SAT prep book, beside a framed photo of gap-toothed seven-year-old Carly as she smiled into the camera. A wave of sadness gripped Teri's body which immediately transformed into frustration and anger. When had she lost her daughter?

"Well, as you say, it's your ankle. And now you have to live with it the rest of your life." Teri turned to go and froze with her hand on the door as Rozlynn's words suddenly echoed in her ear, ...*that was my last word—bitch. Something I have to live with for the rest of my life.*

With a force of will, she marched into the hall bathroom, flipped on the switch and stared at her image in the mirror. The harsh fluorescent light cast shadows, which exaggerated the dark circles under her eyes into a raccoon-like mask. Her hands were trembling as she opened the vanity drawer and withdrew the scissors. She turned her back to the mirror, pulled her shoulder-length hair into a ponytail and whacked off several inches, one large clump at a time. With closed eyes, she clutched the top layers and whacked ... again ... and again and again, feeling elated and in control as thick auburn locks fell to the floor. Finally, the trembling stopped. She placed the scissors back in the drawer and without looking at herself turned out the light and headed for the den couch.

12

LEN

GRETCHEN SEEMED PARTICULARLY agitated today, so Len made his face as still and blank as possible. He sat quietly, waiting for her to begin. Her legs were crossed, left ankle shaking rapidly. Len watched, imagining her shoe flying through the air. It had yet to happen in his office but Marilyn once had a nervous client's sandal bean her in the head.

"I've got to ask you something." Gretchen's voice was trembly. "I mean, I probably shouldn't even ask this. It's none of my business. And it doesn't have anything to do with *us*, I guess."

He waited in silence, smiled with lips clamped together. He'd long ago learned most clients were more forthcoming when he remained quiet.

"It's just, well, it's okay if I say it?"

"There's nothing you can't say here, Gretchen."

"Well …" Her foot had begun to shake again and a lone tear slid down her cheek. "My roommate told me your wife killed someone. I told her I didn't believe it, but she said your wife killed her in an accident and they let your wife go free. Is it true?" She continued to sit ramrod straight for a moment then exhaled and slouched into the seat cushion. Her crossed leg dropped to the floor with a resounding thud.

Len struggled to control his dismay. "Gretchen, let's take your questions one at a time. Yes, it's true, my wife was in a car accident. Her car skidded and a young woman died. My wife was not charged because she committed no crime. It's been in the newspaper. I'm surprised you didn't know about it."

Her voice came out a hoarse whisper, "My roommate said it was during Thanksgiving. I was gone, remember?"

Remember? He couldn't remember anything but that weekend, and Gretchen bore absolutely no part of the memory. He nodded.

"Well, so, is it weird being around her?"

Len sat forward, resting his elbows against his knees. "Who?"

"Your wife. I mean if someone I knew killed someone, I think being around them would totally freak me out." She had grown pale and was visibly shaking.

"Gretchen, let's talk about why this is upsetting you so much. It would be helpful if you could reflect on this. As you said, it's not really about *us*."

"But it is about us. Don't you see, Dr. Berger." She reached across to the side table and grabbed a tissue. "Oh, this is just so hard to say."

He waited.

"See, I finally understand why you don't pay attention to me anymore. I thought you were just bored with *me*. I guess whatever I have to say must seem pretty stupid now, doesn't it?" She was leaning forward, speaking quietly and earnestly.

He knew he should be alarmed and even ashamed, but all he felt was a desire to put his head down and let her pat his shoulders in comfort. He envied her freedom to jangle her foot, to cover her eyes with her palms. He coveted her place on the couch. But he'd learned his trade well: Dr. Berger stayed still, his face blank, providing quiet assurance.

Gretchen seemed to relax. "Whew. I said it. I feel better. I've just been so worried."

"I would not be here if I thought I couldn't give you my full attention." He hoped he sounded sincere. "There have been some rough days, but when I am here, I am truly here. Believe me, Gretchen, what you say matters very much."

"Really?" She was tilting her head, a cross between vulnerable and coquettish.

"Really."

She smiled and leaned back. "Hey, I like your new needlepoint."

He glanced at the gift given the day before by a terminating client. Cross-stitched gratitude bearing the message: *There's No Place Like the Illusion of Home.*

"Speaking of which," Gretchen said, "I need to talk to you about what happened this week with my mom."

❧

"ANYONE HOME?" Marilyn poked her head in, then opened the door wide. "Well, don't you look like crap. You're gonna tell me people pay *you* for advice."

"Not a funny thing to say today."

"Oh, sorry." Marilyn slumped into the nearest chair and swung her legs over the side of the arm. At five foot ten and broad-shouldered she filled the chair. "So tell the doctor, Doctor. What happened?"

"Nothing. Just tired."

"Leonard Berger."

The cleaning service had finally washed away the dead spider. He closed his eyes.

"Len?"

"I've been waiting for months and it finally happened. With Gretchen, no less. The bulimic woman I consulted you about. Apparently, her roommate told her about Teri's accident. Gretchen says now she understands why I don't pay attention to her anymore."

"Ouch."

"Hey, don't look so sad. You're supposed to be cheering me up."

"Cheering you up? You mean I should tell you to just snap out of it. Or would you rather I say you're a piece of shit therapist so you can feel even worse? Len, your family has been to hell and back. Of course you might not have the attention span now. But when the clients start playing doctor, it's time to see a doctor."

He wanted to plug his ears shut with his fingers, the way his kids used to do when younger. He put his head down on his desk. "It never fucking ends."

"Tell me the truth. *Do* you pay attention?"

He glanced up. Her expression was studiously neutral, but in her eyes he saw empathy and concern. "I don't know. I'll be listening to some client's story and I'm right there with her one minute, and I've drifted home the next. I can't get all the … the … stuff out of my head."

"What specifically?"

He smiled. "You're doing it. We're not supposed to treat each other."

She looked sheepish, shrugged. "Oh, well. So tell a friend."

Len stretched his legs to the edge of the desk and began to talk, and once he started, it all spilled out. How Teri continued to swing from being remote to short-tempered or tearful yet was unwilling to get on meds or talk to a counselor. How even before the accident, she seemed at loose ends, but now it was much worse. He felt as if he were married to a person he no longer knew. How they were bickering more than ever before. How Carly was never around and when she was home she was either sassy or deeply irritated about something, and, yes, she was a teenager but this seemed more like a response to all the tension in the house. How Jimmy sometimes pissed his bed at night and had taken to spending all his time in his room. How the ghost of Elise seemed to be an accusatory presence in every corner, in every conversation.

"And as if this isn't enough, my mother-in-law has decided to re-enter our lives."

Marilyn sprang up in her chair, wiping her brow in a grand gesture. "Now I'm worried."

"Yeah, actually me too. Seriously."

"You are serious."

"I am. It's been over a year since our terrible fight and I must say I haven't missed Selia a bit. But even far away, she's like poison, only she's the kind that tastes fine and is odorless, so you never know you're being asphyxiated until it's too late."

She chuckled. "C'mon, Len. With all you've got to worry about, this hardly seems a list topper."

"You've never met my mother-in-law."

"Has she contacted you guys—after all this time? Does she know about the accident?"

"Last question first. Selia smells trouble the way a good hunter smells fresh blood in a weak wind. Believe me, she *knows*. As for contacting us, well, don't laugh, but for the past couple of weeks she's been calling home and hanging up on whoever answers."

"So how do you—"

"We know. Even without caller i.d., we know." He bit back a scowl. "There's always a long silence, this kind of intensity only Teri's mother could wordlessly send across a thousand miles. She's the green sky before the tornado."

"Well, she certainly brings out the poet in you," Marilyn said with a smile. Then her face grew somber and she reached her hand out and lightly touched his arm. "I'm sorry, especially about the kids. That's tough. And, of course, Teri." Her voice changed to the well-modulated tone of professional concern. "Len, remember what we learned in psych 101—about intervention? Well, I'm intervening. Your family is suffering from post-traumatic stress. You all need to be in therapy. Or at the very least, Teri. You know that. So stop jacking around."

"I'm telling you, Teri refuses to go. And I keep thinking, any day everything is going to be better again."

She shook her head up and down in small movements. "It will. But not tomorrow. And …"

He was instantly alerted by the change in tone. "What?"

"I don't want to add pressure."

"Say it."

Her mouth contorted. "Word is out, Len. We haven't gotten a new referral in months. This office needs you to be here when you're here."

He drew in his breath and only seemed to exhale once Marilyn walked out. She was right. Len's practice had been limping along since the New Year. He was already done for the day. Light schedule tomorrow. He groaned, sinking his head into his palms.

The phone rang. He looked at his watch—five-forty. The line would be forwarded to voicemail; this had to be his private back number. He answered. Static.

"Hello. Hello?"

The silence was loaded. Len felt a sudden prickly itch along the back of his neck. "Selia."

"Yes, Leonard. I called to give you advance notice about my travel schedule."

"Travel? Are you going somewhere?"

"Don't be coy. I've decided to forgive and forget and come help out."

Len sputtered into the phone. "Forgive? Who's forgiving whom here?"

"We don't have much time, Leonard. If I'm going to come all the way up from Boca, I have a lot to do to get ready. Frankly, I'm shocked you haven't called me for help. I read the story in the *St. Louis Post-Dispatch*. About the accident." A pause, as if waiting for a response, then she added in a voice filled with Selia hubris, "Yep, I taught myself how to read the *Post* online in order to follow your wife even if she didn't bother to do the same for me."

"*Do. Not. Come,*" he hissed. His hand shaking, he placed the phone on the cradle. He stared, his mouth opened in horror, waiting for it to ring again. When it did he grabbed the receiver and barked, "God damn it! What?"

"Len? Hello?"

"Teri?" She was crying. "Honey, what's going on?" He could hear the muffled sounds of whimpering. "Teri!" She wasn't making sense, and then she wasn't there anymore. He grabbed his keys, turned off the light and rushed out the door.

13

TERI

PERHAPS THE MOST SURPRISING THING she ever did was to get behind the wheel immediately after the accident. Another person might not have driven again. But two days later Len and Teri went to Enterprise Leasing, where she rented a small Ford Escort. In the months since, Teri left the house as infrequently as possible. Yet when she had to, she still drove.

Even today, she'd driven here with no problem, as if her car was not a killing machine, but a mode of transportation. Like anyone, she'd shaken her head at the gas prices, filled her tank, paid outside by credit card, opened her car door, and sat down.

But suddenly, she couldn't seem to fit her key into the ignition. Every time she tried, her fingers and the key leapt, never catching their mark. Her heart, too, was shaking jaggedly, as if it was leaving her chest for someone more deserving. And the shrieking in her head. Or was it the shrill of a useless ambulance?

Okay. She knew what was happening. Come on, Teri. Panic won't kill, it just feels like it will. Call Len. That's right, press two, auto-dial. "Len?" Voice barely audible. "Hello?"

She could picture his face, how his bronze eyes turned golden, like melting honey. Or like a tiger's eyes? Len was shouting. She dropped the cell phone into her lap and finally, blissfully, allowed her head to flop to the steering wheel. *Oh, Len. Just let it go. Just … let … go …*

❧

THE HOLLOW KNOCK startled her. Teri opened one eye and winced from the shaft of bright sunlight. "Go 'way," she muttered.

The knocking persisted, jackhammer rhythm. "What?" she yanked her head up.

"Ma'am? You okay?" His voice was muffled by the closed window. She watched his lips move, fascinated by the brown tint of his bottom teeth. "Ma'am?" Reluctantly, she lowered the window. He stuck his head in so far their noses nearly touched. "You aw right?"

Aw right. That was exactly what she was. She wanted to laugh, but was too tired. She started to slump back down, but he knocked again, this time on the roof with a force which caused the car to tremble.

"You been sitting here a long time since you filled your tank. We got worried."

Joe, the name on his red-striped pocket read. Of course. Can't get a job as a gas station attendant if the name on your shirt exceeded three letters. Ter, her shirt would read.

She forced her lips to move. "Yes, Joe. I'm just a little tired."

His shirt was stained with black stripes of grease, matching the inked fingerprints he'd left on her window. He was young, nearly as young as the cop who'd handcuffed her.

She looked out beyond the pumps, down the block. There. Right there was the spot where Elise was killed. So goddamned close to this gas station Teri could see it. Why the hell didn't Elise walk here for help? Lazy ass kid, too lazy to even pay attention to babysitting directions. And that smirk she wore on her young face as Teri gave last minute instructions. Some babysitters seemed to hang on to every word. Not Elise. Everything was a big joke. Just go and leave me alone, her jutted hip seemed to say. She'd chew her hair while Teri talked, her eyes veiled and hooded, her shoulders hunched as if holding something dark inside. Though not at that moment. At *that* moment the drenched blonde Elise had stretched her arms outward, her hands waving toward the sky.

Teri stuck her face out the window. She inhaled, remembering the sour stench of fresh blood and spilled intestines. Today the air was clean, a thin early-spring day. She put the car into drive. With extreme caution, she backed out of the station lot and pulled onto Ballas Road, turning left at Olive Boulevard.

Len would come. First he'd go home, see her car missing, then on instinct drive up to the corner. Though they'd never discussed it, he would know this was the corner that continued to draw her back, one block from the accident, a south field unable to resist the pull north.

As she turned into the parking lot of the nearby Drury Inn, she saw his green Volvo drive by. He was on his way to save her. And she was already gone.

❧

THE FIRST TIME TERI RAN AWAY she was eleven years old. Some older kids on the bus had selected her as their victim, tripping her as she walked by, and laughing when her books scattered. She made the mistake of coming home crying.

The next morning, her mother marched her down to the bus stop. Dread made Teri's breakfast thick inside her throat. When the bus arrived, Selia elbowed her way to the front, climbed up the two steep stairs and proceeded to dress down the busload of students. Waving her arms, Selia cried out with the verve of a preacher, "Confession time. Who is bothering my daughter, Teri Meyer?"

When no one stepped forward, Selia began to walk up and down the narrow aisle, stopping at every seat to point her finger directly into the face of each student. Teri stood outside the bus until Selia stomped down the stairs and with blazing eyes insisted she get on. Teri sat immediately behind the driver. She felt, more than heard, the twittering whispers.

That afternoon, when the bus came to take the students home, Teri was not among them. She had slipped out of the playground and started running in the only direction where she didn't know her way. She ran and walked, and stopped and cried, and ran until she started shivering from her sweat. Then she fell and with bleeding elbows and knees sat on the curb until eventually a policeman drove by and took her home.

There was an incident in high school, too, when Selia went to the home of the boy who had just broken up with Teri. She demanded he come and apologize to her daughter. Hours later, Teri snuck out the side door and hitchhiked from St. Louis to Jefferson City. She was gone fourteen hours before hunger and fear overrode pride.

Interestingly, Selia didn't get mad when Teri ran off. In fact, she responded with smugness. *She* had the power to push her daughter beyond the edge. *She* had the power to bring her daughter crawling back. Now, with adult reflection, Teri wondered if there hadn't also been a third element. Selia's daughter had the backbone to leave.

Teri knew the reaction of her husband would not be the same. For two days she had sat in her hotel room repeatedly picking up the cradle of the phone only to lower it back down. Each time her heart would beat wildly in her chest and she would think, *Not yet, not yet*. For the first time in months, Teri could sleep restfully. It was nearly all she did. She had aching moments of missing her kids, no, not missing, but wondering, worrying, experiencing the sense of having left a piece of herself behind. But this morning, peering in the mirror—ragged haircut and all—she almost recognized herself. She was right to have come. She would never have believed she'd actually leave, but here she was.

She dialed Len's office number. He answered on the second ring. "Dr. Berger."

"It's me."

The intake of his breath filled her ear. The output seemed to hiss.

"You got my message that I'm fine, didn't you? I'm sorry I haven't called again, Len. I couldn't. And my cell phone's dead." She stopped, waiting for a response, and finding none meekly said, "I, uh, the charger's at home."

"You're sorry? Gee, Teri, I guess that makes everything just fine, doesn't it?"

She willed herself not to hang up. "How are the kids?"

"Why don't you call them and find out?" His anger clipped his words. A nervous giggle escaped her lips, which Len chose not to comment on. She looked around her quiet, empty room and reluctantly said, "I'm at the Drury Inn." She waited and when he remained silent added, "If you need me."

"Do you plan to stay there?"

She'd never heard him so angry or distant. "Please don't be mad. I'm trying to recover, I really am." Silence, and for the first time she wondered if she had pushed too far. Then she looked at her solid gold band, the simplest matching bands they could find, and she said in a voice husky with years of intimacy, "Len, you're the one who says you've got to take care of yourself before you can take care of anyone else. I just need some time to clear my head. Alone."

Again, no comment. She thought he might have placed the phone down. She couldn't even hear him breathing. She was about to hang up when he said, "Take whatever time you need. But don't expect things to be the same when you come back." He hung up first.

She stared at the phone in her hand, as the silence turned into a series of clicks and a recording told her if she needed help to dial the operator. Instead, she crawled back into bed.

❧

"MA'AM? MAY I HELP YOU?"

Teri startled back to the present. The Nordstrom sales woman was staring at her, head cocked, not a hair out of place. Teri looked down and was astonished to find a peach-colored terry cloth exercise outfit in her hand. She didn't remember picking it up. She peeked inside the label, a medium, and looked at the price tag. Seemed a bit pricey for workout clothes, ninety-eight dollars, but she hadn't bought anything like this in so long, maybe that's what they cost now.

She watched as the sales woman slid Len's charge card through the small machine, waited, frowned then began to punch in numbers. She glanced at Teri, a half smile in apology. Teri shrugged and stepped away. As she heard the machine begin to whine out its acceptance, she fingered another pants and jacket set, in a soft shade of green. This one was even more expensive. "Here, if it's not too much trouble, I'll take this too." The sales woman's smile broadened.

Teri kept one hand on the crisp white shopping bag as she drove back to the Drury Inn. The stiff paper felt full of promise. She'd forgotten how restorative *retail therapy* could be. She pulled into a parking spot and sat for several moments. She'd done it, driven without extreme anxiety to a mall, purchased underwear, a nightgown, toiletries, work-out clothes, and impersonated an average woman on an average errand. There had only been one bad moment, the blackout at the cash register when all she saw was the stunned face of Elise.

She grasped the bag to her body. Tomorrow's forecast called for warmer weather, a good day to take a long walk. First, she'd need to get new walking shoes, maybe even one more outfit. Instinctively, she looked at the dashboard clock and smiled to herself. So what if it was five-thirty? She raised her arms in a long stretch, her fingertips brushing the velvety nap of the inside roof. She could feel her whole body uncoil, languid with freedom. No carpool to drive. No dinner sliding into the oven. No mess to straighten, or dishes to wash, or homework schedules to arrange.

She brought her arms back down to rest in her lap, felt her neck go jellylike when, as quickly, she imagined Jimmy's face. Her chest tightened. Maybe he was crying right now. Or sitting alone in the den missing her. Teri sat upright. "Hang in there, sweetie." The scene changed. Carly swept into the room. This would be her chance to shine, to boss with gentle irony, to sigh just loudly enough to make sure her father heard. And Len, he would come through. Dr. Berger Knows Best.

In fact, they were all probably having a better time without her: No anger in the house. All that guilt aired out. Fresh breezes sweeping through with early-spring fragrance. Teri felt herself a ghostly presence, as if she'd always been gone and was never coming back. And for an instant, she experienced a sadness so deep it sliced through her then left her light and airy. *"Of course I love them. I'm their mother,"* she'd blithely said to Rozlynn, maintaining the charade of simplicity.

Every family has its secrets—the ones time covers but does not erase. Len had been the one to push for children. "We're so happy, just the two of us," Teri would argue, unwilling to admit aloud what felt like a monstrous truth: what kind of woman didn't want to be a mother? Eventually, Len wore her down. Her one consolation throughout the pregnancy was that she convinced herself the baby was a boy. When the doctor held up the healthy, seven-pound Carly, Teri had blurted, "Where's his penis?" Everyone laughed, but Teri had felt a tingling dread. The only role model Teri had for mothering a daughter was the exact model she did not want to replicate.

For the first ten months, long after the *baby blues* should have passed, every time Carly cried so did Teri. It was never a case of not loving her baby, in fact, just the opposite. Teri was afraid to love the baby too much, afraid to be too involved, too controlling, too smothering. Even with Jimmy, Teri held herself back, determined not to mimic the worst of Selia.

Tacitly through the years, Len was the parent to whom the children looked for nurturing. Teri packed their lunches, Len remembered to put the little notes inside. Teri bought their clothes, Len brought home surprise toys. They pecked Teri on the cheek before going to sleep, they wrapped their arms around Len in a tight bear hug. She was the primary caretaker; she knew the babysitters' numbers, the pediatrician's office hours, the teachers' conference times. But, always, it was Len who knew their hearts.

When Teri brushed aside twelve-year-old Carly's concern for the fresh crop of new acne dotting her chin, the pre-teen had screamed, "You care more about how the house looks than how I look!" The accusation had taken Teri by surprise. Didn't Carly realize how liberating it was to have a mother who didn't notice and comment on every single aspect of the child's life?

She sighed as she turned the ignition back on, exhaling sorrow and inhaling freedom as palpably as if the breath itself could flip the switch. She'd go buy cross-trainer shoes, maybe a cute hat to block out the sun. Afterward, she'd catch another nap before a late meal in the downstairs restaurant, and then, alone in her room, she'd order a pay-per-view movie and a decadent dessert from room service.

14

LEN

OH, LENNY,

I know things have been rough between us recently. Maybe we both just need to prove we're each right. What I did was wrong but if you would LISTEN and let me explain my side, you'd understand better. I'm writing because lately when we try to talk, we wind up fighting instead. This may be one of those times when we have to agree to disagree and get past it. I still love you and I assume you love me. So what do you think? Can we put this behind us?

Love,

If you don't know who, then we're in worse trouble than I thought.

"Dad?"

Len grabbed a book and placed it on the letter. "Yes, Jimmy."

"Never mind. You seem busy." He leaned against the door jamb looking waif-like in his too-large jeans and oversized t-shirt. Len felt a clutch of concern; had Jimmy always been this thin?

"I'm not busy, son. Come on in."

Still, Jimmy stood in the doorway. A rivulet of blood was trickling down his arm.

"Uh, Jim, you're bleeding."

Jimmy pressed his arm to his t-shirt, leaving a red splotch on the white shirt.

"Cut yourself?"

"A while ago." Jimmy's expression turned sheepish. "It's fun to play with the scab."

"Here, let me see."

Jimmy shuffled in but stood several feet from the desk. Len reached across and caressed his thumb up and down his son's thin arm, taking care not to touch the wound. It was developing a thick-skinned lump around a small open area. "How long have you had this?" At Jimmy's shrug, Len pressed. "Since before Mom left?" Jimmy's eyes opened wide as though startled by the candor of the question.

"You better leave it alone or it'll get infected."

"Dad, how long will Mom be gone?"

Len shook his head. "I don't know."

"Did she leave 'cause of me? For oversleeping so much?"

"Oh, Cheese, God no." Len sprang up and embraced Jimmy. The boy seemed to have grown an inch since Len last pulled him into his arms. He heard Jimmy sniffle and was infused with fury. How dare Teri do this to them?

"Dad, you're hurting me."

Len loosened his grip and immediately Jimmy stepped back into the doorway. Len's office had always been sacred territory given the confidential nature of the patient files he brought home to study. The result, he realized now with regret, was his own son didn't feel comfortable entering the one room where Len spent most of his at-home time.

"Your mom's leaving has nothing to do with you. Nothing. She's just trying to come to grips with the accident."

Jimmy's eyes were downcast and his lips trembled. Len could almost see inside his eleven-year-old head as he tried to process their conversation. There was so much Len wanted to say: to offer false reassurance, to voice his own frustrations, to soothe, to share. But he remained silent, giving Jimmy the space he might need to respond.

Jimmy cleared his throat. "Uh, Dad, are we having dinner tonight as a family?" Before Len could answer, his son continued, "Because Alan invited me to eat there. He keeps apologizing. I guess he's trying to be my friend again. So, I probably should go. But I don't have to if you don't want me to."

Len glanced at his watch. With the change in season, the room was still bright, but sure enough it was after six. "That's fine. I'm glad you two are buds again." Then to Jimmy's rapidly retreating back, "But come home right after dinner."

Len heard the back door creak and braced himself for the storm Carly had become. Instead, he was greeted by an immediate and sudden silence. It must have been Jimmy leaving. Len rubbed his temples, trying to staunch the oncoming headache. How much easier it was to be Dr. Berger, to hear with dispassion and feel only professional concern.

With a heavy sigh, he shoved aside the book and picked up the letter from Teri. There was no date on it. It had been startling to find the letter in his lower left drawer and he had almost seduced himself into believing it was freshly written. Ha. Teri contrite? He hadn't heard a word from her since their one conversation and he sure as hell was not about to call her. She owed them all a lot of explaining and a lot of apology.

He had no memory of the fight, which would have precipitated this letter. They used to write to one another when they couldn't resolve their issues by discussion. But this went way back when their kids were still toddlers. What had they fought about then? What had they even fought about last year? Before the accident? Anything, everything—all of it now seemed trivial by comparison. A client had recently said that next to a day in Iraq nothing was difficult. Len had kept his face expressionless while internally churning with recognition.

He heard a crash in the kitchen and, grateful to leave his musing, scurried out, pulling shut the office door. "Why are you so late?" he groused. But instead of his daughter, Len was greeted by a splattering of glass shards, a puddle of milk, and the startled hissing of their neighbor's gray cat as she tiptoed across the sink to the counter.

"Get out of here," he swatted. The cat bounded down, landing in the small clearing between glass, liquid, and boxes. She meowed once, sounding annoyed, and glided out the back door, which Jimmy had left open. Len looked around the mess and smelled a sour stench. Dishes from yesterday were piled high in the sink. A line of ants crawled across the counter. And multiple boxes cluttered the floor because they still had no cabinets.

Damn her! Len kicked the wall and felt a piercing pain. "Shit!" he screamed into the empty room. The sound seemed to bounce back and slap him against the wall, scaring him with the force of his anger. He thought of the letter, the "*Oh, Lenny,*" and felt his eyes well with tears as he began to laugh with hilarity at the idea of Dr. Leonard Berger crying over spilled milk, a maniacal sound that would greatly alarm him if emitted by a patient.

As he walked out in search of rags, he passed the clock—six-twenty. Where the hell was Carly?

❧

HE AND TERI met in high school junior year, honors English, and they disliked each other instantly. She was everything he found distasteful in a girl: too pretty, too aloof, too good. He would slump in the back row, a Lit book propped in front of whatever novel he was actually reading, and study her as she effortlessly moved among her peers without truly connecting to anyone or revealing anything about herself. She both repelled and fascinated him, with her self-containment and careless beauty, thick auburn hair, and eyes nearly black, the darkest eyes he'd ever seen. Only her teeth were crooked, not terribly but certainly not perfect. He couldn't believe with such an ass-kicking smile her parents hadn't sprung for braces.

He knew she was equally put off by him, by the unsociable attitude he wore around his shoulders as constant and shabby as his Grateful Dead t-shirts. One time, they were forced to work together on a school project. During the two weeks of collaborating they talked almost nightly on the phone. Once, he let his guard down and confessed his fears about his dad's lung cancer and how tough it was to be a new transfer. They had moved from Kansas City so his dad could go to Barnes Hospital. He sensed a glimmer of connection as Teri expressed what felt like genuine understanding. But as teens, theirs was a world in which apolitical conformists and political activists dared not mesh. She sent him a note when his dad died— nice gesture, perfunctory message.

Seven years later, at a Washington University interdisciplinary graduate seminar, Teri tapped Len on the shoulder. "Excuse me, but didn't you go to Ladue High School?" He looked into eyes almost black. Little else was recognizable. Her long hair was now cropped shorter than his own. Drawn cheeks dimpled tight by her mouth, and the crooked teeth seemed larger in her shrunken face. But the coal eyes were the same, duller, but still the color of obsidian.

"Teri Meyer?"

She smiled and for a moment he saw a glimpse of the attractive girl she'd been. He wanted to say, "What the hell happened to you?" Instead, he replied, "Yeah, I went to Ladue—Len Berger."

"You look great. I barely recognized you." A giggle. "That didn't come out right. I mean, you looked great before. I mean ..." She offered a rueful smile then her expression turned quizzical as though she was trying to decide something. "My dad died last year. I remember when your dad died. It sucks, doesn't it?"

The door opened and the professor strolled in. Len asked, "Hey, want to grab a drink after class?"

"I don't know. You were such an asshole in high school. Are you still?"

When he called his best friend, Jack, seven months later to say he was going to marry Teri, Jack was incredulous. "Teri Meyer? But, Berger, she's a *nice* girl."

❧

NOW, LEN STOOD outside the Drury Inn room, forcing himself to remember the *nice* Teri, the girl of his youth. He lifted his hand and with taut knuckles knocked. He could hear rustling in the room. He knocked louder. Footsteps. An eye peering out. Then the almost sighing of the door itself as it very slowly swung open.

"You're here."

He had anticipated she would be haggard, unkempt, depressed. Instead, she seemed well-rested and, well, healthy—no—more than healthy, almost glowing. Her face had good coloring, her hair had resumed its luster. If she were his patient, he'd be relieved.

She stepped aside and motioned him in. "Want some tea?"

"Tea?"

"They have a little coffee maker in the room and I bought some wonderful raspberry tea in the gift pantry. I just heated water." She shrugged, a cross between apology and pleasure.

He stumbled to the nearest chair and sat down. "You look wonderful."

Teri blushed. "Well, hardly wonderful, but better. I am better."

Len's eyes swept across the room, which had the feel of someone settling into a place not her own. She had doubled two pillows and stacked them against the headboard, leaving a vacant space to the left where his pillow should have been. A satiny blue nightgown, one he'd never seen before, was draped across the top of the sheet. A paperback was opened on the nightstand next to a ceramic mug.

"What do you do all day?"

Again a shrug. "I've been shopping a little. I'm reading a lot. Oh, and I've started power walking…" she halted against his sharp silence. "I still need time, Len."

"A month? A year?"

With jerky motions she poured the hot water into two cups, dripping some onto the table and floor. She dunked the tea bag several times, then busied herself with sopping up the spill.

"Jesus Christ, Teri, you haven't even called the kids."

Her face drained of color. "I know you'll call me if something is wrong."

"Wrong?" his laugh tasted of bile. "Oh, nothing's wrong—other than Jimmy being completely miserable and Carly never around. And I'm fantastic."

"Len, let's not do this." She waved her hand as he opened his mouth. "See why we have to be apart? We make it worse for each other."

"This isn't just about us. Our family needs to stay together, to get past this accident."

Her retort was immediate. "You seem to want to snap your fingers and put it all behind us. Is this what you tell your clients?"

He modulated his tone and spoke slowly, the way he might to a child with a hearing impairment. "I do not expect you to *snap out of it.*" He could hear the sarcasm in his voice and he checked himself. Teri resented sarcasm. Dishonest anger, she called it. "But I do think we have to go on. Somehow."

She cradled both hands around the cup, blew against the heat, sipped. With exaggerated care, she placed the cup back on the table while staring out over his shoulder.

A low moaning could be heard through the wall, then rhythmic banging, slow at first and growing faster and louder. The guttural animal sounds of intimacy could not have been more ill-timed. Len grew prickly with embarrassment as he shifted his chair further away from this woman with whom he'd shared a bed for over two decades.

"Len?" She waited until his eyes met her own. "Do you remember the night Carly was born?"

"Of course."

"I panicked; afraid you'd never need me again, since you had her. I didn't realize there was more than enough neediness in every family to go around. I thought maybe you ... parceled it out ... to those you loved."

He sat completely still, having no idea what would come next.

"Obviously, I was wrong to have been scared. Of course you still need me. Only now—" she twisted her wedding band, "now I don't want you to. It exhausts me."

"Poor, poor Teri."

She flinched at his harsh tone. "We promised if it ever quit working for us we'd let each other go." How unlikely the promise had seemed ten years ago when many of their friends were divorcing and starting new lives. Teri continued, "You want me to be someone I'm not. I don't know if I ever was her. And since Elise—" Her hands flailed in the air. "Let me go. Please. It will be easier for everyone."

Her voice was so quiet he almost missed the despair, hearing only his own hurt and rejection. But something, years of love, years of professional listening—his ear caught her hushed appeal. *Don't let me do this*, she seemed to be saying. He squared his shoulders. "No."

She covered her face with her hands and began to cry—quietly at first, then with loud hiccupped gulps. He sat still. He knew not to touch her. After several minutes she looked up. Her face was puffy and peppered with red blotches.

"For better and for worse," he said.

She smiled wryly. "This worse?"

He walked over to the window. Scarce buds were beginning to break through on the trees. It had been an intermittently frosty, early spring and the plants seemed unready to acknowledge March. Len begrudged them their ability to stay cocooned, temporary as it was. He had a sudden image of himself standing in front of a roomful of applauding peers accepting the St. Louis Therapist of the Year Award. Was that only a year ago? How could he have had the temerity to take hold of the plaque as though he knew the answers to family issues?

He turned to Teri. "I get that you need space. You've always needed space." He paused. This was the moment they might have once quipped about growing up with Selia, how Teri and her dad used to build little invisible walls around themselves to block out the noise. But her face was pinched tight and he sensed what he said now might direct the future. He clenched his fingers, digging them into his palms, stalling. After several moments, he once again met her eyes, saw in their darkness his wife. "Teri, I don't want you to be anyone else. Not before the accident and not now. I know you've been restless for a while, even before … all of this. But you'll figure it out, what comes next. Except we have to do this *together*."

She was quiet so long he wasn't sure if she would answer. The noise in the next room mercifully had stopped, though it made the silence between them all the more apparent. She rose from the chair, crossed the room and stood over the bed, resting both hands on the mattress with her back to him. "I need to tell you something," she said, barely above a whisper.

As if by instinct, his whole body tensed from knowing he did not want to hear whatever she was about to say.

"Years ago when your mom was dying and you were gone so much, well, I used to call Elise to babysit." She lowered her head, continued, "Sometimes I left the kids alone in the house to go pick her up, figuring it was less than ten minutes each way. They were too young to be alone, but Len, remember how it was? I had to get Jimmy into the car seat, and Carly always needed her favorite doll … By the time I got them ready, I could get Elise and be back. She lived so close."

He clasped his hands together, willing himself to show no emotion, not dismay, not judgment. Not until she finished.

"I never went anywhere special. I just needed time alone, maybe to shop or walk around somewhere." She grimaced as if in physical pain. "I'd wait until I knew the kids would be asleep and then come home and leave them alone again to drive Elise back."

He waited for more. When it became clear she was done, confession uttered, he asked, "Is there anything else you've never admitted?"

Something flittered across her eyes, but was gone as quickly as it appeared. She shook her head no.

"Teri, what do you expect me to say?"

"Nothing. *Please* say nothing. I just needed to finally tell you. So you understand that …"

"That?"

"That I was so goddamned stupid and selfish—and lucky. Lucky nothing bad happened. I mean, well, you knew we used her a few times. But it was more times than I ever told you about. And, Len— oh this is so awful—I continued to call her even when I realized she was using drugs. I'd pick her up and could smell pot, and who knows what else on her in the car, and I just ignored it. When I think about it, now ..."

A surge of emotion exploded in his head. *She left our young children alone! She used Elise—Elise!—as a babysitter multiple times without telling me, not at that time and not since.* The temptation to lash out at Teri was so palpable he could nearly taste it. But as she continued to stand hunched over, miserable and wracked with remorse, he recognized that this accident was much more complicated than he might ever understand. *It was Elise Horowitz, their babysitter, who died. Their drug-using, rehab-needing babysitter who the kids didn't even like. Who Teri snuck over. Who Teri killed.*

He should run! Yank open that hotel door and tear ass out of there, away from all the fucking sorrow. But when he looked at Teri, this woman he loved, the impulse dissolved as quickly as it had come. With a barely contained sigh, he wrapped Teri into a hug, his arms tight against her rigid body, saying nothing. He had no words that could be both honest and soothing.

Finally, she pulled away. "Thank you." She clasped her fingers into a steeple, reminding Len of when his clients needed to draw upon inner strength. "And, Len, I will come home. To you. To our children. Only," she held out her hand as if to halt anything he might say or do, "not quite yet."

15

CARLY

"CARLY, LET ME SEE IT AGAIN. That is just so major."

"Shh. I still don't want anyone to know." Carly yanked her jeans leg down, taking care to keep the material away from the skin.

Becca peered at her own bare ankles. "And your mom didn't even punish you? You're so lucky."

At Carly's grimace, Becca put a hand on her shoulder. Carly pulled back, banging her head against her locker. Everyone was always touching her lately, even Becca. She hated it. Best friend or not, Carly wished she would keep her hands to herself. Jason too. It was so gross the way he kept rubbing her tits wherever they went—in the car, in the school hall, every date. It would be nice if she could ask her mom about it, only that was impossible since her mom hadn't bothered to come home for five days.

"You going out with Jason tonight?"

"I guess so."

"What are you guys doing? Or should I say where you doing it?" Becca winked, then licked her lips.

Carly forced a laugh and winked back. Everyone assumed she and Jason were screwing. She let them think what they wanted. "Shit, here comes Melanie. I can't deal with her today. Sorry, I'm outta here."

Becca grabbed Carly's arm. "My mom said you could stay with us while your mom is, uh, gone."

Carly felt her face flush. She used to be able to talk with Becca about anything. But here was Becca, with this perfect family, and Carly with her mom a total mess. It was bad enough when she was in the newspaper apologizing for killing that girl. And after that, every time Becca or someone came over, her mom was sitting in her pajamas or dirty sweats in the middle of the day. Now her mom had run away from home like some half-ass teenager. *She* was supposed to be the one pulling that shit, not her mom.

"Naw. My dad's with me. And I've gotta help with Jimmy." She walked away as fast as she could, her head down, watching her feet move. It's what her dad said to do; just keep putting one foot in front of the other. Stupid cliché, which actually seemed to help.

"Whoa, watch out." She banged hard into the burly chest of an Old Navy sweatshirt just as she felt a hand creep under her sweater and grope her left boob.

"Hey," she sprang back and looked up. "Jason, we're at school. Jesus."

He leered. "Sorry, baby. You're too sexy. Is that bad?"

"But not here."

"Well, guess what? My brother Brad is going out of town this Saturday and we can have his place. Can you tell your dad you're spending the night at Becca's?"

She scrunched her eyes shut, trying to hide the alarm she felt, and nestled against his chest. His body warmth and the fresh smell of onions and burgers were reassuringly familiar. "Okay. I can do that."

"Gee, don't sound so excited."

She stood on tiptoes, kissed the rough underside of his chin. "I'm psyched," and when he didn't look convinced she pressed closer, added, "I can't wait."

~✦~

HOW MANY STUPID MOVIES had she seen with this exact scene? Here she was, lying with the sheet drawn up to her chin, sticky gunk all over her stomach, her butt on a bloody wet spot, a knot closing her throat, and Jason snoring next to her. She'd never before hated anyone as much as she hated Jason right then. Not even her mother.

Carly shivered under the sheet. She reached around for her underpants until she found the lacy silk. What a waste. He hadn't even noticed.

In the dark, she stumbled across the room to the bathroom, where she dampened a towel and started scrubbing her stomach. The more she rubbed the stickier it felt. A trickle of blood had dried on the inside of her left thigh. She left it there.

She made her way in the dark, unfamiliar hall to the kitchen and opened the refrigerator, suddenly hungry. Inside were a can of tomato juice, some limp celery, and a bottle of Merlot. What an asshole; even she knew you didn't chill red wine. She shut the door and crept across the kitchen to the wall phone. She punched in the numbers in the dark.

"Hellooo?" Becca's voice was slurred and thick.

Carly whispered, "Bec? Did I wake you?"

"What's wrong?"

"Shit, I did wake you. Go back to sleep. I'll call you tomorrow."

She could hear Becca sitting up, instantly alert, that priceless radar of a best friend.

"I'm up. Spill the beans, Berger."

"No beans."

"Bull. What time is it anyway?"

Carly leaned close to the small clock on the stove range. "Uh, four-forty. Oh, man, I'm sorry. I thought it was later. Or earlier. I've been up all night."

"What's doin'? If you're gonna wake me, at least tell me."

Carly glanced down at her ankle, at her "lucky charm." She put the phone against her mouth, her lips sliding over the bumpy holes. "We did it."

"Did what?"

"*It*, Einstein. Screwed."

"Screwed!"

"Yeah, and it was horrible. I hate him. You think I can leave?"

"Wait, wait, Carly. Back up. I thought you guys had been at it for months. You told me."

Carly could hear the hurt in Becca's voice. She sighed. She'd known this was coming. "Well, I don't know. I—I guess I didn't really want to talk about it."

"With me? Not with *me*? I thought we tell each other *everything*."

Carly ran her fingers across the tattoo. She liked to touch it, feel the rough scaliness of the healing skin.

"Listen, I'm sorry. There's just so much going on. Jason's been pressuring me, and I was afraid you'd tell me to do it and I didn't want to. I don't know. It's not like I lied to you. I just didn't really tell you the truth." And she still wasn't telling the whole truth—that she'd assured her mom she would wait until she was at least in college, but what was the point anymore?

The silence grew, and she knew Becca was fighting conflicting emotions. Carly struggled for patience, then answered Becca's unasked question: "No one else knows." She could almost see Becca's shoulders relax—her territory sacred.

"So what happened?"

"It was horrible."

"Yeah, well, it always is the first time. Remember me and Jeff? Totally gross."

The line of dried blood along her thigh looked like a fresh scar. "I just thought it would be different because Jason and I are in love."

Becca snorted in Carly's ear.

"Hey, you can't laugh or I won't tell you." She wrapped her arms around her bent legs, the phone cradled against her shoulder, the stiff mouthpiece shoved against her chin. She could feel where a new underground pimple was forming. "I got here and he was high."

"Where?"

"His brother Brad's. He's gone for the weekend and said Jason could use his apartment. Oh, yeah, if my dad calls, I'm supposedly spending the night at your house."

"Okay. Now get to the story."

"Anyway, I've told you how Jason gets when he's high. If we mess around, he's done pretty fast and it's no big deal. Literally."

Becca laughed. "Oops, sorry."

"Anyway, I didn't want to like give him a blow job. I just wanted to do it and get it over with. But Jason kept shoving his thing in my face. So finally I put him in my mouth, only—" Carly began to laugh, a giggle which grew until she was laughing so hard she put the phone down on the table. She could hear Becca calling her.

"Carly, get back on."

She picked up the phone.

"Go on."

"Only I hadn't thought we'd do that. And, and … Becca, you have to swear you'll never tell anyone. Even if we quit being friends or if I die tomorrow or anything."

"Carly."

"Swear."

"Okay. I swear. Come on, what happened?"

"Well, uh, I had gum in my mouth. And it kind of turned into little pieces of gum, you know what I mean? And the pieces got stuck on his dick and in his hairs."

"No way."

"Way."

"What'd he do?"

Carly unfolded her legs. The kitchen floor was cold under her heels. "He was so out of it I don't think he even knew. But he pulled out and this, like, string of gum kind of stuck from my chin to his dick. I swear I'm never chewing gum again."

"This is hilarious!"

"Sure, you think it's funny. I think it's like permanently on my chin." She touched her face. Her whole body was becoming gluey. She felt spasms of the giggles coming on, first quietly, and then she was laughing so hard drops of pee wet her new silk panties. "Stop, I'll wet my pants."

Becca laughed even louder. "You can't lose your virginity and pee in your pants on the same night."

Like a blanket falling across a light, Carly immediately sobered. "Yeah. You're right."

Becca quieted and in a low voice said, "Hey, I'm only kidding. I don't care." But the mood was gone.

They were silent for several moments. "Carly, you okay?"

She took several deep, full-body breaths. She'd read in Cosmo about it, how it chased away those butterflies which seemed stuck in her chest. "Anyway, we did it. He lasted about one second or less."

"Uh, I hate to ask but you did use something, didn't you?"

"Duh. I made him pull out."

"*That's* what you used? Are you a total idiot? Why didn't he wear a rubber?"

"Well, I had one but Cheese stole it from me, long story, and Jason forgot to bring any. I almost made him go to Walgreens, but I decided it's cool. I just ended my period."

Carly waited for a *Cosmo* quote; instead, Becca quipped, "You better keep your fingers crossed."

She lifted her head. The kitchen was growing lighter. The sun was beginning to dawn. "Thanks for waking up for me."

She could picture Becca's expression; her face twisted sideways, kind of sad in the way people looked at Carly since her mom's accident. "I gotta go. Remember, if my dad calls, I'm in the shower or something."

"I love you." Becca's voice was husky.

Carly's own throat began to close. "You too."

She reached and hung up the receiver then studied the kitchen for the first time: dishes in the sink, no pictures anywhere, a pile of dirty clothes on top of a small washer/dryer unit. The linoleum floor was filthy with scattered crumbs and large muddy shoe prints. Jason was so proud of his brother's "bachelor pad." Forevermore, this would be the image she'd have to carry for the first morning of the first day of the rest of her no-longer-a-virgin life.

16

JIMMY

THE WATER WAS MURKY and there were clumps of green algae growing along the sides. Where were the bottom dwellers? Oh, there was one sucking a rock. Where was the other? Jimmy stood to the side of his aquarium but the water was too cloudy to see the fish. He lifted the lid and a whiff of warm, stinky air filled his nose. The water level was a couple of inches too low. He needed to fill it except he'd have to go into the kitchen to get a big pot and he'd see Carly.

He dipped his hand into the tank and swirled. Two zebras swam over and through his fingers, their yellow and black stripes nearly glowing as their velvety fins tickled his knuckles. No one among his family and friends thought fish were real pets, but Jimmy talked to them all the time and he knew they cared. His fingers brushed against something slimy, the silken body of the other bottom dweller. He yanked out his hand and flicked the drops of water across the room. "Gross!"

"Jimmy, get your butt down here. I need help," Carly shouted from downstairs.

"Hold on," he yelled back. He could hear her banging pots and slamming drawers. Well, big surprise, she was pissed about something.

He got the net and swished it until he caught the dead fish. As he walked to the bathroom to give it a proper burial, he looked closely at the bloated body. A familiar wave of sadness washed over him. Sometimes, paying attention to algae, PH, water level, and the balance of fish populations seemed so pointless. They just died anyway. All the time. He'd go weeks without a death then three would die at once.

"See ya, buddy," he said, dropping the fish into the toilet and flushing. He watched the little black-dotted body swirl around several times and disappear. Back in his room, he noticed that he'd sloshed water all over his Hebrew workbook. Hebrew school, something else to worry about. All his Jewish friends were in Hebrew school every Sunday morning to have a Bar Mitzvah in two years, but nobody else seemed to struggle as much as he did with learning the weird alphabet. Carly said the strange letters and backwards reading would click at some point but he wasn't sure. "Well, this sure is problematic," he said aloud. *Problematic* was on this week's vocab list and he was supposed to use each of the ten new words in conversation every day. According to his teacher, the vocabulary exercises were preparing the fifth graders for middle school. Alan's older brother said middle school was a waste of time except to prepare you for high school, which only had the purpose of preparing you for college, which prepared you to be an adult. But now, his mom said you're never prepared for what life hands you. "That's problematic too," he laughed. Nine words to go.

"Hey, Curdled Cheese, get down here now!"

He shoved the workbook under the bed to dry and warp. "What's curdled mean?" he asked as he stomped down the stairs. Carly hated when he stomped.

"God, you walk like a hippo. Have you got cement in your shoes? Why don't you go for a swim?"

"Like you should talk, Elephant Legs." He marched into the kitchen, clomping so hard it hurt the bottoms of his feet.

She turned her back to him and began stirring something on the stove.

"Tell me what curdled is or I'm not gonna help." He would get extra credit if he brought in a new word and shared how he used it in a sentence.

"It's cheese that's spoiled. Like you." She stirred so vigorously red sauce splashed out of the pot and all over her sweater. He watched in horror as her new pink sweater, a birthday present from Jason, became smeared and spotted with bright red like a summer rash.

"Oh, damn it." She tore the sweater off and began rubbing it under water. The spots quickly spread and turned pinkish orange. "It's ruined! And it's your fault."

Jimmy stared. Her boobs were falling out of her tank top like those women on HBO.

She glared at him. "Don't be such a pervert. Get me a shirt, will you?"

He didn't move, but he did turn his head. Who wanted to look anyway? He stared at his shoes for a moment then was startled as she suddenly dropped to the floor and began to cry, holding the dripping sweater against her face.

"Carly? You okay? You're acting weirder than usual. And that's really bad."

"Chee-ese," her growl made the sound of a grinding disposal.

"Geez, Car. Okay." He was extra careful not to make any noise as he went up the stairs, avoiding the center of the third step, the creaker. He pulled a denim shirt out of her closet and tip-toed back down.

She was leaning against the refrigerator looking paler than the white door. He sat across from her and stretched out his legs. She smiled as she took the shirt. "Thanks."

"You on drugs?" He meant it to be silly only as he said it he grew worried. Maybe she was.

"Don't be a dork."

They sat on the floor without talking for a long time, like five minutes or maybe just one or two, while he waited for her to do or say something. She was still holding the wet sweater and now her pants had big splotches all over them, which didn't seem to bug her. Finally, she wadded up the sweater and aimed across the room. The sweater landed smack in the middle of the sink.

"Nice shot."

They high fived and she smiled. "Hey, sorry I yelled at you. I've just got a lot on my mind. And Jason's going to go crazy when he hears about this. I think he spent like an entire paycheck on my present."

Her switch to calm seemed—what was that word—oh yeah, eerie. BINGO! Another vocab word. He waited to see which Carly appeared next. His dad said she was just going through hormonal changes and it would happen to him, only differently since he was a boy. His dad would wink at him, a guy-thing wink, whenever Carly went totally bizzerko.

"Jason won't be mad. He's so cool. I bet he'll buy you another one."

"Hrump." She was standing and stirring the sauce again, this time with slow, robotic movements.

Jimmy reached into the largest box on the floor for dinner plates. The cardboard side was beginning to tear along the seam, but when Jimmy told his Dad to tape the box, he'd just given a really angry scowl and walked out of the room.

"Get four plates, Cheese. Dad called from work. He said he's going to try to convince Mom to come home today."

"Mom? Today?"

"Hello? Is there an echo in the room? Anyways, I bet she won't show up. I wonder if she'll ever bother to come back."

He sank into the kitchen chair, feeling like his breath had disappeared. Their mom had been gone almost a week and he could barely remember how she looked when standing in this kitchen. "Maybe she will. Should we go out to eat? Like to celebrate?"

"Well, that's a dumb idea." But Carly's voice was soft and he could hear it crack the way it did when she was scared, yet trying to act big sister brave.

"Is she okay?"

Carly walked over to the sink and looked out the window. The slant of the sunlight made her face striped. "Dad said when he saw her she seemed a little *troubled*. But supposedly, she really misses you and me. Or at least it's what Dad says." Tears were trickling down her face and she didn't seem to notice. Suddenly he wanted to cry too.

Slowly, Carly reached out and placed her hand on his, the way his mom sometimes did. He bit his lower lip as hard as he could stand, and she didn't say anything about him fixing to bawl his eyes out, didn't swat his head or call him a baby-freak. She kept squeezing his hand so tight it hurt.

"Cheese, are you scared?" she asked.

He started to answer no, but suddenly realized he was. "Of what?"

"Of her. Of us, our family. I mean what's gonna go wrong next?"

He began swinging his legs, hitting his heels against the underside of the chair. Then he remembered how much Carly hated that and stopped mid-air. He flexed his calf muscles and decided to count how long he could hold them up.

"Yo, you freakin' out on me?" Her tone was teasing. He plopped his feet to the floor.

"Just trying for a mind escape. Or that's what Dr. Dad would say."

"Dr. Dad. I like that. I wonder what Dr. Dad does have to say. I mean, really."

They grew silent. What *was* his dad thinking? Did he still love her? What kind of mom leaves her family? Mrs. Rubin never would.

"It all seems a million years ago, doesn't it?" Carly's voice was far way.

"What?"

"When Mom just acted like … Mom."

"Yeah." He'd already forgotten that mom.

Absently, Carly picked at a loose thread on her shirt. "I used to hate it. The way she was so boring."

"Guess we can't say that anymore."

"Hah!" she laughed, a sound somewhere between a donkey's bray and a hiccup. "Sometimes I hate her. Do you?"

He pictured how soft his mom's cheek was when it brushed against his own and how cool her fingertips felt when she pushed back his hair. His lungs seemed to squish together with missing her. "Naw. Not really."

Carly stared at him with such seriousness he was afraid of what she would say next, when she whispered, "Do you remember *her*?" When he didn't answer, she spoke the name no one ever said but they all constantly thought: "Elise."

Before he could stop the words, they slipped out, "I didn't like her." He clasped his hands to cover his mouth. His whole body went cold. It was wrong to say bad things about people who were dead. He wanted to swallow the words back but didn't know how.

"Well, I kind of hated her."

A memory popped into his head. "Remember the night she made popcorn and taught us to play Old Maid?"

Carly tilted her head, thinking. "Oh yeah. I forgot about that." Her face brightened. "It *was* fun. And you were losing each hand, but she let you win."

"So?"

"I just mean it was really nice of her. She taught me how to play War one time and she always let me stay up late without tattling to Mom or Dad." She shrugged a little, as if confessing a secret. "Sorry she never let you do that."

He'd thought Elise hated him. She would usually ignore him, pretending to do homework but mostly staring off into space, frowning without seeming to be aware of it. Was she really sad or was he too annoying? Before he could decide whether or not to ask Carly, she began counting out silverware, setting three sets on the table, and holding the fourth in a tight fist.

"Cheese, we better get ready. Even if Mom doesn't come home tonight we need to start trying, like Dad says, '*to act normally*.'"

"Oh, so you'll be mean and horrible?"

She spun around and with lightning speed grabbed the kitchen towel hanging over the chair and whipped it across the air, snapping against his upturned palms.

"Ouch. I was just kidding."

"And I was just practicing at acting normally."

17

TERI

WITH A FEELING that seemed suspiciously like excitement, Teri stepped outside. She had downloaded new music on her iPod in the hotel's computer center, and wore her new shoes and the peach outfit the saleswoman assured her would "breathe." To the tunes of Annie Lennox's plaintive refrain "*Why*?" Teri began to swing her arms the way she'd seen power walkers do.

She headed in the direction of a neighborhood behind the hotel. It was an older area of ramshackle houses on small lots, not unlike the street where Teri had been raised. She looked up at the vivid blue, cloudless sky sensing, as she sometimes did, the presence of her dad. She didn't believe in an afterlife, yet on a day like today, when the air was soft and the flowers budding, it seemed he must be sharing her space, just as he seemed to be at her side in her darkest moments. How else to explain that in the first hour after the accident he had draped his arm around her, offering the strength she would need in this new life. "I'm here, Teri," he'd whispered into her ear, the way he had when she was a girl, and he would come home late every night from January to mid-April. He'd sit on her bed, smelling of cigar smoke and musty papers. She hated tax season, hated the way clients robbed her of her daddy, leaving her alone with a simmering Selia, who harped on Charles the moment he walked in, telling him where to set his briefcase, how to remove his shoes. Charles would shrug off Selia's needling, shake his head free of numbers, and engulf "his girls" into his arms.

Teri halted her step, stabbed by a sharp pain in her side. She stretched out her arms one at a time and bent at the waist to work out the knot. As she palpitated, she felt the familiar ache of loneliness and regret that accompanied most thoughts of her parents.

How many memories she had of standing back with her dad, and watching as her mother swept into and out of people's lives, telling neighbors when to mow their lawns, commenting on how their home-baked cookies had too many nuts or too few chips, and offering "suggestions" about the minutia of their lives. "Doll," Selia would drawl into the phone, affecting a fake southern accent as though she were not St. Louis born and raised. "I've got the most marvelous yard man. Don't need one? Hmm … have you noticed how tall your hedges have gotten? Well, sure, but doll, yesterday I stood next to them and they reached my neck. I'm short? Ha! You're just too funny. Hold for a sec, I'll get his number. In fact, why don't I call him for you?"

Her mother had been beautiful, with pretty features and smooth creamy skin that never lined until it leatherized in the Florida sun. Had Selia aged during these months of estrangement? It was odd. Teri could clearly picture her father–stuck forever in the early droop of middle age—but Selia was vapor.

A car honked and startled Teri out of her reverie. The car whizzed by, full of teenage boys. She waved, causing them to shout out catcalls. Teri sucked in her stomach and tightened her butt, a bemused smile remaining on her lips long after their tail lights disappeared.

She entered a newer neighborhood where million-dollar homes sat on lots once occupied by three houses. A black, wrought iron fence ran the length of a manicured back lawn behind which an in-ground pool sparkled in the spring sun. Teri thought suddenly of her kitchen, the holes, the boxes. No! This was her time. She'd deal with the rest later.

Her eyes lingered on the pool. She and Len, newly engaged, had been driving home from a movie one summer night and on impulse had parked their car, climbed a fence, shed their clothes, and skinny dipped in a stranger's pool. They'd stepped into the water quietly, one slow limb at a time, then swum with languorous strokes, playing their bodies off each other until finally Teri had entered the circle and wrapped her legs around Len's torso. With their skin warm in the cold water and Len inside her, she'd paddled them both to the shallow steps, as his pumping created gentle waves. The danger, the liquid chill, the goose bumps on her damp breasts in the summer air … It was a night, that even years later, they whispered about, bringing new heat to their bed. Teri felt a sudden hunger, like the aftertaste of something strong, hot, and spicy. How long had it been, anyway? How long since she'd lost herself in Len's touch?

Her steps slowed and she looked down and groaned. A dead possum lay in the middle of the road, its fur strewn in clumps, bared yellow teeth, spilled guts. A circle of flies buzzed around the carcass. Instinctively, she averted her head, walked several steps back, and stared. In spite of herself she had briefly glanced at Elise, noted a mouth locked in an O, wavy blonde hair soaked red, an inked snake on her broken neck.

Teri started to run, felt the out-of-shape heaviness of her body and slowed back to a walk. She hadn't even asked Carly where she'd gone for her tattoo. Somewhere clean and safe? There was that terrible story about the group of high school seniors who all got tattoos during their Cancun spring break and came home HIV positive.

She snapped her teeth in frustration, stomped the sidewalk, and closed her eyes, face upward so the warmth of sun created bursting black spots under her lids. Teri stumbled to a grassy hill and sank down. Len was so angry when he called this afternoon, and she'd pleaded for more time. Why did they have to keep having the same tiresome conversation over and over? He'd hung up on her. She'd called right back, but it went straight to voicemail.

She pressed her knees to her chest, suddenly overcome by the weight of loneliness. "Oh, Mom," she whispered. "I think I need you." For a moment, she felt her mother's presence, felt the relief of cleaving into Selia's take-charge energy, of letting go and holding on. Felt herself collapse into older arms and complex memory.

Charles Meyer had been working on a particularly thorny accounting issue when he experienced a thundering herd in his chest. He tried to reach across the desk to hit the office intercom button but his hand lurched away. He had two distinctive, final thoughts: Teri! He wouldn't see her grow into adulthood. And Selia! She would be furious with him for leaving her a widow.

Or at least that's how Teri always imagined her father's last moments. No one could know for sure. What they did know was at three-fifteen on Tuesday, September twenty-first, Marge entered her boss' office to take dictation. She found Charles slumped over his pile of papers, hand stiffly twisted inches away from the phone, his face the color of ash.

Teri was studying for her graduate entrance exams when her mother phoned with the news. Her first thought, with the GRE less than a week away, was she didn't have time for this. She also had tickets to a Fleetwood Mac concert the next night, which she'd now have to miss. With her third thought, reality hit.

She didn't realize until more than a year later that she was just going through the motions and clamping shut all emotion. She cried at the funeral and at the gravestone unveiling eleven months later. The rest of the time Teri trudged through the hours of the months believing she was fine because what choice did she have. She entered the master's English program at Washington University, started dating Len, fell in love and finally began to thaw. At night, Len would hold her so tight her ribs ached as she maneuvered through the minefields of mourning. Once she started to cry she felt as though she'd never stop. Without thinking it through, and shrouded by the malaise of grief, she dropped out of grad school and got a job at Borders to pay the bills while Len pursued his doctorate in psychology.

Eventually, she realized that adjusting to her father's death did not mean filling in the gap but learning to live with it. Teri walked down the wedding aisle alone; no one could take her dad's place.

When Carly was born, Teri followed Jewish tradition and gave her the Hebrew name of Chaya, feminine for her father's Hebrew name, Chaim. Six years later, Jimmy emerged from Teri's body wearing his grandfather's face. With a bittersweet stab, Teri had looked upon the oversized ears, thick eyebrows and aqua eyes and realized for all their resemblance, this baby was someone new. Her father was *not* coming back. She would never stop missing him since she would never see him again. But life went on.

Selia's mourning process forged a different path. There were times when Selia seemed to swoon with grief. At the funeral, both Selia and Teri were given the traditional piece of black cloth to wear for the seven days of *shiva*, the torn garment, which symbolized the rip in their own lives. The seven days came and went and Selia continued to wear her cloth. Daily she would discuss her horrific loss with shop clerks, waiters, and neighbors. It wasn't that Selia was only about drama. Teri knew her parents had truly loved one another in a strange, mismatched way, and that her mother genuinely grieved. But they had been so different—Charles quiet, passive, unassuming, and Selia a windstorm that sucked out all the air in any room she occupied.

During the early months after Charles died, Selia re-focused all her attention on Teri. By now Teri had her own apartment in the Central West End and it wasn't unusual for her to come home from class and find Selia watching TV and waiting for their dinner to finish baking in the oven. Teri wanted to feel close to her mother, but the relationship was too suffocating for them to maintain any sustained connection.

The year Teri and Len married Selia put her house on the market, the home where Teri grew up, in the poorest neighborhood of the wealthy Ladue school district—a purchase of "brilliant foresight" about which Selia had routinely bragged. Sure enough, the house sold for the asking price within three hours. She raised a ridiculous amount of money during her estate sale by *shmoozing* with all the visitors, swapping stories and winks as she convinced them to buy the junk she no longer wanted. Within two months of making the decision to leave, Selia moved to Florida where being widowed was a state pastime. As a well-kept, attractive woman in her late fifties, living among widows decades older, Selia became the hot commodity of the Boca Raton dating scene. Over the years, she attached herself to a number of lonely men but she never loved anyone but "her Charles" again. She did, however, develop a close and lasting friendship with a woman in her building, Harriet, and together they frequented all the early-bird specials, which Teri would hear about two hours later during her own dinner time.

Four times a year, every year, Selia flew back to St. Louis: for the Jewish High Holidays, for Passover, her birthday, and Mother's Day. She would move in for a week, and for one week, Teri and Len would hold their breath, roll their eyes and count the hours until the visit was over. Selia had an "I only say this out of love" comment for everything—the way Teri cooked, the drapes she hung, the clothes she wore, and the way Len folded the newspaper. Little Carly was the prettiest, most gifted child ever. Yet, Teri could see that even Carly was just another person for Selia to try to control while in St. Louis, and another photo to flash in Florida.

Then Jimmy was born, with his startling resemblance to Charles. Without invitation or permission, Selia's visits lengthened from one week to two. She found delight in everything the baby did, for once seeming to enjoy another person as someone truly separate. Jimmy was not merely Selia's grandson, Jimmy was Jimmy. On his fourth birthday, she handed Teri a gold pocket watch, which had been given to Charles by his own father. "Put this away somewhere for Jimmy when he's older." Charles had prized that watch, wearing it on special occasions, fingering it lovingly whenever he took it out. Teri had asked for the watch when Charles died. It was the only thing belonging to her father she really wanted. Selia had said no. She was keeping it for herself. After all, it was *her* husband who had died.

Perhaps what transpired was inevitable? It was during one of Selia's birthday visits. Teri and Len were taking Selia to one of her favorite restaurants, known for its authentic Italian food, but located a half-hour away in a crime-ridden area of north St. Louis city. They had seven-thirty reservations. At seven-fifteen Len called, apologetic, a client emergency. Could they drive themselves and he'd meet them there as soon as possible? Selia was furious. It wasn't safe. It wasn't right. Where were his priorities? It was her birthday. Teri shrugged, which seemed to incense Selia more.

Carly had gone out with friends for the evening, but in front of Jimmy, in front of the babysitter—of all people, of all times, the sitter she rarely used, Elise Horowitz—Selia shouted, "Open your eyes. Do you really think all those late nights are about clients? Have I raised a daughter as gullible as that? Your husband is probably having an affair with some desperate client. Or with what's-her-face, Marilyn, his partner."

"Mom, how *dare* you say those things? It's not true."

Jimmy's eyes had popped open. Elise stared from mother to daughter, amused and smirking.

"Well, dear, you can believe what you want. As always I'm just trying to help you."

"No, Mother! *As always* you're only trying to *help* by controlling everything and everyone."

Selia had spun on her heel and walked out, turning her head briefly at the doorway. "I'll plan to eat alone. And you can plan to eat your words."

Len was furious when he heard. Teri, for the first time in their marriage, wondered at the true source of his fury. She resented her mother for planting a seed of suspicion where none had existed before. What *were* all those late nights about?

They waited up, and when Selia returned, Len immediately confronted her. Where did she get off, talking about him that way? She knew nothing about him and from now on he intended to keep it that way. Selia had stood frozen in all-knowing smugness until Len was so infuriated Teri had to move between her husband and her mother because she feared one might swing at the other.

The next day Selia left early in the morning and didn't return until dinnertime. Something prompted Teri to check. Sure enough, the gold watch was gone. "Where is it, Mom?"

"It's with someone who will appreciate it."

"Someone?" Teri sputtered. "Who?"

"Henry."

"Our old yard man?"

Selia jutted out her chin. "Yes, the yard man. I knew he would enjoy having something special from your father. After all, he took care of our lawn for over fifteen years."

Teri had sunk into the nearest chair. "But what about Jimmy?"

With no sense of irony, Selia retorted, "Sometimes children suffer needlessly because of the actions of their parents. Oh, and changing the subject, dear. Something about the babysitter from last night doesn't seem quite right. I'm not sure she should be trusted with my grandkids."

That night after Len threw Selia out of their home, after the taxi had come and taken away her mother, Teri lay in bed numbly staring at the ceiling. Self-centered, yes, full of self-importance, always, but she'd never known her mother to be cruel.

More than a year had passed. Without a conversation, without a letter, without a visit. Teri and Selia had matched stubbornness. The kids had grown into adolescence. Len had never given Teri reason to distrust him. And the sitter about whom Selia had offered her final advice had been killed by Teri.

Teri opened her eyes and scratched where the grass tickled her ankle. She needed a nap.

As she walked slowly back toward the hotel, she glanced across the outer road to the highway. So many cars zooming by, inside each one a driver lost in thought, talking on the phone, brushing off crumbs, selecting new music, reaching for a tissue, eating a sandwich, sipping coffee, putting on makeup, knotting a tie, feeling under the seat ... every single one of them with minds elsewhere.

She pushed through the hotel revolving door, waited impatiently for the elevator, and finally reached her room. She tried Len once more but the phone immediately went to voicemail. As she slid the window aside, she remembered her father's oft repeated and favorite proverb: *When a door closes, a window opens.* She inhaled. The air smelled thick and damp. A storm was coming.

18

CARLY

"GRANDMA?" She looked like her grandmother—sort of. This woman had bright carrot-orange hair, which swathed her scalp in tight ringlets of curls, as garish as a clown's wig. Her face was caked with powder and foundation, ending in an abrupt orange line just below her chin. She was considerably thinner than how Carly remembered, but instead of appearing slim and fit, she resembled a shrunken, shriveled walnut.

"Ech. That sounds so old, and look at you. You're nearly an adult. Time to call me Selia, dear." She stepped into the doorway and motioned behind her. "Can you give me a hand or two?"

Carly peered over her shoulder at the mismatched luggage lined from the porch to the sidewalk. "Wow. You staying forever?"

Selia threw her head back and laughed. Her curls didn't even sway. "Long enough."

Carly started to brush past Selia, but her grandmother gripped her forearm. "Actually, let me see you first." Selia turned Carly a few inches at a time until she'd completed a full circle. She ran her hands along Carly's arms and down her spine, nodded once, an affirmation. "You've gotten prettier. That's good. Now be a doll and grab a couple of those bags, will you?"

Carly bent to retrieve the two medium-sized suitcases, preparing to groan, and instead flung them into the air. They felt empty. She gripped both handles with her left hand then picked up the largest case, also nearly weightless, in her right hand. She turned sideways, banging into the doorframe as she struggled to enter.

"Oh, dear, let me get that." Selia held the door open, blocking the entrance with her body.

"Grand, uh, Selia, you've got to move."

"Of course." She stepped back and allowed the screen to slam against the protruding corner of the largest case.

Carly banged through the door, one clunk at a time, twisting and turning until she and the three cases stood in the foyer. She was panting from the effort.

"Let's just leave the others for now, yes? They'll be safe out there?" Selia smiled wide and Carly immediately recognized her grandmother underneath the horrible hair, layers of makeup, and Florida-browned body. Selia's front teeth were oversized, wide, and long like the wax teeth kids shoved into their mouths on Halloween. Even years before, when Selia had been an attractive, fuller-figured woman, her teeth had seemed to belong to someone twice her size. According to her mother, Selia was proud of her smile.

"I almost didn't recognize you for a minute. Your hair. It's so … orange."

Selia patted her scalp, beaming with obvious pleasure. "I just hate gray. Don't you?" She ran her fingers through Carly's fine, straight hair, also reddish, but no closer in shade to Selia's than a pumpkin to a rosa plum. "I could color yours too."

As Carly gasped, Selia belted out a laugh. "Oh, my dear girl. I have missed you. It's been too long, yes?" When Carly didn't respond, Selia glanced around the room and cooly asked, "Is Mom home?"

"Uh, not right now."

"Oooh," Selia's lips curved down, but Carly couldn't tell if it was a smirk or a grimace. "Where is she?"

"Dad will be home soon."

"Yes, well … Leonard."

Carly felt her spine stiffen. "And Cheese should be here in about twenty minutes. He's at a friend's house."

"Cheese?"

"Jimmy's friends call him Cheese. You know, Berger."

Selia grinned, "And you're Ham?"

"I'm just Carly."

"Carly Jane." Selia's eyes softened. "Carly, named for my beloved Charles." Her voice caught. "And Jane, my mother's name, may she rest in peace."

"Yeah, Mom's told me."

Selia caressed Carly's cheek. "Great-grandma Jane wasn't as pretty as you. Not that a girl today needs to be pretty anymore. Smart, yes. And maybe a little sensitive. Of course, your mom's too sensitive. That's why everything hurts her so much. Don't you agree, Carly Jane?"

Carly could feel her face flush. Unsure how to respond, she stepped away from the wall and moved past her grandmother toward the stairs. "Should I take these up to the spare room?"

"That would be wonderful, dear, though, aren't they too heavy for you to carry upstairs?"

"Actually they're pretty light," Carly said. "Are they empty?"

Selia laughed loudly, again throwing her head back. "I don't like to over pack a bag. Everything gets too wrinkled. So I never put more than four or five items in a suitcase. Give it some thought. You'll see it's smart."

"Don't you have to pay for each suitcase?"

"Sure, honey, but it's important to always be prepared. Now be a dear and take my things to my room."

Carly put the two smaller cases in front of her body, dragged the larger one behind, and thumped up the stairs, one awkward step after another. She stopped in front of the guest room and kicked the door open with her foot. The place was a mess, the pillow flung to the floor and blankets half off the bed. No one had been in here since her mom left home. Carly dumped the cases in the doorway and scrambled to straighten before her grandma noticed.

"Hmm ... Who's been sleeping in *my* bed, asked Mama Bear?" Selia was eyeing the room with the laser-like intensity she'd been giving Carly since she entered the house. Carly could feel the same itch along the back of her neck and into her hair her dad said he got whenever talking to Selia.

"I'll change the sheets for you. Sometimes, uh, when Mom's here, if she can't sleep, sometimes she comes in here for a while. Or goes on the couch."

"Well, your mom never did do well with death."

"Who does?" Carly squeaked.

"Hey, sugar girl, from our very first gasp for air we all begin to die. It's a fact, whether you accept it or not." Selia flung the largest suitcase onto the bed next to Carly. Inside were a beige blouse and a red one, a half-slip, a brightly flowered skirt and one pair of white pumps.

Carly felt a giggle starting somewhere deep in her throat.

"Go ahead and laugh. I don't know what's so funny, but I don't mind if you think it is." Selia's voice had none of the hurt Carly would have expected, none of the pain her mom's voice would have had. The urge to giggle abruptly halted.

Selia opened the next case. It too, was barely filled. A neon pink terry cloth jacket and matching pants, several brightly colored shirts, size extra-small petite, and a tape recorder and unopened six-pack of cassette tapes. Before Carly could comment, Selia said, "I record books for the blind. One must always do what one can to help others. Don't ever forget that."

She wasn't sure if she was supposed to agree or ask a question or offer a compliment, but Selia clearly was expecting some response so Carly asked, "You want me to get your other stuff?"

Selia smiled, her oversized teeth stretching her lips to a straight line. "You are precious, aren't you? Always were. Or am I confusing you with Bacon?"

"Bacon?"

"Your brother. What's his silly name now?"

"Oh, you mean Cheese." Carly looked at her grandmother, who already seemed to take up so much space. "Uh, I'll go get those cases now." She started to walk out then turned. "And, no, it wasn't Cheese who's the great kid. It's me."

She could hear Selia's appreciative laugh all the way down the stairs.

19

TERI

"MOM?" TERI FLUNG OPEN THE DOOR. "Oh, it's you."

"Sorry to disappoint you. Think I could come in anyway?"

Teri stepped aside to allow her husband and a suitcase to pass through. She watched as he took in the sight of the hotel room. She'd bought herself fresh flowers yesterday and had rearranged the small table and chair for a better view of the blossoming trees. She squared her shoulders, prepared to defend herself.

Len scowled, his face creasing into folds. Still clasping the suitcase, he crossed the room, sniffed the flowers, then opened the closet door.

"I'm feeling better, Len."

He studied the new outfits, fingering the sleeves, reading the price tags, pushing each one slowly aside.

"The kids are okay, aren't they?"

He shut the closet door and set the case down by her feet. "What made you think I was Selia?"

"You promise not to laugh?"

"I don't imagine there is much I'm going to find funny right now," he said.

"I know it sounds insane. The past two days I've been thinking non-stop about my mom. Crazy, I've actually wanted her to be in town." She watched for the ironic grin but Len's face stayed stony.

He pulled back the drapes and glanced out. Several days before, he'd leaned into this same window for long, tense, silent moments. This time he spoke immediately. "Well, guess what? Your wish is true. Selia's back."

Teri gasped. "Seriously? Have you seen her?"

"Carly has."

She started to reach for Len, feeling the need to put her hand on his body somewhere, a shoulder, a cheek, but his face was so hostile, his eyes cold and remote, she stopped in her tracks, let a moan escape, and slumped onto the bed. "Is she staying with us? Uh, with you guys?"

"Teri, get this straight. There's no 'you guys' in this scenario. There's us or there's nothing. I will not let that woman stay in our house if you don't bother coming home."

He motioned to the suitcase. "It's your decision. I'm going for a cup of coffee. I'll be back in a half hour."

The moment the door shut, she sank against the pillow. A spring breeze whistled through the screen. The scent of fresh flowers wafted across the room. Teri closed her eyes, trying to savor this last bit of peace. She inhaled several times then stood and began to pack.

JIMMY'S HUG WAS SO TIGHT it took away her breath.

Gently, she pried his arms off her body. "You're hurting me, sweetheart." He looked stricken. She tousled his hair and forced a smile. "I'm glad to see you too."

Carly was leaning into the corner, eyes shifting in wary glances toward her and quickly away.

"Carly?"

With exaggerated reluctance, Carly heaved her body from the wall and shuffled over to Teri. They hugged stiffly, but as Carly was pulling away, Teri grasped her. For a moment, Carly relented, allowed her body to mold to her mother's, and then moved back. Teri had read once that until children reach a certain age, they are willing to forgive their parents anything. What was that age? How much was anything?

"Is Grandma here?" Teri tried to sound nonchalant.

"She went to the grocery. She said she'll make us dinner." Jimmy's voice trembled as he spoke. He looked taller, thinner, paler. Carly's face was a little fuller than before. The den was more crowded than Teri remembered. She understood how a bird must feel when, after being allowed to fly freely, it is stuffed back into its cage.

Three expectant faces seemed to be waiting for an explanation. The suitcase was heavy in her hand. Teri offered the best she could: "I'll go unpack."

❧

THROUGHOUT THEIR MARRIAGE, Teri had consciously struggled not to mimic her parents' relationship. Theirs would be a true partnership with mutual compromise and consideration, and equal say in decisions. Teri would admit when wrong and she expected the same of Len. As a mother, Teri had struggled even more to eschew the patterns learned in childhood. She allowed Carly and Jimmy to make their own mistakes without trying to fix their small stumbles. She didn't launch an interrogation when they brought home new friends. She gave her children privacy, space, and freedom.

But as she sat frozen on her bed with the sounds of her mother's and her daughter's voices traveling up the stairs and into her room, she found herself paralyzed with fear about how she would mother—or be a wife—from now on. No guiding principle seemed to fit. "How can you, of all people, be so selfish?" Len had hurled into the phone during her initial call home from the hotel. The insult had hung in the air, filling her with a sense of shame and exquisite discomfort.

With an ache that seemed to burn inside her chest, she yearned for the anonymous peace of the white-walled hotel room, which asked nothing of her. But "there's us or there's nothing," Len had warned. Sighing, she glanced in the mirror, pinched her cheeks, bit her lips, and finger-styled her hair. May as well get the first awkward moments over. She navigated the stairs as slowly and as quietly as possible, hoping to catch sight of Selia first. She should have known better. Dishtowel in one hand, dripping pan in the other, Selia blocked the kitchen doorway so Teri was forced to make the initial move.

"Hello, Mom," she said with feigned calm as she offered a self-conscious, brief hug.

Selia continued to stand in the doorway, unabashedly examining Teri from head to foot. "You look better than I expected, except what happened to your hair? Did you cut it yourself?"

Teri's lips stretched into a mock smile. "You're wearing yours differently too."

"Your daughter almost didn't recognize me. But it has been so long you really couldn't blame—"

"Mother. Stop. Not yet."

They stared at one another for several moments, neither blinking first.

"Mom? Everything okay?" Carly stood behind Selia, both their expressions startlingly similar: heads slightly cocked, eyes questioning, mouths pursed in expectation.

She might as well have thrown her arms up in defeat. That fast, Selia was back.

"Yeah, everything is great. Your grandma is here."

Selia bared her teeth in pleasure. "Well, girls, we better get going on dinner."

Later, lying in her own bed for the first time in over a week, Teri listened to the sounds of family, Carly on the phone, and Selia reading aloud with Jimmy. Len's fingers sought her own and she lightly gripped his in return until his thumb and index finger wrapped around her wrist. Instantly, she was there: those fifteen minutes in handcuffs, the echo of the siren in her ear, the sticky blood at her feet. Teri shivered at the memory and slid her hand free. As subtly as possible, she scooted to the far edge of the bed as Rex Martin's words echoed in her head: *In simplest terms, this was a car accident.* No! A bent fender, *that* was a car accident. This was the taking of a life. It could never be pounded out or painted over. Elise was gone. Forever. And, yes, she had come home to *us*, but it was *she* who was the murderer.

20

TERI

SELIA STOOD NOT SIX INCHES AWAY in the small dressing room as Teri struggled to try on the gray, wool-blend suit jacket without jabbing an elbow into her mother's side. "Uh, Mom, think you could step back?"

Instead, Selia leaned closer, inspecting the material first with her eyes then rubbing the lapel between her thumb and forefinger. "It's a nice quality. Now turn around and let me see how it sits on your shoulders."

Feeling ten again, Teri moved as far away as the cubbyhole allowed, and turned slowly while Selia appraised her from shoulder to knee.

"I still don't see any reason to buy a suit for me. I'll never wear it."

Selia pulled a carrot-orange curl up and away from her forehead, watching in the mirror with satisfaction when it immediately sprang back into place. She turned that same smile to Teri as she ran her hands over the outline of her daughter's arms, hips, and rear. "It's a good fit. But you're too skinny."

"Hardly. And you didn't answer me."

"Every woman in today's society needs a serious suit. Surely you realize that."

Selia's voice carried a conviction that was undeserved—how could she possibly know when she had never held a job? Still, it was easier to nod yes than to engage. Teri had forgotten how exhausting her mother could be. And to think, just days before she'd yearned for Selia to knock on her quiet hotel door.

"I wasn't trying to compliment you, by the way," Selia said. "You've gotten too thin."

As Teri appraised herself in the full-length mirror, she saw what she'd closed her eyes to these past several months. Her face was hollowed, with protruding cheekbones, and her eyes and teeth had become disproportionately large, telling signs of stress-induced weight loss. Loose skin sagged from her upper arms and even her hands had grown bony.

She turned her back to the mirror as she dressed. Then, having lost the battle to pay for it herself, she stood childlike behind her mother while the cashier rang up Selia's charge card for the two-hundred-sixty-dollar suit. Teri managed to mumble her thanks, recognizing both of them believed they had done the other a favor.

"Hold your handbag closer to your body," Selia whispered as they exited the Dillards Galleria door. Teri swallowed back her annoyance and hugged the purse to her ribcage. Forty-four years old and evidently she still didn't know how to hold her purse.

"This is so much fun," Selia said, settling into the car and pushing her seat back to be even with Teri. "Where to now?"

Teri couldn't quite imagine going anywhere else, but she knew Selia well enough to know their "girls' day outing" was barely beginning.

"We could get your hair cut in a decent style. It looks like you chopped it off."

"Only if you dye yours back to a natural color," Teri quipped, reaching out to pat Selia's ring of stiff curls.

"Okay, let's go kitchen shopping. Think how satisfying it will be to unpack those dishes together, and use your space more efficiently." Selia's smile was wide toothed, challenging Teri to either mildly disagree or actually argue, depending on whether she preferred to lose quickly or after a prolonged discussion.

In the past, Teri would have taken the bait or conceded. This time she did neither. "I can't look for kitchen stuff. That's what I was doing … that day. I, uh, I just can't. Please don't pressure me."

Selia's eyes welled with tears, an immediate and genuine reaction, which seemed to startle them both. Teri rested her head on her mom's shoulder, and left it there for several comforting moments, before sitting up straight and putting the car into drive.

"Any other suggestions?" Teri asked.

"Well, if you're up to it, I'd like to go see Charles."

They drove without speaking, feigning interest in an NPR story on Wally Lamb's newest collection of essays written by women prisoners. Teri found her mind drifting as the interview droned on until she realized the theme of the story, and snapped back to attention. She clicked off the radio and they rode the rest of the way in silence.

Surprisingly, Teri remembered the exact spot. After meandering the cemetery's narrow road they pulled against the grass and shut off the engine. Selia stared out the window, sighed, and opened the door. Teri waited for a couple of minutes, giving Selia time alone before joining her at the gravesite. Again, Teri felt the urge to nestle her head against her mother. Instead, she leaned close and clasped her hand.

"You're standing on my grave, you know."

Teri instantly jumped away, horrified to realize what her mother said was true and that Selia was standing on that very same ground herself. She stepped back a few more feet then, and with effort, looked directly at the tombstone. The surreal slab of granite read the full English and Hebrew name of her father, his birth date, the day he died, the fact that at one time he'd been perceived as a "Beloved Husband, Father and Son." But not yet a grandfather. She stared at the grassy mound trying to channel her dad's spirit, feeling nothing except a yearning to feel something. Of some consolation, the other half of the tombstone was blank. At the time of Charles' death, without discussion, Selia had agreed to the funeral home's offer of a special discount if she would add her own name and date of birth when they were engraving Charles' half. Upon finding out, Teri begged her mom not to go through with it. "I can't bear to see your name too," she'd said, and without an argument Selia had uncharacteristically acquiesced.

"I guess I'll miss him forever," Selia said.

Teri nodded; she would too. She walked several steps away searching the ground until she had retrieved a handful of small, round stones. She offered some to Selia and together they placed the stones alongside the curved top of the headstone, a Jewish tradition, like so many that Teri observed without having a true understanding of why.

Across an acre of varying tombstones, two groundskeepers were filling in a new gravesite. Their music was just loud enough to break the heavy silence of death. One of the men caught her eye and quickly turned off his radio. In the whine of the early-spring wind Teri could hear the thud of dirt hitting the coffin and with it, George Horowitz's plaintive, "No. No. No." Abruptly she turned on her heel, calling over her shoulder to Selia, "Take your time, Mom. I'll wait for you in the car."

Minutes later, Selia climbed in the passenger side. She retrieved a tissue from her compact, black, patent-leather purse and blew her nose several times until the tissue crumbled into little balls that dropped to her lap. She brushed them to the floor mat, shrugged in a bit of apology. In a voice of clearly forced cheer, Selia said, "Okay, now you pick where to next."

"As long as we're this close I probably need to stop in at the nursing home. They have a paycheck waiting for me—from December."

"They should have mailed it … you should have told them. Though maybe they're waiting for you to return to work. When are you going back? You loved that job. Unless, of course, you stopped loving it during that year you didn't talk to me."

Teri stared straight ahead, not bothering to respond. Selia's mood shift from supportive and loving to, well, to Selia-like, caught her off guard. Even as she recognized it was her mother's classic self-defense against her brief show of vulnerability, Teri couldn't keep up. Clearly she was out of practice.

She pulled into a vacant spot at the Delmar Gardens. "Hey, Mom, did you ever go see that gerontologist? The name Len got for you?"

Selia visibly stiffened. "I don't know what you're implying or why you would think to say it *here*, but, no, I most certainly did not because I don't need to see that kind of doctor."

She could push; she should push. During the last visit over a year ago, Selia had exhibited signs of particularly illogical thinking that concerned Len. But Selia's mouth had tightened into the grim line Teri knew all too well; nothing productive could come out of a conversation at this time. Instead she asked, "You coming with me?" as if there were any chance Selia would choose to stay in the car.

As they entered the lobby, Teri was hit by an unexpected flood of emotions. In many ways, this had been an ideal job, one in which she brought and received much joy from the seniors. How often she'd laughed with them about the foibles of her children, her husband, her own beginning signs of aging. With the residents, Teri had felt an easy kinship and a willingness to share she rarely experienced with her peers.

Now, however, what stood out was the stench of soiled diapers and persistent illness. She walked toward the business office, face down, hoping not to see anyone she recognized, as Selia headed in the other direction to the public restroom. She stopped in the office and retrieved the one-day December paycheck, and was almost back to the lobby when she heard, "Teri! Is it you?" She felt something inside her melt.

Esther Fishgolde was slumped sideways into her wheelchair, the droop of her left side more pronounced than Teri remembered. But her eyes sparkled with obvious delight as she reached out a hand. Teri grasped the cold, bony fingers between her own and squeezed.

"You bring me a book?"

Teri laughed. *No, hello. No, where the hell have you been?* As Esther had once told Teri: "There's no time to waste, no time for niceties. Best damn part about my age!"

"Uh, no. I'm just here to pick up my paycheck."

"We miss you. When are you coming back? I haven't read a decent book since you were here."

Teri looked closely, and seeing no sign of judgment answered as honestly as the question deserved. "I don't know if I am …I don't know if I can," she added in a soft whisper, putting her lips so close to her old friend's ear she inhaled the smell of unwashed scalp, and found it surprisingly inoffensive. She'd learned from Esther, and others like her, that as long as they had their minds they were still there and the rest was just physiology.

"Not coming back?" Esther's voice carried, and, sure enough, that was the moment Selia re-appeared.

"Of course she is. And, hello, I'm Selia Meyer, Teri's mother. You are—?"

"Esther Fishgolde." She smiled, clacking her dentures together. "Teri's other mother!"

Teri stepped back and watched Selia turn on her charm. She began by complimenting Esther's best feature—a full head of hair more silver than gray—and going from there to discussing Esther's favorite topic—the latest books that would be "ideal for a beach if only I wasn't in this blasted wheelchair in this blasted nursing home with these blasted useless legs of mine." Selia, predictably, threw her head back as if the comment was truly humorous, and Teri stepped away giving them wide berth.

She walked to the end of the hall and poked her head into Esther's room. On top of her bed stand was a pile of library books. Teri felt a clutch of both relief and regret. Despite what Esther had said, someone *had* already taken her place and was supplying the voracious reader with her "reason to keep living." Draped across the back of the corner chair was a navy blue, polka-dotted dress, the one Esther wore whenever her son took her out. The fact that it was still on the hanger did not bode well. Too many times Esther's son had issued empty promises, something which used to fill Teri with vicarious frustration, and during this past year of estrangement, more than a little bit of her own guilt.

Beyond Esther's half of the room, the area was stark, the window-side bed stripped of linens and blankets, the closet door opened to reveal several empty hangers and nothing else. Teri fought a sudden choking sensation, turned and raced out. She grabbed hold of Esther's arm, shoving Selia aside. "What happened to Margaret?" she cried.

Esther seemed to take in Teri's panic at a glance. In a voice both soothing and matter of fact, she stated the obvious. "She died, honey. About a week ago."

"Oh, Essie. Oh, no." Sudden tears filled her eyes, tears she'd held back at her dad's gravesite. She kissed Esther's cheek and without saying goodbye, blindly walked away, hurrying past a line of residents parked in wheelchairs against the hallway wall. She could hear Selia puffing behind her, telling her to slow down, but Teri couldn't catch her breath until she was once again outside inhaling gulps of fresh air. She shuffled, shoulders slumped, to her car and sank into the seat. When Selia started to speak, Teri waved her hand for silence, eyes forward seeing nothing, fighting to control her body's shaking.

Finally, she found the words. "I can't believe she died." Facing Selia, without bothering to wipe away the tears that were streaming down her cheeks, she sobbed, "Everybody keeps dying."

"Esther said the woman was ninety-two. Of course she died."

"I can't do it, Mom. Don't you see? All that death."

She put the car in reverse and slowly backed out, pulling past an ambulance parked in front of the nursing home, lights flashing without sound. For once, Selia respected Teri's privacy, keeping her hands folded in her lap and her legs crossed at the ankle, not even commenting when Teri drove straight home, their girls' day outing at an end.

As she turned off the car and hit the remote control to lower the garage door, Teri spoke. "How come you never had another child besides me?"

Selia's mouth gaped open in surprise. "What kind of question is that?"

"Just wondering. I think I've always wondered."

"You were enough."

Teri locked eyes with her mother, searching for more. "It's irresponsible not to," Teri muttered, barely loud enough to be heard. "Everyone should have more than one. Everyone."

"Where are you going with this, Teri?"

She could taste the bitterness as the words left her mouth. "This way if someone kills your kid, you've got an heir and a *spare*." As she got out of her car, she barely noted Selia's paling face. Without waiting to see if her mother needed assistance, without bothering to bring in her new suit, without grabbing her purse—the same purse she didn't know how to hold correctly—Teri trudged into the house, discarding her shoes and her jacket in the kitchen as she made her way past the boxes of dishes on the floor toward the stairs that would lead to her bed.

21

LEN

THE SMELL OF GARLIC and raw onions assaulted Len as he walked into the packed deli. He looked around the room, scanning the rows of booths. He nodded at a couple of familiar faces, not sure if he knew them from his building or elsewhere, and spotting an empty booth in the back of the deli, he rushed toward it.

"Hey, jerk-off, watch where you're going!" The woman's voice was blistering. Without thinking, Len shoved his weight, sending her off-balance. They looked at each other and simultaneously reeled back.

"Gretchen. I didn't mean to knock you."

"Dr. Berger. Jesus, I'm sorry. It's just so crowded here. I mean, I was kind of rushing and some guy comes barging by, well you, and I thought you were butting in line and I was hurrying, you know, so I could get to my appointment on time—with you." Her face had grown redder as she talked and her voice had the forced sound of air escaping the lips of a balloon.

"No, I'm the one who's sorry." Len swiped his hair off his brow. "Uh, well, I'll see you after lunch." He walked past, feeling how stiffly he held himself while trying to assume a normal gait. He sat at the booth, keeping his back to the front of the deli where Gretchen stood. He ripped a napkin in half as he plied it loose from the overstuffed metal holder, wiped his brow, and wadded it into a soggy clump just as Marilyn slid into the opposite bench seat.

"Man, this place is crowded. They giving lunch away? I practically had to knock half the people down just to walk back here." She slipped her blazer off and laid it on the seat by her side. "What's up? You look like you swallowed a fishbone."

Len leaned close. "Did you happen to notice a woman wearing a bright red jacket—dark hair, early thirties, extremely thin?"

"Maybe." Marilyn peered up.

"She's not one of the ones you knocked aside, is she?" Len asked.

"Should I have?"

He shook his head, winced. "What's a therapist's worst nightmare?"

"Gee, where do I start? Worst? Hmmm. Flicking off another driver only to realize it's your client?"

"Close. How about purposely shoving against someone in a crowded restaurant and then staring smack into the face of a client in the throes of transference?"

Her mouth turned downward with exaggerated empathy. "You didn't break her leg or anything?"

He grunted.

"Well, in that case, she'll be back."

"Knowwhatyouwant?" the waitress shouted above the din, her pencil poised over a hand-sized order book. "LookI'llcomeback."

"Wait!" Marilyn raised her hand. "I'll have—uh—"

"I'llgetthenexttable—"

"Corned beef on rye, with sauerkraut and mayo. Light on the mayo." Len scrambled to get the words out before the waitress abandoned their table for other customers.

"Same for me. Only make the mayo heavy."

"Youwantpickles?" At both their nods, the waitress grunted and hurried off, leaving Marilyn and Len to exchange a bemused smile.

They sat in comfortable silence, observing the shifting crowd of people. He studied his partner's defined profile as she people-watched, and wondered, as he had on many occasions, why she had never married. Marilyn wasn't pretty, at least not in the conventional sense. Broad shouldered, her hair tightly styled in upswept waves reminiscent of Len's "old maid" aunt, her attire always somber and conservative, navy blue suits with starched white blouses. But all Marilyn had to do was flash a smile or turn the doe-like warmth of her hazel eyes upon someone and she became, if not beautiful, at least unexpectedly attractive.

"Twocornedbeefryesauerkrautmayoonelightoneheavy." Their waitress shoved the plates down and was gone, a waft of sour pickles in her wake.

Marilyn lifted the side of the bread and slid her plate across the table. "Switch with me. Why do they always assume the woman wants the light mayo?" She took a large bite of sandwich. A piece of sauerkraut stuck to the outside of her lip. "So, the woman you knocked over, do I know about her?"

The sauerkraut danced as she talked. Len motioned to her lip, flicking his own in pantomime. She licked her lips all the way around, managing to miss it. With a grin, he grabbed several napkins and repeatedly swatted Marilyn's mouth until they were both laughing and bits of paper were scattered across her plate.

"Uh, Dr. Berger?" Gretchen's cheeks were flaming. "Excuse me. I just wanted to tell you I may be a minute or two late because I need to run over to the post office." She kept glancing from him to Marilyn and back.

He dropped the napkins onto the table. "That's fine."

She stood there, shuffling awkwardly from one foot to the other. "Have you met my partner, Dr. Bunn?"

Gretchen mumbled against her coat collar, "Oh, hi. Well, I'll see you around one." She shuffled away, head bent, shoulders sagging.

Len sighed. It was going to be a very long fifty-minute hour.

GRETCHEN WAS UNUSUALLY FIDGETY and Len found himself rolling and unrolling his shirt sleeves while they sat, he looking at her, she looking at the ceiling. He waited, leaning back into the cushioned chair, feeling impatient but struggling not to show it. After several minutes of silence, she spoke. "You love her, don't you?"

"Who?" he stalled.

"That Dr. Somebody. Man, right? Dr. Man? She kinda looks like a man. She's so big. Too big."

"Gretchen," he paused, checked the note of irritation in his voice, more evenly said, "She's my partner. She's a very skilled therapist."

"But you love her."

He closed his eyes and sat back, thinking how best to respond. Then he leaned forward, knees on his elbows, chin in his palms.

"Why don't we explore why it's important for you to know how I feel about her?"

"Jesus!" Gretchen shot her hands into the air and stomped her foot. "I hate when you give me that bullshit. Why don't we explore why *you* can't answer *my* question. It's *my* dollar." Her nostrils flared and her face had turned crimson, a deeper red shade than she'd been in the deli.

He answered carefully. "You're right. This is your hour. So I'll answer. Dr. Bunn is my business partner and friend. I am married and I love my wife."

"But your wife killed someone."

He couldn't stop the grimace.

"Oh, geez, I'm sorry. I don't know what's wrong with me today." She bowed her head and spoke quietly, her chin against her neck. "I do know what's wrong. I hated seeing you. It made me feel totally nervous and I don't even know why. I mean, at first I was embarrassed because I called you a fuck face ..."

"Jerk-off."

"Oh, yeah. Well, that's not so bad." They both grinned, lessening the tension. "I couldn't decide whether or not to go talk to you and I could barely eat because I kept thinking about it and I was so afraid you'd come by and talk to me. The whole thing is stupid, isn't it?"

He kept his gaze steady, waiting.

"Anyway, I thought, what the hell, how much worse could it be than us practically slugging each other in line? So I walked to the back looking for you and there you were playing facey shmacey with this enormous woman, who wasn't the same woman in all those pictures."

He raised an eyebrow.

Gretchen flushed and in a rush said, "Well, I looked up some articles from, you know, the accident last fall. Is that okay?" She was slumping further and further against the chair. He watched, waiting to see if she'd actually slide right down to the carpeting.

"Your wife is really pretty. And a normal size. Not like that Dr. Man."

"It's Dr. Bunn, not Man."

"Okay, Bunn. Wait, you guys are Berger and Bunn?" She laughed. "Hey, Doc, I'll have a pickle with my Prozac but hold the onions."

He smiled; he'd heard it all before.

"Anyway, it was so weird seeing you. Sometimes I imagine when I go places that I'll run into you and I look all around and when I don't see you, I'm not sure whether to be relieved or disappointed. Is that sick?"

"No, Gretchen. It's not sick. Right now your therapy is an important piece of your life. It's normal to wish to extend it to other places."

She took a deep audible breath, as though to dive underwater, then abruptly shifted topics. "I've been thinking a lot about my dad. Sometimes I think I see him and I go creeping up to someone and it's never him. Wow, is that weird? It's kind of the same as with you. I'm always, like, disappointed and relieved." She cackled. "I mean how Freudian is that?" She resumed talking into her collar. "I dreamed about my dad two nights ago. He was in this yellow car and driving too fast. I kept screaming for him to slow down, but every time we hit a curve he sped up until two wheels were off the ground. Suddenly I was flying out the window, only it turned out I was almost drowning in the Atlantic Ocean. I kept wondering why nobody warned me about how cold the water would be, and then I woke up. I felt buzzed all day and I couldn't stop eating, and I threw up before bed. It had been almost a week since I puked. So see why I felt so shitty when I saw you at that deli? You were having all this fun. I mean, I want you to be happy. But maybe not *that* happy." She smiled and waited until he returned the smile.

That moment of giddiness with Marilyn *had* felt good. When was the last time he and Teri had laughed together?

" … and I thought, ok, I'll do what Dr. Berger suggests and try to take control over my own life. I told my boss I'm quitting. Now he's begging me to stay. But I've got to get out of there. I can't stand the way he stares at my ass. I mean, it feels like the right decision. But it's scary to think about leaving. I hate *him*, but the company is awesome. The thought of looking for a new job totally freaks me out …"

Teri had announced to him last night she'd decided to start hunting for a "real" job, something with young people, full time. No discussion, no soliciting of his opinion. Apparently, she had already quit her library-book delivery job and didn't bother to tell him this either, though she managed to let him know Selia supported her decision. And when he dared to question whether or not this was the right time to take on something new, she'd left without saying goodbye and had walked the neighborhood for over an hour.

"... so I tell my mom I'm going to look for another job and she says, get this, she says, 'Honey, unless he's fucking you, what's the harm in a little peeking?' Can you believe it? Rick, you know, my brother, he was there and I thought he'd go through the roof. He started banging his fist against his other hand and saying he was gonna beat the shit out of my boss. I was crying and said he better not make any more trouble. My mom starts screaming at Rick, I don't even know why. He stormed out without saying anything. And the minute he left, take a wild guess what I did? I went searching through every pocket in the closet and finally found a cigarette in Rick's winter coat. I'm so mad at myself. After three months, one fucking cigarette and I'm hooked again. I bought a pack. Can you tell? When I walked in today, did I smell like smoke?"

You want smell, Gretchen, smell my house. Selia burned cabbage rolls last night. Poor Carly had turned green and rushed off to the bathroom. When she finally came back to the dinner table, she was sweating and pale. Even this morning, the lingering odor made him gag.

Gretchen was still talking. "... well, I thought, what the hell. Everything else is going wrong. And I'd had that dream. So I called my dad. He answered the phone too. Didn't recognize my voice at first. Do you know how awful I felt? But pretty soon I'm telling him all kinds of shit, like he's going to suddenly care about the details of my life."

It had taken less than a week for Selia to return to a brasher-than-ever Selia. Telling Carly how to wear her hair, Jimmy how to eat, Teri how to dress. He shouldn't have been surprised, but there was no humor to his mother-in-law when he couldn't share it with his wife. He'd tried, had even hoped Selia might inadvertently be the conduit back to his marriage. But Teri just shrugged when he complained and whatever opinion she had regarding her mother stayed clamped between tight lips.

"So what do you think about all this?"

What did he think? He wondered why she would think he could help.

"C'mon, you're the doc." Gretchen's voice was a blend of sarcasm and plea. She was perched on the edge of the couch.

He intertwined and squeezed his fingers together, summoning energy from a depleted reserve. "Well, Gretchen, I wonder why you turn your anger at the men in your life into self-destructive behavior. I wonder if you've ever forgiven your father for walking out on you and your mother. Or if you've ever forgiven yourself."

She jerked upward. "Forgiven myself? Me? What did I do wrong? I was four years old. What could I have done? God, I hate this shit. Is it time yet? I've got to go. If I'm late again, I'll lose my job. Hah. That's a laugh. I'll quit but the bastard better not fire me. Is it time?"

"We've got about five more minutes."

Gretchen collapsed against the couch, heaving her coat over her lap. She looked wildly around the room. Her eyes settled on the bookshelves behind him. "You know, I remember the day he walked out. It was raining." A derisive snort. "Figures, huh? Movie material. You know, pitch dark sky, rain, and scared little girl. I kept crying for my dad. He always came to me during storms—not my mom. She thought I was too old to be afraid. Four fucking years old. Anyway, I was shouting for him and then I heard some noises. I ran downstairs. My parents were screaming at each other in the kitchen. My dad picked me up; only I peed on the floor. My mom started yelling at me, but my dad hugged me anyway and got my piss all over his coat. He carried me upstairs and he put me in the bed and said he'd be right back with clean pajamas from the laundry room. Only I kept waiting and waiting and finally I think I fell asleep. When I woke up, my whole bed smelled like piss and I was so upset that I threw up. I shouted for my dad. Finally, after a long time my mom came in. She told me my dad had left and I better go grab clean sheets. I guess I did, though I don't remember. Pretty weird, huh?" Gretchen's face was pinched together and her eyes squeezed shut.

Their time was up, but Len sat quietly, waiting. After more than a minute she blinked, startled, as though coming out of a deep sleep. "It's time?" Her voice was calm.

"Yes."

A soft opening of the door, and she was gone.

He leaned back and raised his head to the ceiling. It was raining the day Elise died. There was static when he called Teri's cell phone to say he'd be home late, had an emergency five o'clock client appointment. They had barely spoken when he heard a crashing sound and Teri's sudden hysterical screaming. "Oh my God. I think she's dead!"

"Who, Teri? What's going on? Where are you?"

She must have dropped the phone. For several heart-stopping minutes, all he heard was a door slamming, Teri crying, and then the piercing wail of sirens. Finally, Teri picked the phone up and in a voice deadened by shock said, "I'm at 270 and Olive. You better get over here."

In a panic, he had hung up, reached for his coat, and scurried out. Hours later, he realized he'd forgotten to cancel his emergency appointment. Ironically, the client had called back and left a message, she didn't need to see him after all. There had been no reason to call Teri.

He opened Gretchen's file and jotted down a few cryptic notes about today's productive session, shaking his head at the lunacy of his field; the more miserable his client was when leaving his office, the more "progress" she was making.

22

SELIA

HIS FISH-BELLY WHITE and hairy stomach protruded from under his sweaty, Create-A-Kitchen uniform shirt. His teeth were nicotine-stained, his eyes rheumy. And his stench was worse than his appearance, sour sweat and soiled clothes. Selia swallowed her shudder and produced the toothiest smile she could. "What can I get you for lunch?"

"Nuttin, ma'am," he grunted.

"Oh, no, that won't do."

"Uh, thanks, but we ain't allowed to eat on the job and anyways I've got something in the truck the Mrs. made for me." He scratched where his naval bulged like a dented can.

Selia patted his sweaty arm. "Well, I guess we just won't tell anybody, will we?" She laid out a full spread: leftover calves liver, reheated corn on the cob dripping with butter, sliced apples, and lemonade. She sat with him while he wolfed down the first plate, asked for seconds, and licked his fingers.

She kept up a steady chatter, telling him about her condo in Florida, her tips for cheating at gin—wink—even a few shared secrets—I know I can trust you. She told him about her dear friend Harriet's deadbeat daughter, LuAnn, and how Harriet was considering pulling her granddaughter, Amy, out of the house at one point a year or two ago. Now Amy was going to college in the fall, having graduated high school early so she could take an out-of-town spring internship. Mostly she just wished Harriet would see a doctor about her labored breathing and take off some weight.

When his eyes started to droop and before he might plop his head onto the plate, she sprang her idea, because, after all, it was just so disconcerting—his eyes crossed at the multi-syllabic word—well, upsetting, to have *only* this beautiful new countertop finally installed thanks to his work. And she so appreciated he'd moved them ahead of the two previous orders. Of course, she promised to make sure no one ever found out. Listen, she'd told him about Harriet's daughter, hadn't she? And the *mishegas*, you know, craziness, with LuAnn was certainly nobody else's business, but how silly for them to wait *two more weeks* for the cabinets when, instead, she didn't mind waiting right here for him if he would zip back to the warehouse and pick up the cabinets today. She'd never tell, not ever.

Just think, Ralph, oh, Reggie, sorry, so just think, Reggie, what a great surprise for Teri to come home from her job interview, she'd already told him about that hadn't she? And almost certainly Teri wouldn't get this job either. Well, what do you expect, a middle-aged woman who hasn't worked but two days a week in well over a decade? Of course, she wouldn't dare tell her daughter, though she would have thought Leonard made enough money so Teri could just volunteer to give her life some purpose, the way Selia herself recorded books for the blind. But that's another story, and what a marvelous surprise for Teri who had had such a difficult year, poor thing, she couldn't shake that whole terrible incident, as if she was the only one to ever have a car accident. And, yes, it was especially awful that she knew the girl, but that's another story. Anyway, as she said, what a great surprise for Teri to arrive home—did she mention the dishwasher man was coming later this afternoon?—and find her cabinets installed, her countertop in place, and the kitchen nearly done. That way, little Jimmy might start having friends over again, and Carly too.

Oh, he would do it? What a wonderful man, so kind, so caring, how fortuitous—uh, lucky—that he was the one sent out for the job. She'll be right here waiting. How long? Oh perfect, just long enough for her to have some cookies ready. She didn't have to? Well, of course she'd make some cookies. Did he have a favorite kind? Ah, same for her, nothing beat a warm Toll House, but he'd better get going so they'd still be warm—wink—and another pat on the arm—shudder—and he was gone.

She sprayed the room with Lysol and opened the windows, though there wasn't much point in trying to clear out the air since he'd be back in an hour or so. But how surprised Teri would be to come home to a nearly finished kitchen. She opened the pantry and retrieved a half-empty bag of Chips Ahoy, placed the cookies on a dinner plate, sprinkled a few drops of water on a paper towel, covered the plate and popped it into the microwave. His truck was noisy enough; she'd surely hear him coming in plenty of time to zap the cookies so they would be soft, chewy and warm. She threw the wrapper in the trash.

She called Harriet's number and when no one answered, tried Amy. Still no answer. It had been a week since they'd last talked and Selia hadn't liked the tight quality to Harriet's voice. If she didn't reach Harriet in the next day she was going to have to call the good-for-nothing LuAnn and see if she'd bothered to check on her own mother.

The room seemed larger without Reggie in it. She felt again that familiar afternoon malaise, when loneliness settled inside her chest and between her eyes. Every widow she knew agreed that three p.m. to seven p.m. were the killer hours. All those years of frenzied cooking, car pools, piles of dishes, and bowing to the needs of others. How she had longed for quiet and peace; how lonely the quiet felt now. She shook her body, flung her arms into the open space. Years ago, Leonard had taught her that, the flinging away of sorrow.

Selia stepped outside on the porch to wait for Reggie. Phew, the man did stink. And he was hardly a challenge; a little liver and fruit, a bit of a chat, and he was a blob of putty in her hand. Selia smiled and was stretching out her fingertips toward the sun, when someone came hurrying forward, swinging her arms, swaying her hips, her gait like a rocketeer shot out of a cannon. Selia never could figure out those "power walkers." Either run or stroll, for God's sake. If they knew how ridiculous they looked, they'd surely stay home and get a treadmill. The woman was tiny anyway, what calories could she possibly need to burn off?

Selia sauntered across the lawn, as though toward the mailbox. Something about the walker looked familiar and just as she slowed to move around Selia, who'd managed to block the sidewalk, the woman halted mid-step. She pulled her earphones off without turning down the music. Strains of wailing men–good lord, the Bee Gees—spilled out. The woman was dressed in all pink, from sweatband to ankle socks. She had on bright pink lipstick and smelled fragrantly of something pinky expensive. Selia felt a visceral dislike, but pasted on her huge-toothed smile, the one that startled adults and had been known to frighten young children.

"Excuse me, but don't I know you?"

"Hi! I'm Stacy Rubin." The woman thrust out a small, dry hand, which Selia chose to ignore. Of course, Stacy. Selia remembered her from previous visits. Even when she and Teri could find nothing agreeable to discuss they always had their mutual dislike of Stacy to fuel a pleasant conversation. The mother of Jimmy's friend, the one who thought herself all the kids' pal. Selia never did trust the motives of a mother pretending to be otherwise. She stretched her lips wider.

"I remember you, Stacy. You don't know who I am?"

Stacy squinted then grimaced in embarrassment. "Oh, sorry. Of course, you're Teri's mother." She hesitated. "You look different."

Selia patted her hair, watching as Stacy's eyes traveled up then abruptly away, the way one might consciously look past a deformity. Selia separated a single curl knowing it would spring immediately back into place. "I do so hate gray. You too, I see."

Stacy flushed, running her fingers through hair that obviously received a more delicate dying process, yet still had the perfect uniformity of color nature never bestowed. Selia winked. "I won't tell."

Stacy forced a grin that closely resembled the grimace of a moment before. "How nice to have you visiting. It's been a *long* while, yes? Teri must be so pleased to *finally* have you here." She yanked her sports bra strap, drawing it out and letting it snap against her concave shoulder. "I know how much Jimmy has missed you. The poor child has been through so much." She matched Selia glare for glare, until, as though suddenly remembering herself, she dropped her eyes demurely.

Selia threw her head back and laughed. She'd be damned. The woman was a dishonor to pink. "Well, go on ahead now. I'm sure we'll be seeing more of you. And I hate to keep you from your exercise program." She glanced pointedly at Stacy's thighs, noting with delight that though tight, they bore the inevitable cottage cheesing of age.

Selia hummed to herself as she hurried up the walkway to zap the cookies before Reggie—or *was* it Ralph?—returned. Those pesky nouns kept eluding her lately. But whatever his name, it sure felt good to be back, to be putting everything in order the way only she could.

23

CARLY

HIS TONGUE TASTED LIKE EARWAX. "Gross," she gagged.

"Gross? My kisses?" He slid as far away as he could, hugging the car door.

"Oh, Jason, don't be mad." When he didn't respond, Carly added, "You kissed my ear and you tasted like my ear. I was just kidding about the gross part." She reached out but he yanked his arm to his side. "Hey, you know I love you."

"Yeah? You sure don't act like it lately."

She noted with shame his downcast eyes. Swallowing a sigh, she leaned across the console and tugged until he finally relented. She licked around the outside of his ear, stuck her tongue into the middle part, then into his mouth. Rather than pull away, he sucked harder on her tongue and started panting. She opened her eyes and when she saw his were closed, rolled hers. Sure enough, he reached up and pawed her boob, squeezing until it hurt. She let him feel both her boobs through her bra until she couldn't take it any longer. "Jason, we've gotta go. Someone's gonna see us." She gently pushed him, taking care this time to let her fingers linger against his arm for a few moments.

He sank back against the passenger seat. "When can we get together? Tonight?"

She hesitated. "I've got a shitload of homework." At his hangdog expression, she added, "Let me get my books at my house then I'll take you home and go to the library. Maybe I can get done early."

He kept his head on her shoulder during the three-mile drive from school to home. As they pulled into the driveway, he surprised her by palming her cheek until she was forced to directly meet his eyes. "I love you. This isn't just about sex." Her eyes watered, but he wouldn't let her look away. "Carly? Is everything okay with us?"

For just a moment, she imagined the freedom in telling him how she really felt. But he was being so sweet, so earnest, she couldn't do it. "Yeah, we're cool," she said, then grabbed and squeezed his hand. "Come in while I get my stuff."

Her grandma and brother were in the den, watching Judge Judy. Selia immediately jumped up. "You must be Carly's boyfriend. And, silly me, I've forgotten, what's your name, dear?"

"Jason, ma'am."

"Ma'am? Oh, please call me Selia." She stood on her tiptoes and traced her finger along his profile. "Hmmm. You're a hunk, aren't you? You're not Jewish?"

Jason sought out Carly, alarm written across his face. "Uh, no. Episcopalian."

Selia smiled, her large teeth stretching her mouth into wrinkles. "Beautiful features, your people."

He shifted from leg to leg then turned to Jimmy. "Yo, Cheese, wanna shoot some baskets while we're waiting? I'm not gonna let you beat me like last time."

After dropping Jason off with the promise to call soon, Carly turned east onto Olive and began to drive aimlessly. She flipped through radio stations, forcing herself not to think and not to feel. As usual, she glanced away from the 270 and Olive overpass where her mom had the accident. She continued past Brad's apartment where she and Jason first screwed, and past the street leading into Becca's neighborhood. She kept driving, staring ahead, stopping for red lights until she was miles from home and no longer able to block out Jason's question.

What *was* wrong with her? It wasn't that she didn't specifically love Jason anymore; lately, she didn't love anyone. Even Becca got on her nerves, the way she kept playing Joe Psychologist, telling Carly it was just all the craziness with her mom's accident, her mom running away, and her grandma coming to live with them. She even showed Carly a *Cosmo* article titled *Can Love Survive Trauma?* as some sort of proof that Carly's moodiness was a normal response. The only thing the stupid article did was make Carly crabbier. In fact, lately, Carly felt totally pissed off all the time, except when she was crying for no reason.

She entered the Loop, a stretch along Delmar Boulevard filled with bars, restaurants, head shops, and used-record stores. It was almost five and Jason had already left two voicemail messages, and Becca one. Carly headed further east and only as she passed the tattoo parlor and continued driving did she allow herself to accept where she was headed and why.

She crossed Skinker, leaving behind the county and entering the St. Louis city limits. Almost immediately, the landscape changed as she turned left and went north, passing boarded-up vacant buildings, and street corners with clusters of dark-skinned men and teens. Briefly, she considered turning around. Instead she drove past several more streets into an unfamiliar area until she found a Walgreens. There she pulled in and parked between two old, rusted cars. A skinny woman carrying a baby in her arms and dragging a toddler, got out of the car next to her.

"Ernest, get your butt moving. Now." The toddler skipped to his mom and grabbed her shirttail. She shrugged him off. "Don't tug on me!" She glanced at Carly, her dark face pinched and tired.

Carly sat in her car for a few minutes, trembling. Finally, she entered the store and, in a daze, wandered up and down the aisles until she came face to face with an entire shelf of test boxes. She forced herself to study the multitude of brands, prices, and instructions. This one gave results in one minute, this one five, this one you peed against a stick, another one into a cup. Prices varied from eleven dollars to twenty-two. She unzipped her jacket, looked down at her swollen chest, and zipped the jacket again.

EPT, EPT Plus, Encore, Assure. Which one would give her a "negative"? She reached for the cheapest one, some generic brand, and stumbled toward the line at the cash register, sweating and feeling faint.

"You okay?" It was that mother again. Up close, Carly could see she was not a *woman* after all but about Carly's own age.

"Ha," glancing at the package in Carly's hand. "You ain't gonna be okay for a long time!" The girl's cackle held a note of angry glee.

Carly started fanning her neck and face.

"Mama, c'mon, let's go." The toddler was yanking his mother's sleeve with both hands. She swung so fast the toddler fell on his backside and started shrieking. The teen mother pulled him up and pushed him toward the door. She looked over her shoulder at Carly, a smile playing her lips into a sneer. "See what you got to look forward to."

"Next."

Carly moved up to the register. She watched her fate being scanned.

"Eleven sixty-eight"

As she struggled to unclasp her wallet, she felt a voice against her ear before she heard it. "Uh oh, looks like someone's been doing more than just getting a tattoo."

Carly recoiled, moving away from the warm breath in her ear and staring straight into the fawn brown eyes of Markieta Banks.

"So what brings you to our part of town? They don't sell those tests where you live?"

She hunched her shoulders, trying to hide the wad of dollar bills and her dad's credit card. She offered a ten and a five-dollar bill and rushed out without waiting for the change.

The key danced against the lock as she opened the door, climbed in, sank into the driver's seat, and closed her eyes. A knock reverberated against her window. Carly lowered it an inch and hissed, "Are you following me?"

"Girl, you're in *my* neighborhood. I live here. What's your excuse?"

Markieta fingered her ear, where Carly did a quick count of seven earrings from top to lobe.

"Hey, I didn't mean to give you shit back there. I've been where you're at. If you need a number or something, call me." Markieta pushed a scrap of paper through the narrow opening.

Carly watched it flutter to her lap. "A number?"

Markieta didn't respond.

"Oh." She shoved the paper into her purse. "Why are you being nice to me?"

"I told you. I've been there." Markieta started to step away and, instead, leaned back into the window. "I know we're not friends, but

I always thought you were more real than most of those other girls."

As she drove back home, Carly's thoughts kept returning to the incredible coincidence of again running into Markieta, a voluntary transfer student who was bussed from an urban city neighborhood to Carly's suburban school. Carly had always sensed Markieta was a loner and until now, they'd never had a reason to connect—disinterest more than dislike. How bizarre that Markieta would offer her friendship. As though they shared some secret bond—as though the test would be positive.

TWO FORTY-NINE. Two fifty. Two fifty-three. Just do it. Piss, find out. Not going to sleep anyway. Maybe, maybe if she closes her eyes and promises not to open them for ten minutes, maybe she'll sleep, wake up, blood on her underpants. She felt an unlocking of hysteria rising in her throat. Please, please, please, please. She'd never be mean to anyone again, not even her mother. She'd never yell at her brother and she'd do her homework the minute school was over and set the table every night without being asked. Please, please, please. Okay. Close your eyes, no peeking for at least ten minutes. Just relax, it will be okay. Everyone knew the surest way to get her period was to waste money on a pregnancy test. Everything was fine. Go to sleep. Don't look. Two fifty-seven. Shit.

Carly sat up and threw her blankets off in an angry huff. She fumbled in the dark and pulled the small rectangular box out from under the mattress. She tiptoed down the hall to the bathroom—a bubble of dread dulling everything to pale gray. It was her body, but somebody else seemed to be opening the box.

All those instructions. Unwrap stick. Wipe carefully. Pee in toilet, stop, now hold stick near body and pee again, soaking the bottom half of stick. Why can't she stop sweating? Her boobs aching and tender as she leans forward. Stop, keep stick upright, don't drop it in the toilet. Place stick on box on sink. Wait. Result might take five minutes. The first window shows immediate line. Throat closes in dread—no—just the test window. Doesn't mean anything, except test is working. Head in hands, cold and sweaty. Finally, open eyes.

A heart.

Look at instructions: Blank window, negative. Heart in window, positive. Bring the stick next to eyes. Peer closer. Oh fuck … Fuck! A heart.

A jangle, a noise, an opening, a brightness of new light. Through the fog of shock, a halo of orange. A scramble to hide the stick as Selia mutters "oops" and closes the bathroom door.

24

TERI

TERI HAD BEEN NERVOUS for days, ever since the call in response to an ad she answered last week. Now, looking around the dimly lit office at the oversized, makeshift desk in an otherwise nearly empty room, she felt a rush of panic. She knew the problem: she wanted this job too much.

"Mrs. Berger? Sorry I'm late. What time is it? Oh, my goodness, I am sorry." A broad-shouldered, big-bellied, balding man with green eyes and full, fleshy lips appeared as though from out of nowhere, and immediately took up the expanse of space behind his desk. He extended his hand. "Bernard Kollen, everyone calls me Bud." As he sank into his chair with a lack of grace, dust spots rose and flew in the stream of sunlight. "Let's see now." He picked up her resume and held it within inches of his eyes, placed it back down and smiled. "I left my glasses at home. You know what, why don't you just tell me about yourself."

"Well, uh, thanks for meeting with me." Teri could hear the squeak of her own voice, though Bud seemed not to notice. He continued to recline against his chair, hands crossed behind his head, elbows jutting east and west. Teri glanced at the framed desk photo of two young boys sitting on either side of a golden retriever, presumably his sons. A small oscillating fan was perched in the corner providing brief bursts of air, and next to the fan was a stack of books on education, and a teetering pile of folders. She didn't know whether to be alarmed or calmed by the program director's casual and stark office.

"I guess you want to know about my background. I don't really have much … background I mean, when you consider—"

"Mrs. Berger," he shifted forward and steepled his pudgy hands as if to pray. "Just tell me why you're here. What are you looking for?"

"You do have an opening, right? I saw the ad, actually I saw it months ago, but I finally called. I mean I was interested then, but I haven't been sure for a while what I'm looking for, except—well, anyway, is there still an opening?"

"Yes, we are looking for an assistant. I asked what are *you* looking for?"

"Oh. Me." Teri could feel sweat pooling under her armpits, no doubt soaking through her silk blouse, which, thankfully, was camouflaged by the new suit jacket. She wrapped her arms across her middle, pulling her skirt down and her jacket closed. Immediately, she realized that made her seem aloof, and, as inconspicuously as possible, she readjusted her clothes and rested her hands against her lap. Throughout her fidgeting Bud remained still, continuing to present a friendly face that invited her to speak. She took a deep breath. "I guess I'm hoping to find a job where I can give something back. My children are older and I want to return to work and do something meaningful."

He leaned forward encouragingly. "Tell me more."

Tell him more. Where should she start? With the decision, made with barely a second thought, to drop out of grad school? With the uninspiring job as a Borders bookseller she gladly gave up when her kids were born? With the inane decisions of *that day* last fall that changed everything?

"I have an undergraduate double degree in English and creative writing from Washington University, and I took some graduate classes there toward a Master's in English." She hesitated, trying to decide how to frame what came next. "For personal reasons I didn't finish. Mostly, I've been a stay-at-home mom. I mean I have been working a little, just two days a week, at a nursing home. I don't do it anymore. And now my kids are both teens. Well, my son is only eleven."

Bud smiled the smile of a parent with small children who doesn't yet realize how quickly it all disappears, all those knee-high adoring hugs. "Tell me more about the nursing home work."

She felt her face flush with embarrassment. "There's not much to say. I went to the library and checked out books for seniors." To Teri, selecting books specific to each resident's taste had carried the intimacy of gifts of jewelry, only better. But that was before. "Now I'm ready to work full time. My resume may not show it; however, I'm extremely dependable." She flashed to Len standing in her hotel room furious she hadn't called Jimmy and Carly. And the disappointment in the Delmar Gardens manager's voice when Teri finally called and stated she would not be back.

Bud was clearly waiting for more. Teri gripped her thighs, leaving damp prints on her skirt. "I believe I'd be a good tutor or mentor, or whatever you call it. I love to read and I want to pass that passion on to kids. And writing, I haven't written in years, but in college I really enjoyed creating stories, and at one point I dreamed of writing a novel. Over the years, I've even tutored a few of my daughter's friends in writing. Oh, and if you want, I could help put together new programs too—" She stopped, horrified to realize she was babbling in a high-pitched voice and was probably stepping way out of line. "I mean," she said more quietly, "if that's what you're wanting? I'm not sure I really know."

"As a matter of fact, it's exactly what we need. Fortunately, we've received more grant money for a full-time opening, so your timing is perfect. But I'm curious. You've been working with senior adults and now you want to switch to teenagers. Why?"

"I don't know. It just … feels right."

His gaze was penetrating. Did he suddenly realize why her face looked so familiar? Had he read the articles? Teri retrieved her purse and began to stand.

"Wait." He raised and lowered his hand. "Mrs. Berger, when I began Mentor Write five years ago, I had a lot more questions than answers. The scale is still tipped by the questions. However, one answer I've grown to trust is my instinct. Assuming everything checks out, I'd like for you to join us."

She tried to keep her response calm and professional, but sensed her eyes betrayed her surprise.

He mistook her reaction. "Look, I know this may seem unusual, my offering the job so quickly. I've always run my organization based on gut feelings. And so far …" he grabbed his rounded middle with both hands, "it seems to be working." His face relaxed when she burst out an appreciative laugh—the recognition of two strangers finding an immediate connection. And when she nodded, as though she were deserving of this job, he clapped his hands together.

"I can't pay much. The hours will be demanding and some of the tasks are a son-of-a-bitch. We go into underserved schools in lousy neighborhoods where the problems are insurmountable. But everyone who works here came with the same qualification—a desire to reach beyond his or her own skin. So, if you want the job, it's yours."

The room seemed suddenly to hum. "Yes," she croaked. Len didn't even know she was on a job interview today. Surely he would understand; he would need to understand. Louder, she repeated, "Yes!"

This time when he held out his hand, Teri grasped it fully with both of her own. "Thank you," she whispered.

"Thank *you*, Mrs. Berger, for coming to us. Though I must further warn you," he gave a wry shrug, "now that you've accepted. I'll need you to work with teenagers who are often prickly and unpleasant. Okay?"

Well, there's one fewer in the world now. Teri tried to cough away the thought. It came out sounding like a gasp for air. Bud was watching her intently, his expression still friendly but curious.

He knew. Teri didn't know what, but enough. Could she trust a man who would willingly hire damaged goods? Then he offered a nearly imperceptible tilt of his chin, which seemed to say, yes you can. She walked out with her head high, quietly singing "Hallelujah."

TERI SET FIVE SPARKLING DINNER PLATES on the table, waving one in a show of appreciation to Selia. She had yet to discover the full details of how her mother had achieved the one-day kitchen installation—dishwasher, countertop, cabinets—but Teri had long ago learned most of Selia's stories were best left untold.

They had barely all sat down when Jimmy blurted, "Mom, it's so cool you got the job." She shot him a quick *shush up* glance, but it was too late.

"Well, dear, you didn't tell me. What kind of job did you get?" Selia held the serving knife mid-air; a clump of meatloaf hung from the blade. No one in the family liked meatloaf except Selia, who had prepared it four times in the past three weeks.

Teri shrugged, wanting to hug her news close and not place it under family scrutiny.

"What job, Teri?" Len echoed.

Stalling, she went over to the refrigerator and began scrounging around for something else to eat. She lifted the lid off an old cottage cheese container, nearly gagged, and walked back to the table empty handed.

Everyone had stopped eating and was staring at her. "I'm going to be an assistant at Mentor Write."

Selia sniffed. "How much does it pay? You know, women are always underpaid." Again the voice of authority from a woman who had never earned a paycheck in her life.

"Mother, that's hardly an appropriate question to ask someone."

"Someone?" Selia peered over the edge of her half-rim glasses. "I would think my daughter is more than just a *someone*."

"The job," Teri continued, turning her body pointedly away from Selia, "will involve going into various underserved schools in the city and doing writing and reading residencies, some schools for a week or so and some one or two days a week for a full semester. I might even get to design new programs."

"Do you know how to do that?" Carly asked.

Teri flushed, remembering Bud's unexpected gut feeling about her. "I'll learn."

"Will you be able to drive me to my soccer games?" Jimmy asked.

"I assume you're only going to work part time? I can't stay here cooking forever you know. I *do* have a life in Florida." Her mother.

"Will you need the car *everyday*?" Carly implored. "You mean I'll never get to borrow it?"

And Len, "What are your hours going to be?"

Teri looked at the faces of those who were supposedly the closest people in her life and saw a table of strangers. The first night she had eaten alone in the Drury Inn's Applebee restaurant, she had felt like that; alone among a room full of people. The second night she brought along a new novel and found a corner table she liked. By the third night, she was making eye contact with familiar faces as she walked past.

"We'll figure it all out. Other mothers work, you know."

Carly flounced her hair over her shoulder. "Where's your office, Mom?"

"Well, it's in kind of a rough area, a few blocks northeast of Delmar and Skinker. But it's right near a Walgreens and a couple of small stores, so there should always be people around."

Carly suddenly blanched.

"Honey, what is it?" Teri reached her fingers across the table, but Carly pushed her hand away. "What's wrong, Carly? I'll be safe. Mr. Kollen says no one has had any problems since he started the program. It'll be okay, I promise."

"I know. I'm not a baby." Carly stood, knocking her chair against the wall, and rushed out of the room.

"Well," Selia huffed. "I wouldn't let a child get away with that."

No one answered. Jimmy was stuffing forks full of ketchup-soaked meatloaf into his mouth.

Len sighed, "Who's Mr. Klellen?"

"Kollen. Not Klellen. Bud Kollen. And he's my *boss*." The word resonated in her ears, the connotation of a separate life. The word seemed to slice through Len.

As Selia reached to clear the table, Teri waved her to stop. "You cooked, I'll do the dishes." Selia stood, plate in hand, her brow wrinkled as if trying to decide whether or not to say something, but before she could, Teri said, "Thanks again for the gray suit, Mom. It brought me good luck."

"Humph," Selia said, clearly pleased. She placed the plate in the sink, pointedly surveyed the finished kitchen with smug satisfaction, offered a backwards wave, and sauntered out.

Instantly, Len and Teri both laughed, the sound filling the room and seeming to turn the lights brighter. She eased back into her chair, feeling her spine relax even as her body was gently humming with something that, amazingly, felt like excitement.

"You're excited," Len said and she nodded. For years, whenever one knew exactly what the other was feeling or about to say, they'd joke about being married too long and it was time for a divorce. She didn't say it now. Still, it was nice—the connection. It had been a long time.

"The kids were kind of rough on you tonight. I'm sorry about that. But they'll adjust."

"Thank you." She stood to clear the table and passed Len. He reached for her hand and she planted a kiss on his head.

Hours later, they were stretched out taut in their now-usual far sides of the bed, back to back, and separated by as much space as the queen size allowed. Teri felt Len's foot, warm and long, tentatively touch the tip of her calf. She started, then relaxed.

"So you're pretty thrilled? About the job?" His voice was a husky whisper. To better hear, Teri scooted her body nearer to his, taking care not to touch him.

"Yeah."

He flopped over, moved closer, and curved to the same spoon shape as she. Teri could feel the heat from his body, though his skin remained inches from her own. His lips brushed against her earlobe. "It feels kind of weird, you going to work full time. I hope this is what you want."

When she didn't respond, he pressed up against her; instinctively, her body pressed back. "I hope so too. I have a good feeling about it." She could hear the bedroom timbre in her own voice.

"Hmmm … speaking of good feelings." Len's whole body was slowly molding to Teri's backside, his legs curved inside her curve, his chest enveloping her back. A cloth-covered hard mound pushed against her. She extended her hand and withdrew him from the opening of his boxers, feeling his body gasp. The touch, for so many years, familiar and routine, was now filled with intimacy and mystery. Gently, she lowered his boxers, rolled down her underwear, and guided him between her legs and into her body. As one, they both inhaled. He slipped her gown over her head, laid a soft palm against her breast. For a moment, neither of them moved. Then he began to slowly slide in and out, whispering against her ear, "Maybe this will take us forward."

"Yes, maybe, yes." Every sensation was heightened, as if woken from a deep sleep.

He reached between her legs, his dancing fingers knowing exactly where to go. "I love you so much, Teri."

Teri's eyes immediately stung. She waited for the now-familiar sense of burden, of an unwanted responsibility, but it didn't come.

She felt her nipple harden and thrust out against his hand. "Oh," she moaned. "Lenny."

"We're gonna make it. We're gonna survive. God, this feels good." Len's breath warmed her neck, her ear. Her body was squeezing itself around him, with vice-like tightening. He was arching his back, *not yet*, she wanted to say, but at that moment, her whole body began to tremble, and her mind left, taking her somewhere else inside this moment of nowhere. Just sensation. Just body.

Then it was over. But wondrously, the usual grayness had lifted. She could feel the smile playing across her lips, as they lay still, moist skin to skin. He stayed inside her, his right arm nestled between her breasts. Within minutes, Teri heard a quiet snore against her ear. Soon his body felt heavy, his arm dug into her ribs, her legs cramped. But she didn't dare move. She had no desire to slip away.

25

CARLY

CARLY OPENED HER LOCKER and gazed at the photos lining the inside door. One of her and Becca wearing matching lime-green shirts and black leggings. A two-inch picture of Jason, which she'd kissed with raspberry-colored, lipsticked lips. A photo she'd taken of her parents and brother last year. Her mom looked pretty and still normal. Her dad and Jimmy seemed so happy. She'd taped the pictures up a couple of weeks ago after her mom told her about Elise's mom's refrigerator.

She caught her breath at the thought. Every once in a while it hit her that Elise was dead. Mostly she dwelled on how the accident had changed everything for her own family. But Elise was *dead*.

She'd still seen Elise occasionally, even after Elise quit babysitting. They went to the same middle and high schools, three years apart and in totally different social circles. The few times Carly spotted Elise she was either alone or hanging outside with a group of other senior girls, similarly dressed in all black, wearing dark make-up and smoking right out in the open. One time Carly waved and Elise, almost shyly, waved back. But the next time Carly waved, Elise mouthed "twerp" and that was it. Two years passed without a sighting then, by coincidence, they'd been at the same party this past Labor Day weekend. Jason's older brother was best friends with Elise's new boyfriend. There had been a lot of drugs, but Carly had settled for a beer. She was sitting in a corner, bored, when Elise stumbled over with a clear drink in one hand and a straggly, nearly emaciated cat in her other arm.

"Well, if it isn't little Carly, acting all grown up. Does your mommy know what kind of parties you go to?"

Carly had not bothered to answer. It was clear from the slurred words and dilated pupils Elise's rehab treatment hadn't done much good. Elise had lurched away into the crowd. It was the last time Carly saw her.

"Are those your parents?"

Carly turned swiftly from the locker and knocked against the body of Markieta Banks.

"Your mom's pretty."

"It's an old picture." Carly slammed her locker shut, and began walking down the hall.

"So?" Markieta was keeping perfect step alongside her.

"So, what?"

"Yes or no?"

Carly searched for signs of smugness; seeing none, she said, "Yes."

"Well, fuck!"

"Yeah, you can say that again."

"Now what?" Markieta's breath smelled like onion rings.

Carly felt a wave of nausea. "I don't know." She stopped in front of Mr. Clark's math class. "I'm here now. Where do you go?"

Markieta looked at her watch. "Science."

"You're gonna be late."

"I know. But I've been wondering how you're doing."

"Why?"

"I told you. I've been there. And I had no one to talk to."

Carly forced out a whisper, "What did you do?"

A line creased Markieta's forehead. "I did what I had to do."

"How will I know what I have to do?" Carly's throat felt like when she'd had strep and couldn't swallow.

"At some point you just do whatever." She tore off the corner of a piece of paper and wrote down a number. "Here. Our phone's been cut off, so you can't call that other number. But if you call my auntie, she'll get me the message."

Carly stood, her mouth thick and dry, and watched Markieta hurry away. She slumped against the wall for a few moments, feeling faint.

Two girls walked by, talking about the upcoming spring dance. Carly wanted to scream. It was not fair. All these girls screwed their boyfriends. How come *she* had to get pregnant?

"Miss Berger, are you planning on joining us?" Mr. Clark was standing in the doorway, his arm raised to close the door. She lowered her head and shuffled in, clutching her books against the pea-sized fetus that was ruining her life.

"OH, THAT'S SO CUTE. Hold it up, Carly." She lifted the tiny yellow sweater, the size of her math book, with penny-sized bunnies dotting the front. It was hard to imagine the baby would have to be at least three months old before it would be big enough to fit into this impossibly small sweater. Carly put her hand on her stomach, felt the baby's foot pressing against her palm. She looked at the table full of packages wrapped in bright pastel papers with rattles and pacifiers hanging from ribbons of yellow, and selected the next gift, a box the size of a pen set. It stood out among the large packages, such big boxes for such a small person. Carefully, she unwrapped the paper. Inside was a bottle the size of a thimble with a label marked "Poison" on it. Was it perfume? She brought it up to her nose and breathed in the pungent fumes of turpentine. Immediately the room began to whirl. Some of the Poison had leaked out and was dripping down her lip. She extended her tongue, caught the droplets, and let them slide to the back of her throat. She could feel a hot scorching as the drops melted pieces of her esophagus, traveling beyond her heart, circling the baby, immediately turning its downy white skin to charcoal. "My baby!" she screamed. "You've killed my baby."

Carly bolted upright. Her heart was pounding in the dark room. Her jaw ached; she must have been grinding her teeth again.

"Carly Jane? You all right?" Selia slid into the darkness.

"I guess I had a nightmare." She lay back, sinking her head into the pillow.

Selia wiped Carly's brow, a gesture immediately reminiscent of her mom. "Tell me about your dream and I'll interpret it for you." Selia's words were soft, caressing the darkness.

"I don't remember. Probably about school."

"Then why," Selia leaned close, her voice low, "did you scream, 'my baby'?"

Carly felt her body go rigid. "I don't think so. I might have said 'my body.' Yeah, now I remember, it was 'my body,' because some kids were shoving me against my locker."

Selia cupped her hand against the small swell of Carly's abdomen. "I know, Carly Jane. I may be a bit older but it doesn't mean I don't recognize a pregnancy test when I see one."

Carly opened her eyes and was startled to see her grandmother's face only an inch beyond her own. Without thinking, she threw her arms around Selia's neck and began to cry. "What am I going to do?"

Selia unlocked Carly's arms. "What do you want to do?"

"Go back in time. Never screw Jason."

"What does Jason say about this?"

Carly hesitated. "He doesn't know."

"He is the father, isn't he?"

"Of course he's the father, Selia! You think I'm some kinda slut?"

Selia threw her head back and laughed, the full-throated laugh Carly remembered from the day her grandmother arrived. With a start, Carly realized she must have already been pregnant.

"He's so dense."

"Honey, you want a man, you better accept dense. Comes with the nuts."

Carly snorted, then clamped her hands against her mouth. "Shh. I don't want Mom to hear us."

"Speaking of your mother—"

"No. You have to promise you won't tell her." At Selia's frown, she continued, "You don't know how it's been around here. Mom will probably run off again."

"Oh, phsaw. All that nonsense happened before I got here." She patted Carly's arm. "Let's focus on what's important." Selia placed her cheek on Carly's stomach and held it there for several moments, as if trying to hear a voice. She kissed Carly through the thin nightshirt and sat up. They stared directly into the eyes of one another. There seemed to be a third presence in the room. Carly felt her heartbeat quicken. It was a *baby*.

She turned her face away and let the tears trickle down her cheeks. Becca's niece had those perfect little toes and those huge green eyes. Jason's eyes were blue.

"So what's your plan?"

"Well, that's pretty obvious, isn't it?" She tried, unsuccessfully, to keep the self-pity out of her voice.

"You weren't thinking of killing it? Oh, Carly, you don't want to do something you might later regret."

"Selia, don't do this to me. It's not killing—exactly. I mean, it's not even a person yet." Carly clenched her jaw. She hated Jason. Spurting jerk! Everything was so easy for guys.

"Is it less a person than you were at this point, or Jimmy, or your mom or dad?"

"But I'm only seventeen. I want to go to college. I want to have fun."

Selia winked. "Seems to me, you've already been having fun."

She rounded her body into a fetal position, wrapping her arms against her knees, trying to squish her middle as tightly as she could. Maybe she could squeeze it to death.

"Shh … let's close our eyes, Sweetheart. I know this is hard. And nothing has to be decided yet." Selia scooted next to Carly and whispered, "I'm here for you, Carly Jane. I'll help you figure something out."

They lay together for a long time, Selia's soft humming the only sound in the pitch-dark room. Slowly, slowly, Carly could feel herself relax as she edged closer to her grandma's knobby warmth, until the humming changed to steady, deep breathing.

Carly unclasped her hands from around her knees, trying to imagine being *really* pregnant. She would have to deal with Jason's reaction, whatever it would be. What if he wanted to break up … or get married? Her parents would be totally freaked. And all her friends. She'd be the talk of the school like that cheerleader last year who had to quit the squad, and afterwards dropped out of high school. And she'd have to take her SAT test in a maternity outfit. If she even went to college.

She sat up, decision made. She stood to go to the bathroom and immediately dropped back to the bed, her legs too shaky to hold her. How creepy would an abortionist be? What if it hurt? What if she bled to death?

Then she was six again, sitting in the den with her grandma, waiting. She was trying to write a letter, one painstaking, misspelled word at a time. "I lv yu grnma." Occasionally Selia would glance distractedly at the paper. Finally, they heard the key in the door and in a burst Carly's entire world changed. She sat rigidly in her chair as Selia bounded across the room and grabbed Jimmy out of her mom's arms. Her grandma's face immediately softened into something Carly couldn't identify. She only experienced the moment as a forgotten first child. Now Carly realized it was the expression of awe and joy from the miracle of a new baby.

She placed both palms against her stomach and kneaded the doughy skin, trying to touch the hard part underneath. *Is it less a person than you were at this point? Or Jimmy?* Carly stumbled to the bookshelves. She grabbed her Oscar the Grouch doll, buried her nose against his musty fur and cried.

26

SELIA

SELIA SQUINTED, trying to see through the glazed front door windows. Piles of papers and shoes were scattered all along the foyer. She was still peering in when the door suddenly opened. Selia stumbled backwards, startled and annoyed. She hadn't even knocked yet.

"Jesus, you look like hell," Selia blurted.

"And who the hell are you? Marilyn Monroe?"

Selia straightened her shoulders. "Actually, I'm not Marilyn Monroe. I am Teri Berger's mother, Selia Meyer."

Rozlynn eyed her for a few moments, saying nothing as Selia stared back. Rozlynn's hair hung limply to her shoulders. Her face was puffy with dark, bruise-like shadows. She was dressed in a soiled, man's t-shirt with a hole at the neckline, and too-tight pajama bottoms that pulled at the hips, revealing a roll of flesh bulging out of the waistband. Selia struggled to mask her alarm.

Rozlynn scratched her armpit, and slowly, deliberately, sniffed her fingers. "Yeah, I coulda figured it was you," she drawled.

"Have we ever met?"

"No, but you look just like her. Or I guess she looks like you."

Selia flushed with pleasure. Most people thought Teri resembled her father. She liked the idea that she'd made her mark on her daughter's face.

"You may as well come in. If you're anything like her, there's no getting around a visit, is there?" Rozlynn stepped inside and the door swung sharply against Selia's knees.

She hurried in and locked the screen door but kept the front door open. The house needed fresh air, that was obvious. She ran a finger across the foyer table, needed a dusting too. Selia retrieved a tissue from her purse and swiped the surface.

"What are you doing?"

She held up the black-tinged tissue. "The table was filthy."

Rozlynn's mouth unhinged. "How *dare* you."

"I would think you'd appreciate my efforts."

The two women glowered at one another, unblinking. Then Rozlynn turned and walked away. Selia felt a momentary rush, followed by disappointment. There was little joy in a triumph so easily achieved. She placed the tissue on the table and followed Rozlynn into the kitchen.

"So, Teri Berger's mother, what brings you to my happy little home?"

"I am up from Florida visiting my daughter. I thought I'd stop by and see how you're doing."

Rozlynn was rustling through her purse, pawing like a puppy in search of a buried bone. Her face twisted into a sneer, her eyes bearing a hint of desperation. "You smoke?"

"No. Thank God. Ball and chain."

"Yeah, well, I've got the chain, but I seem to be out of balls." She continued to dig, pulling out lipstick tubes, a plastic hairbrush, a bulging wallet.

Selia traced her index finger along the greasy kitchen table, even more grimy than the foyer. She rubbed her thumb and finger together, frowned, and reached over the clutter to retrieve a napkin from under a pile of newspapers.

Abruptly, Rozlynn stopped the search, her hands filled with the contents of her purse. "Look, I don't know what you want from me and I don't really give a damn what you think about my housekeeping. I didn't ask for company, not from you, and not from your daughter. Go do your guilt thing on your own."

"Guilt? I have no guilt."

"Maybe you should." Rozlynn flung her fist in the air; a tube of lipstick sailed across the room.

"Did you have control over what your daughter did? Or what happened to her? Of course not. Me neither." Selia paused for effect.

"From the moment my daughter took her first crap she was living her own life. Her accidents belong to her, not to me."

"What are you doing here? I didn't call a cleaning crew, which is about the only thing you've done so far. Or is that it? Do you have Thursdays open?" Rozlynn grabbed a dishtowel hanging from the cabinet handle and tossed it at Selia, before opening the refrigerator and sticking her head inside.

Selia waited, offering no response until Rozlynn faced her, a crusty plate in one hand, the other holding a half-eaten piece of chocolate cake, speared on a fork. She popped a chunk into her mouth and held the plate out in offer.

Selia smiled. "I'm not hungry."

Rozlynn stretched her lips into an exaggerated frown, chocolate crumbs sticking to her lips and front teeth.

"In response to your question, no, I don't have Thursdays open. I'm here to help my daughter, but I'll be going back to Florida in a while. So you'll have to find another crew to clean. And I would recommend you get someone. I'm no neat freak, but this is pretty awful by anyone's standards."

"Anyone's but mine. And since this is my house, I guess it's none of your business, huh?"

Selia could see Rozlynn was having a good time. She knew it as surely as she knew this woman needed a good dose of provoking. Some people just did. Certainly, Teri often did, and even that husband of hers. "Well, actually, I disagree. I think your business is my business."

As Rozlynn's frown deepened, cutting lines in her bloated face, Selia continued, "You know what *mishpocheh* is?"

Rozlynn didn't answer.

"It's the Yiddish word for extended family. The idea is ultimately we're all somehow connected. Like if your brother's wife's sister marries my cousin, you and I become *mishpocheh* and your business becomes my business. That's what's happened here. You lost your daughter because of my daughter. But, lady, I lost my daughter because of your daughter." Selia's heart was pumping faster. "A goddamned accident. And now my daughter is so wracked with guilt she can't see straight. She ran away from home, left her kids, her husband. For what? What did she do wrong? Now she's back and she's

still not back. Her marriage is suffering, her children are suffering."
Selia clasped her fingers together as though trying to squeeze out the
strength to continue.

"You're wanting my sympathy too? What is it with you two?"
Rozlynn walked to the sink, scrubbed her hands for several moments,
then wiped them against her rounded hips. When she sank down,
the chair made a groaning noise.

Selia sought Rozlynn's eyes and recognized the torment of
soul-deep pain. She remembered that look in her own mirror and
the sense that healing was unimaginable. And this was for a *child*.
With resolve, she plunged: "Listen, I do have a reason for being
here. I've got a problem and you've got a problem, and I think we
can help each other." She inhaled deeply for impact and for air. "No
one knows this but—" She looked around the room as though to
check for unwelcome ears then in a low husky voice whispered, "My
granddaughter is pregnant." She waited, expecting Rozlynn to react,
forgetting for a moment this woman didn't even know Carly, much
less give a care if she ruined her teenaged life.

"Yeah?" Rozlynn was losing interest.

Selia leaned forward again, her lips just inches from Rozlynn's
face. "Do you want her baby?"

Rozlynn instantly snapped back, and shrieked, "What?"

Selia nodded several times and folded her arms across her chest.
"It's perfect, isn't it? Carly can have the baby, give her to you, or him,
but I bet it's a girl. You'll have another daughter, my daughter can get
past her guilt, move on, Carly moves on, everyone moves on. It's a
moving on kind of answer."

"Are you insane?"

Selia tried not to look smug. "When I first discovered Carly
was pregnant—she's only seventeen—I thought it was a disaster. I
know that girl. There's no way she's going to give up college or any
of her dreams to raise a baby. And I just can't bear to think about an
abortion. I mean, I'm pro-choice and all, for others. But the thought
of my Carly going through with it … Well, I just can't imagine … But
last night it came to me. It's *bershert*, fate."

Rozlynn continued to stare, her slacken cheeks sagging to her
chin. "You *are* insane."

"I'm not." Selia couldn't keep the pride out of her voice. "I
thought you, of all people, would realize that."

"Me? Of all people? Why would you think you know the first thing about me?"

"Oh I do." Selia's voice dropped several octaves, a voice of empathy and sorrow. "Women like us, who suffer terrible losses, we *know* each other."

Rozlynn turned away, but not before Selia saw her eyes well up. On impulse, she decided to push forward, open a door an inch. "My daughter told me you and your girl had a fight right before she died." She ignored Rozlynn's stiffening. "My husband of blessed memory died with our fight in his ears." She glanced around the room, the piles blurred by an unexpected filming of tears. "I told him I hated him, never wanted to see his ugly face again. I don't recall what we fought about. Something stupid, I'm sure. One of those married moments where you can't imagine living one more hour with the son-of-a-bitch and the next day you can't remember what you were so furious about. I had a vicious temper back then. Matched my hair." At Rozlynn's pointed look, Selia smiled. "I know, it's a little orange—covers the gray. Anyway, the day we fought he stomped out the door. He went to work and I stormed around the house. I got a call two hours later. He'd had a heart attack. They found him slumped at his desk, face down in a mug of coffee."

"I told my daughter she was a bitch."

"I told my husband he was a cunt."

Rozlynn snickered, put her hand across her mouth, and began to laugh outright. In a moment both women were laughing, tears pouring down two sets of cheeks. "Cunt?" Rozlynn snorted. "A man?"

"Yeah, yeah," Selia swiped the tears from her face. "I'm no poet. I admit it." Selia could feel a deep old ache begin to soften at the edges. All these years and she'd never told anybody. "I'm serious about the baby. Sure it's crazy, even I know it. And I'll need to convince my family. But is it crazy? Couldn't this help all of us?"

Rozlynn was quiet for so long Selia almost restated her crusade. She stifled the impulse. She was learning the power of silence from her therapist son-in-law. Rozlynn finally looked up. Her face was twisted into a bitter grimace, but when she spoke, her voice was flat. "So, in other words, you're offering a trade-in? Somebody's baby to take the place of my dead daughter?"

"Well ... " Selia stopped. "I mean, when you put it like that ... " She stopped again, trying to collect her thoughts. Why couldn't the woman see the beauty in the idea? She scanned the room, letting her eyes settle on each of the photos of Elise. "Rozlynn, please understand, I don't mean to be insensitive."

Rozlynn met her eyes. "No, I suppose you don't. But your plan is outrageous, completely inappropriate. And it won't bring back my daughter."

Outside, a siren sounded, followed by a longer, louder one. The persistent shrill seemed to go on and on until cut by a sharp, sudden silence. She turned to Rozlynn. "Tell me something about your daughter, a sweet story."

Rozlynn hesitated to speak for many moments, enough time for Selia to feel uncomfortable, and then in a low almost monotonous tone said, "Elise had a way with animals that was extraordinary. The animal shelter where she volunteered apparently told her she was better at calming abused cats and dogs than any they'd ever seen." Rozlynn shook her head back and forth, as if reaching an epiphany. "I think she saw something in these animals she recognized ... maybe a sense of aloneness. And I don't understand. We loved her, we really did."

Selia reached for Rozlynn's hand, who immediately pulled back. "More than once she brought home some flea-bitten, mangy dog or cat I made her return. Would it have killed us to let her adopt a pet? Would a pet have made a difference? Would she have—"

"Rozlynn!" Selia interrupted. "Stop! Regrets are useless. Which is why, well, I'm just going to say what I need to say. Obviously, this baby won't replace your daughter. Nothing will. But there are all kinds of families nowadays. And I truly believe Carly will never consider keeping the baby at this age. So why not you?" She stood and walked to the refrigerator door, imagining a photo of an infant's face held by a magnet next to a picture of Elise. A sense of loss cut through her—give up their baby? *Was* she thinking crazy? Or what if Teri wanted the baby? No, Teri never would. "Look, I'm fighting for my daughter and for her daughter." She walked back to the table, pulled her chair close. "And for your daughter."

Rozlynn gazed outward, seemingly transported to somewhere Selia couldn't fathom, her expression a strange cross between horror and confusion. It was tempting to keep talking, to fill the empty space with more sound reasoning until the woman was convinced. Instead, she opted for silence, with patience for some minutes then fidgeting impatience. Still, Rozlynn gave no recognition that anyone else was in the room.

"Well," Selia said, reaching for her purse. "I'll stay in touch?"

Rozlynn blinked, turned to Selia and gave a slight dip of her chin. It was enough for Selia. At the entranceway, she picked up the blackened tissue, crumpled it, and stuck it into her purse. She left the door open.

27

TERI

"TODAY WE ARE GOING to start out by sharing your free writes about the most meaningful moment in your life." Teri moved to the center of the room moderating her voice to sound as if she was ready for anything. She had been working for three weeks with eighth graders at Anchor Middle School teaching narrative writing, and she was learning to expect the unexpected. "Who wants to go first?"

Anthony immediately volunteered. An undersized, ostracized boy, Anthony often feigned ignorance to hide what was clearly a nimble mind in a school where it wasn't cool to be smart.

He stood and began to read, his easy fluency giving him away. "The most meaningful time in my life was when my daddy put my brother and me on top of the roof and he made us jump off. We kept crying and saying 'Daddy, no,' but he wouldn't come get us. So we jumped." His smile grew wide, pride shining on his face. "It made me not run away from my fear."

Stunned silence. Then the kids said the things Teri wished she could.

"Man, you jackin' me?"

"Your daddy did *what*?"

"Your daddy crazy."

Teri had to ask, "Was it a one story?"

"Naw. Two story."

"What happened?" Her question was barely heard above the squawks of his classmates.

"Duh, we both got killed. Whadya think?" Anthony pumped a fist into the air. "My daddy caught us."

As he sat down, Cierra raised her hand. Teri tried to mask her surprise. Overweight by at least thirty pounds, Cierra was plagued by acne, which covered not only her face but also her neck and shoulders. She also had spent most of her life in and out of foster care. As a middle schooler, she may as well have had leprosy. Teri had made a special effort to reach out, offering gestures of encouragement that seemed to go unnoticed.

Cierra held the paper directly in front of her face and her voice cracked as she read: "The most important moment in my life was when Mrs. Berger started coming here because she acts like she really cares about me."

"Girl, you are so lame."

"Whadda kiss-up."

Teri mouthed, "I do care," as the bell rang, signaling the end of another day. As the students piled out she reached to pat Cierra's arm, but the girl shuffled ahead of the touch.

When the last of the students left, Teri buried her face in her hands and breathed deeply, fighting off a wave of dismay. Anchor Middle School was located in one of the poorest and most crime-ridden neighborhoods in St. Louis, and the students regularly revealed stories of trauma, abuse, and neglect. Every day, as Teri opened the door to the school she steeled herself for what she might read and hear.

"You done for the day?"

Teri raised her head.

DeDe Cooke glided in with the grace of a dancer, sinewy body and long slender legs, light brown skin, hazel eyes. She'd only recently begun working for Mentor Write, and already all the eighth grade boys had a crush on her, and the girls wanted to emulate her.

DeDe lifted her bottled water and squirted it to the back of her throat. She wiped the dribbles with the palm of her hand. "You look a little rough. Tough group?"

"One forty."

She rolled her eyes. "No wonder." The homeroom classes were a code everyone quickly learned. One-o-eight was the gifted class. Teachers actually looked forward to it. One-o-seven had the "slow" kids, well-behaved but dull, spiritless. One-forty was a daily headache. A roomful of ADD, ADHD, BD, ED kids—the alphabet language of the "shit of the school" as the assistant principal had described to Teri on her first day. "They know they're shit and so does everyone else." Yet, surprisingly, Teri liked them. She liked their spunk, was drawn to their sorrow. They were just kids, after all, big overgrown hormonal babies in sagging pants and tight braided weaves.

"Hey, look at this, my two finest new mentors together in one room." Bud clomped in, heavy footsteps in thick-soled shoes.

Teri felt herself flush with pleasure.

"So how goes it?"

"You make us work too many hours for too little money with difficult kids. What could be better?" DeDe's tone was playful, though Teri noted the worry line that suddenly creased Bud's forehead.

"What about you, Teri? How are you doing?"

For nine hours five days a week, she forgot everything but the moment. "I love this job."

"Well, fabulous, because I have a favor to ask of you both." He ignored DeDe's groan. "We're going to sponsor a series of fundraisers to buy new computers for Anchor Middle. Since you two are going to be at this school for a while," again he didn't acknowledge DeDe's grimace, "I thought you could co-chair the project."

"Of course," Teri answered immediately.

"It will mean a bit of extra work, occasional night meetings and weekends. There will be some traveling in Missouri. In fact, there's a conference coming up in Jefferson City on Title One school technology grants where we can make valuable contacts. I will need both of you to attend. There will be other trips too. Okay?"

Len's disapproving face flickered in her mind as Teri said, "Definitely, I'd like the challenge and I don't mind the extra work."

DeDe looked from one to the other. "Listen, my sister and her girl are staying by me right now. But I'll do what I can."

He clapped his pudgy hands together, making the flat sound of dough hitting a table. "You have no idea how much I appreciate it. And our students will be so grateful." He patted both of their shoulders, leaving in his wake the scent of spicy aftershave.

DeDe waited while Teri packed her book bag, and they walked out together. Teri glanced over her shoulder as she reached into her purse for her mace and key chain. DeDe seemed relaxed, but as they headed toward their cars her eyes glazed with the watchfulness of an animal sensing danger.

"Your family doesn't mind you traveling? Or working longer hours?" DeDe asked.

Teri shrugged. She liked DeDe, but, as with everyone now, she didn't know if DeDe knew about the accident. So she tilted her chin in a noncommittal way that was neither honest nor a lie.

"Hey, by chance do you have a daughter named Carly, who goes to Parkway North?" DeDe asked.

"Yeah. How'd you know?"

"Well, that's crazy. So my niece tells me she's got a new friend finally at her school." DeDe seemed to hesitate, then with a sheepish smile said, "A *white* girl. And when she said her last name, well, I just thought I'd ask."

Teri went rigid but she kept her expression neutral trying not to betray concern or confusion. Hopefully, Carly had the sense with this new friend, whoever she was, not to share family matters with her. Teri gave a half wave good bye. "See you Monday."

Once inside her car, Teri immediately locked the doors. She put her book bag on the floor, out of sight of possible carjackers, and glanced in the back seat. Not a nickel, CD case, or candy wrapper in sight. Nothing to tempt a break-in.

The ride out was three short blocks, stop signs on each corner. She stayed on hyper-alert until she reached a busy thoroughfare, which, though landscaped with liquor stores and broken windows, offered enough traffic to give Teri a sense of safety. As she turned onto the highway, she felt her shoulders relax.

Just last week, a drive-by shooting had occurred one block from the school. Two days later a young woman was accosted in the corner park. The danger was real; Len reminded her of that each time he read about another such incident in the newspaper. Finally, Teri had had enough. "What could be more dangerous than the corner where Elise's car broke down?" For the first time since her return, he'd slept on the couch. Three times last week they'd made love and now, one lousy comment, and he went scurrying off to sulk.

It was so unfair. All those years as the doctor's wife, she never told Len what hours to keep, or where to rent his office. She didn't offer advice or pass judgment. She worked at a part-time job and spent hours making their home beautiful. Well, guess what—she finally had a reason to get up and dressed in the mornings. She finally had, potentially, a career, and it was Len's turn to adjust.

And the kids too. "You're never home anymore. I never get the car," Carly's whine was petulant and self-righteous. Jimmy wouldn't meet her eyes because, poor child, he didn't have Stacy Rubin as his mother. Of course, Selia had plenty to say, none of it supportive. "They need you too," she'd taunted, implying she would go visit her friend Harriet but for these neglected grandchildren.

Except Teri knew better. All she had to do was look in their rooms, at their desk computers, iPods, shelves of books, and closets of new clothes. Did they have any idea how many kids' mothers had to work *two* jobs just to pay the rent? Or the kids who shared rooms with multiple siblings and lived with rats, yet were grateful that at least they had a place to stay.

Teri turned onto her street and slowed, taking in the wide expanse of lawns, two-car garages, and twenty-year-old shade trees. She drove past the Rubins' house and noticed Jimmy's ten-speed bike on the front steps with his bookbag dangling from the handlebars, a reminder that she needed to schedule an appointment with his Hebrew School teacher. Apparently, Jimmy had been neglecting to turn in his weekly homework and had become "too silly" during *aleph bet* lessons. If it were up to her, Jimmy could drop out and not bother with a Bar Mitzvah. However, it was important to Len that his son, as with his daughter, follow the tradition observed by both their generations as far back as anyone could remember. No doubt Stacy Rubin had already booked the room, band, florist, photographer and videographer, and was well on her way to a *theme* for an event two years into the future. In fairness, she too, had obsessed over the material details when it was Carly's Bat Mitzvah party, one day spending a full hour deciding on the perfect shade of maroon tablecloths. An itchy prickle of self-recrimination traveled up her neck. How could she have cared so much about something so totally unimportant?

As she pulled into her own driveway, she slowed the car in the same spot where she had sat for long moments after visiting Rozlynn on Elise's birthday. She rested her head on the steering wheel, and squeezed her arms tight across her abdomen, trying to hold back the wave of despair, which mostly disappeared during her hours of helping strangers' children in a terrible neighborhood that felt like the safest place she went.

Last week, she'd been at Schnuck's on Olive, and had run into two familiar-looking mothers whose sons went to Jimmy's school. They'd pasted on that false smile Teri had grown to expect, the one which said: "How do you live with yourself?" Sure enough, as she walked away the staged too-loud whispers began. "You know she got off scot free ..."

Len was still pressing her to see a therapist to talk through the myriad of intense feelings. She knew he was right. As the days turned into months, it was increasingly difficult to recall a time when her life was not ruled by grief, guilt, and anger. But she couldn't admit what held her back the most—the fear that if she started to cry she'd never stop. And it wouldn't all be about Elise.

28

CARLY

"WHAT A GREAT ROOM." Markieta stood in the center of the bedroom and looked around, causing Carly to see it through another pair of eyes. Orange and red striped vertical blinds hung from the double-width window, matching the two twin bedspreads and throw pillows. The walls were covered in a soft-beige grass cloth, the same shade as her plush carpeting. Bookshelves lined one wall, painted red to contrast with the ash wood of her custom-made desk, dresser, and headboards.

Carly flushed, suddenly embarrassed. "Yeah, thanks. But you should have seen the room I wanted. My mom likes to decorate, kind of a full-time hobby, and she took me with her to pick out the colors. I chose all lime green and black and she nearly had like a cow, and told me she'd just go ahead and do the room on her own." Carly tried to laugh as she mimicked her mom's tone, as though sharing a funny memory, but Markieta clearly noticed the hurt in her voice. "Anyway, she doesn't care much about decorating anymore."

Markieta raised her eyebrows, inviting an explanation. When Carly didn't offer one, she continued her visual inventory, not even pretending to not be checking out every detail until she rested her gaze on the lava lamp, which was beginning to warm up.

"Look how cool this is. My grandma got it for me." Carly closed the blinds. The room was instantly transformed into a reddish glow. Both girls watched as the lava slowly, smoothly slid through the gel, the shapes indistinct and not quite formed.

Markieta turned to Carly. "It kinda looks like an ultrasound baby."

Carly immediately flung open the blinds, letting in harsh rays of sunlight. She turned off the lamp and sat heavily on the bed.

"Sorry."

"That's okay. It's so weird. Sometimes I'll forget until, shit, it's right back again. Did that happen to you?"

Markieta unfolded her hands in her lap. "I never forgot."

Carly felt her phone vibrate in her pocket. "I better get this," she said, putting her finger to her lips for Markieta to be quiet. "Hi, Bec. Can I call you later? I'm kind of busy."

"You're always too busy. Are you mad at me?"

She bit back a sigh. "No. I swear. I'm just—I don't know. I just don't really feel like talking lately. It's me, not you."

"Yeah, well, you better watch out, 'cause Jason said the same thing. And you're gonna lose your boyfriend if you're not careful. You can't just treat guys like dirt." Her voice was creeping louder and louder.

Carly held the phone in her outstretched arm as Markieta's hand flew to her mouth to cover a laugh. In spite of herself, Carly snorted.

"What's so funny? Who's over there?" Becca demanded.

"Uh, you don't know her, someone from gym class. We're gonna study together."

"For gym?"

"I'll call you later," Carly said, hanging up the phone and immediately turning it off. She fiddled with the blinds, making the room darker then lighter, thinking about Becca and the hurt in her voice. "I don't know why I haven't told her. She's my best friend. I usually tell her everything."

"My auntie is the only one who knows about me. And I didn't tell her until it was all over."

Carly turned the radio on and they sat side by side on the bed not talking. It was comfortable, though, with no need to fill the space with words the way Carly felt when Becca was over. She slouched against the headboard so her stomach didn't look so bloated. It seemed bigger, just today. At this rate, soon her jeans wouldn't fit. Suddenly, everything was speeding up: her boobs were all puffy and veiny, her nipples were dark brown, and even her butt was swollen. But the worst part was her exhaustion. Today she'd fallen asleep in two classes. Carly could feel time crunching closed.

"You wanna stay for dinner? My mom's out of town, but I'm sure it's fine with my dad and grandma."

Markieta's features softened in pleasure. "Yeah. I think the last bus leaves at eight. Can someone take me up to the stop?"

"You're going to take the bus all the way home? Alone at night?"

A weird expression crossed Markieta's face. But when she spoke her tone was light and bantering, "Unless your daddy wants to drive me into the hood after dark."

Carly shuddered remembering the boarded-up windows, spray-painted gang graffiti, and no trees anywhere. And that burned-out young mother, who immediately knew what Jason and Becca didn't see. Carly closed her eyes to shut out the image. When she opened them, Markieta was looking at her, chin thrust upward, as though to dare a comment.

"You could spend the night. You can borrow some clothes and take the bus back home after school tomorrow."

Markieta didn't hesitate. "That's cool."

"Do you need to ask someone?"

"I don't know. Maybe later. What about you?"

"I don't know. Maybe later." Carly grinned. Markieta smiled back.

Hours later, lying in bed, Carly felt it again, the quiet ease that signaled a potential friendship. It was funny to see how different Markieta was here than at school. Carly had always thought of her as tough and standoffish: all those piercings in her ear, the cigarettes she smoked, the way she stood off to the side of any group. Today, when Markieta stopped by the locker again and Carly spontaneously invited her over, she wasn't sure who of the two of them was more surprised.

"You're different than I thought."

Carly imagined for a moment that it was she who had spoken. In the dark, sometimes it was hard to remember. "You too."

"Ha ha. With me what you see is what you get."

"Yeah, well, me too."

"I know better, little miss not-a-virgin after all."

Carly flung her pillow across the room. It thudded to the floor. She listened as Markieta leaned over the bed, the springs squeaking in the silent room. She waited, tensed, for the pillow to come soaring back. Instead, it sounded as though Markieta was adding it to her pile. Carly dug her head deep against the mattress.

"Carly? Can I ask you something?"

Carly braced herself.

"What was that thing we had for dinner?"

Carly snickered. "The famous Grandma Selia meatloaf."

"Girl, that was some bad stuff."

"I'm a vegetarian. Wonder why?"

Markieta laughed, a deep rumbling seeming to come from within her chest. Carly could feel her whole body relaxing from the sound. "Markieta?" she whispered.

"Hmmm?"

"Does it hurt?"

"Which part?"

"I guess all of it." Carly stared straight ahead at nothing, her fingers digging into her stomach.

Markieta's voice was husky but flat. "It's this minute of lightning, a terrible sucking noise, some cramping. Afterwards it's like having a really bad period."

"What about—how you *feel* after?"

"Oh. I don't know. I wasn't gonna be a mom at fourteen, even if half my school was."

"Fourteen. Wow."

"I think everyone in my eighth grade class was fucking. A lot of them have kids now."

"But are you ever sorry? You know, that you didn't have it."

"I haven't got room in my life for sorry."

"Please, I'll never ask again. I just need to know more—how it really is—after."

The silence felt suspended, crystal hanging by a thread, ready to shatter everything.

"It hurt. Hurts. I don't want to be a mom. I mean, not yet. It's just sometimes I miss that baby. And when it's over, it's really over. There's no going back and saying, oh shit, I changed my mind. That baby is gone, girl. *Gone.*"

Carly took several deep breaths, trying to loosen the knot closing around her guts. Leaning over, she turned on the lava lamp. It cast a soft red glow into the room. She could just make out the shadow of

Markieta in the dim light. They watched in silence, waiting for the lava to heat, form, separate and float.

"Carly, I told you before, you do what you have to do. And you go on. I know girls who are grandmamas before thirty. It wasn't for me. And you, you've got this whole white-person life ahead of you."

There was a sudden chill in the room and Carly felt like she should be the one to apologize, for her matching furniture or the bus ride home at night or something. Instead, she offered: "My grandma thinks—" then stopped abruptly.

"Thinks what?" Markieta's voice was a drowsy mumble.

"Nothing. We better go to sleep." She nestled into the bed. In the quiet, her mind drifted to last night. Again, Selia had slipped into her room after everyone else was in their own beds, doors closed.

"I have an answer which will work for everyone," she'd said.

Carly could hear the gentle love in Selia's voice. She had felt calmed, as though floating in balmy water. Her grandma had an answer. Everything would be fine.

"Have the baby and we'll give her to Rozlynn Horowitz."

She was sure she misheard. "What did you say?"

"We'll give the baby to Elise's mom to raise. The end of that poor woman's pain, the end of your mother's guilt, and a way for you to move on. It's brilliant actually. I've watched enough years of Oprah to know families do this kind of thing every day."

Carly had squinted, trying to see if her grandmother's face bore the same signs of insanity as her words. "You're kidding, right?"

"It's such a perfect solution. It's a wonder no one else thought of it." She'd smiled, her large teeth gleaming in the dark. "Look, this family has already survived enough shocks to know it's not going to fall apart over something as common as a teenage pregnancy. You finish out this school year barely showing, skip the first semester of your senior year and have the baby. No big deal, a smart girl like you. Nobody even needs to know. Rozlynn and George Horowitz are happy. Your mom is happy. I go back to Florida, and all's well that ends well."

"Except this is the craziest thing you've ever said." A pause, "And Elise is still dead."

"Yes, she is." Selia was quiet for a few moments, her lips pursed and brow down-turned, as if remembering something. Her voice trembled when she spoke again. "But we can help honor that poor girl's memory by giving her parents another child. Even your mom said everyone should have a second child."

She'd lain awake for hours after that, mostly feeling confused and very lucky to have her grandma's love, nutso as it was.

Suddenly she felt a bang against her head, startling her out of her reverie. The pillow. "Thanks," she said and hoped Markieta understood she didn't mean for the pillow.

Carly had drifted to that place which wasn't quite asleep but wasn't awake when Markieta asked, "Carly? Last question."

"Hmmm?"

"Why'd *you* get a tattoo? You're about the last girl I'd expect to do that."

Carly thought for a moment, trying to remember why. "I think I wanted to do something unexpected."

Markieta snickered. "You sure did that!"

29

LEN

LEN HEARD THE OUTER DOOR OPEN and slowly close, followed by the shuffling that indicated Gretchen was sinking into the plush chair he kept in the waiting room. He stood for a moment, his hand on the doorknob, summoning the strength to transform into Dr. Berger.

Gretchen lifted her head from the unopened book in her lap. He noted immediately her red-rimmed eyes and jangling foot. Suppressing a sigh, he stepped away as she walked past him into the room. He looked longingly at the now-empty waiting room then followed her into his office.

She began immediately. "I'm not even going to ask you how you're doing today. I need every minute for myself. Okay?"

He nodded.

"So how are you?" she asked, trying to smile.

He returned the smile. "Fine. How are *you*?"

"Not so good." Her eyes wildly scanned the room for a place to rest. As usual, they settled on the bookshelves. She stared for several moments then began to speak in a monotone. "I quit my job. Just like that." She snapped her fingers, making a dry, powdery sound. "I walked in this morning, saw that look my boss gets whenever I wear a short skirt."

Len glanced at her loose exercise pants and she hurriedly said, "I *was* wearing a short skirt. I don't know why I put it on. I think I must have known he'd look at my legs. Maybe I was hoping he'd stare so I could leave? What do you think?"

Len didn't answer.

"Anyway, he did the thing he does, you know, like practically rapes me with his eyes, and I thought, 'enough!' I told him I quit and walked out. I didn't even stop by my desk, which is so stupid because now I have to go back and get all my things. I wouldn't care except I left my new calculator and all kinds of stuff I sure as shit don't want him to have. What kind of idiot am I? Do you think I was looking for an excuse to return? I don't think so. Do you?"

Len worked not to respond. He could feel his body beginning to slump from the effort, then willed his spine to stay erect. When her silence ensued, he said, "I think something must have happened for you to do what you did. You're certainly not stupid, Gretchen. Why don't you tell me what triggered all of this."

She studied his face for several moments. When she spoke, her voice was laced with concern and anger. "What's up with you? You look terrible. Are you sick?"

In spite of himself, he visibly cringed. "I'm fine. Maybe a bit tired, that's all. But tell me about you."

She held his gaze for several moments before her face pinched together and she squeezed her eyes shut. He remained still, waiting to see if she'd use her time as she should, to focus on herself.

"Every day I go in and plaster on this false smile, swallow all my *real* feelings—see? I'm getting the lingo down—trying to be this person I'm supposed to be. But, man, it's getting harder and harder to pretend. I think I knew today would be the day. I made myself throw up three times this week. I can't keep doing that, can I?"

He looked closely at Gretchen. She did look more ashen, he now saw. He struggled to hide his alarm. Her vomiting didn't upset him as much as his own unawareness of it.

"You didn't answer me." Her voice had turned to a whine.

"I think you already know the answer. We've discussed this before. You can do a lot of harm to your body, Gretchen. But I'm more concerned with *why* you're throwing up."

"I told you why. I can't fake it anymore."

"Let yourself reflect for a moment on how the two are related."

He relaxed into his chair, giving her the freedom of silence. She pressed her palms to cover her eyes. When she spoke, her voice was thick and husky. "Vomiting is the ultimate not faking it. I don't know if you understand, but it's like the total opposite of a smile. I go in the bathroom and put my head in a shit hole and yank out all this nourishment. Sometimes I gag so much my ears pop. Or the puke flies up into my hair. When I feel really horrible, I don't let myself wash my hair 'til the next morning. My boss would look at me like I was this sexy thing he could use and leave behind, and I'd think, *if you only knew.* I guess that's it."

He waited to see if she would continue. She remained quiet.

"I think you're right."

"Maybe I won't do it anymore? Now that I quit my job?" She looked pleadingly at him. Len wished he could offer reassurance.

"My brother left home. Did I tell you?"

He sat up straight.

"I didn't? Well, I guess it was actually since I saw you last week. Seems like a hundred years, but it's only been about ... let's see, oh, I guess just five nights ago. He and my mom started going at it again. Mom was still in her nightgown at dinner and Rick went ballistic, and she told him it was none of his goddamned sorry ass business. Nice talk from a mom, huh? And you wonder why I'm so screwed up. Anyway, he got up and walked out. He does it about once a week. Only so far he hasn't come back. My mom keeps calling me, like I'm supposed to find him. Shit, I can't find my own stockings in the morning."

"Do you think the reason your boss bothered you so much today is because you're more upset about Rick than you realized?"

"Do *you* think so? I hate when you do that. Ask me these obvious questions. Why can't you just say—" her voice dropped an octave and she repositioned her legs several inches apart, her arms folded in her lap, eerily adopting his usual posture—"So, Gretchen, I think you're puking your guts out and quitting your work because it's about trying to control what you can. You can't control the actions of others, but you can control what decisions you make. And, Gretchen—" her voice dropped even lower as she leaned in, placed her chin on her palms, a perfect parroting of how he now sat—"the important thing is to try not to let everyone else's issues become your own."

Len flushed, she was echoing the exact platitudes he had too-often spoken aloud. As surreptitiously as he could, he glanced at the clock behind her head.

She looked over her shoulder, pointedly. "Gee, where did the time go?" Gathering her purse and jacket, she stood.

"We still have a few more minutes."

She glared at him with anger both misplaced and well-deserved. He had been a jackass and he'd been caught.

"Yeah, well, take it off my bill." Her sarcasm was softened by a forced smile. He knew it frightened Gretchen to get too angry with him. He watched her walk out. The moment the door shut between them, he dropped his face into cupped hands.

Suddenly she poked her head back in. "Listen, to quote my loving mother, it may not be any of my 'goddamned sorry ass business,' but I think you need to take some of your own advice, Dr. Berger."

Len couldn't stop the grimace that creased his face before she yanked the door shut.

≈

He could hear the drone of Selia's voice as he closed the garage door and entered the kitchen. She was reading aloud into a tape recorder. "'She tried to fling herself below the wheels of the first carriage as it reached her, but the red bag which she tried to drop out of her hand delayed her, and she was too late. She missed the moment. A feeling of relief coursed through her blood as she crossed herself and stepped away from the train. She felt glorious and at the same instant, she was terror-stricken at what she had almost done. Life! So precious. No man was to be her undoing. Anna got up just as the train hurled by.'"

"Selia, what the devil are you doing?"

She hit the stop button in annoyance. "You have to be quiet when you hear me."

Len shook his head. "Aren't you recording for the blind?"

"Yes." Selia pitched her voice higher in challenge.

He took the book from Selia's lap and began to read. "You're changing Tolstoy?"

Selia sliced the air with her hand. "I never did like the way he kills off Anna. And for a man? It's just so dated."

"Seriously? I swear, only you would have the *chutzpah* to alter *Anna Karenina*."

She stiffened in indignation. "I'm doing the readers a favor. And now I have to read the whole last part again." Shoving the recorder aside, she boasted a wide smile. "I do think my ending is better, don't you?"

He shook his head in amusement, turned on the small light over the sink and rifled briefly through the mail piled on the new countertop. Nothing of interest.

"You're home late."

Len kept his back to her, and started flipping again through the stack of envelopes.

"Can I get you some dinner?"

He opened a letter from Clearinghouse Sweepstakes. He was only one lucky number away from winning three million dollars. And if he subscribed to *Time Magazine* for three easy payments of twelve dollars each, he would double his chances to be a grand prize winner.

"Leonard, sit down. You look exhausted. I'll get you something to eat."

He didn't have the stamina to fight. It was much easier to watch in silence as she scurried about the kitchen. When Selia placed a plate of cold meatloaf and wilting salad in front of him, he only raised his eyebrows. She immediately plopped down a bottle of ketchup and actually had the presence to grin sheepishly.

"It'll go bad if we don't finish it up soon. Seems a crime to waste a good dinner." She sat in the chair across from him and watched until he picked up his fork.

"What do you suppose is grander than three million dollars?"

"Four."

He smothered the meat with ketchup, Jimmy-like, and began to eat. Selia kept bobbing her head rhythmically as he forced in bite after bite. It wasn't half bad with all the ketchup, though he knew he'd pay a price later.

Without asking, Selia opened the cabinet and withdrew an oversized plastic cup, a souvenir from a Cardinals game, which she filled to the brim with ice water. She ran her hand smoothly, deliberately, across the cabinet surface as she closed it. "You never did comment on the kitchen. You like the way I finished it?"

The countertop was a restful green, the name of a spice Len could never remember. The ceramic floor and wall tile were taupe—a shade of gray, or beige, depending on one's perspective. Most importantly, the dishwasher and cabinets were *in*. It was a relief to no longer be living out of boxes. Only the walls needed to be painted. He offered a genuine smile and a much-too-belated, he now realized, "Thanks. It looks wonderful."

Selia continued tracing the edges of the cabinet. "I was surprised. Your wife didn't seem to appreciate my efforts very much. I would have thought—"

"Please, Selia."

"Well, I suppose she's my daughter as much as she's your wife. Maybe I just didn't raise her right."

"I think she's fine the way she is."

Selia's mouth locked in a scowl. "What do you think of this new job of hers?"

He resumed eating, shoving hunks of meat into his mouth until it became obvious she wasn't going to let go. He sighed. "I think the job is great for her. I just wish—"

"Yes?"

He took a large gulp of water.

"Say it, Leonard. You just wish—"

"She didn't work quite so much. Or travel. She's never around. I mean, I know she loves this job. And I'm sure she's great at it. But still."

"I totally agree. A mother's place is in the home. A wife's too."

"It's not that so much. I don't know how we're all supposed to heal if Teri keeps running away." He clamped his lips shut, surprised and alarmed by his candor.

Selia reached across and patted his forearm, suddenly an ally. "Just so you know, Leonard, I'm not very happy with my daughter right now."

"Your feelings are rarely a secret."

"I thought I taught Teri to face problems head-on. I guess this one's bigger than she is." Selia stood suddenly, stared off for a few moments, walked over to the refrigerator and returned empty-handed.

"The girl died."

"I know," she whispered.

Len watched as Selia wiped away a tear, his own eyes dry and stinging. "How's your friend doing? The one who was in the hospital?"

"Harriet? Better. I talked to her daughter again today and the doctors say it was just angina, not a heart attack. She needs to lose weight, but she's back home. And at least her daughter is finally with her." She pulled a curl out and held it, clearly waiting for Len to explore the significance of that last remark. After some moments, she let the curl spring back.

"Teri said you were going to visit Harriet."

The scowl re-appeared. "I miss my friend terribly. And I do plan to go—as soon as Carly and Jimmy regain their mother."

"We'll manage. We have before."

"You mean all last year?"

He felt his neck tighten. "What you did was wrong."

"Everything I do is done out of love."

"Same with a black widow."

She threw her head back and laughed, a little too loudly for just mirth.

"Why didn't you call Teri after you heard about the accident?" Len asked.

"Why didn't she call me?"

Len hesitated, flung back to those early weeks of shock. He could have encouraged Teri to contact her mother. Instinctively, he'd even recognized it might have brought her some comfort and relief. "It's hard to explain what we were going through. I mean, the fact that we knew the victim. That—" the words stuck in his throat, sharp-edged, lacerating, "we didn't like her. Hell, from what we'd heard, even Elise's own parents didn't much like her."

"Sometimes parents screw up. Hey, don't look so surprised, I don't mean *me*. I'm talking about the girl's parents. But if they get a second chance, well, you're the doctor."

His antennae went up, but before he could probe, the doorbell rang. Selia popped out of her chair and rushed to the foyer. Len could hear the chirping of a high-pitched voice, matched by a lilting, "Oh, you're just so wonderful" from Selia. He couldn't distinguish any other words, but the tone was full of saccharin venom. A few minutes later, Selia sashayed into the kitchen, a khaki shirt dangling from her outstretched finger.

"That was your friend and neighbor, Stacy Superwoman Rubin. She heard Jimmy's mother was out of town *again*, so she went ahead and sewed on his new Boy Scout badges in time for the next troop meeting."

"She's not so bad." This time it was Selia who raised her eyebrows and Len who grinned sheepishly. "Jimmy likes her."

"Jimmy's eleven."

Eleven. Yeah, and wetting his bed at night. Len cleared his plate, then, surprising himself, allowed his lips to graze Selia's cheek. "Thanks for dinner. And for being here. The kids really love you." Bemused, Len walked out of the kitchen, cherishing the image of Selia's stunned face.

The second floor was swathed in darkness except for a sliver of light peeking from under Jimmy's door. What was he doing up so late on a school night? Len entered the room prepared to scold his son but instead found him asleep, an open book of riddles sprawled across his chest, Dawg tucked into the crook of his arm. Len marked the page with a scrap of paper. In his plaid boxers and an old camp t-shirt, Jimmy looked particularly long and lean. Len felt a catch in his throat. He placed a soft kiss on Jimmy's forehead, turned off the lamp and tiptoed out.

Len was almost to his bedroom when he heard a whimper. He stopped, standing as motionless as he could. He heard it again, a muffled sob coming from Carly's room—his daughter crying in the dark.

"Carly?" he whispered, opening the door an inch. A father's ear told him the silence was deliberate, her stillness forced. He stood for several moments weighing whether or not to react. Len remembered a time, not so long ago, when only her daddy could slay the dragons of the night, a time when Gretchen's sneer would not have followed him home. With self-disgust Len quietly closed Carly's door, allowing them both to pretend she was sleeping.

There was a name for what Len was experiencing—as Marilyn had reminded him—Post Traumatic Stress Disorder. He'd seen it often enough and not just in his struggling clients but more subtly in his clients' spouses. How they'd be strong and supportive until the client eventually improved, and finally the spouse could let go, exhale. And with that exhalation there would be an outpouring of emotions ranging from anger to sorrow to pure exhaustion.

He undressed quickly, throwing his jacket and pants over the armchair. He'd suffer through another sleepless night and hang his clothes in the morning. He didn't bother to brush his teeth.

30

SELIA

SELIA POPPED OPEN THE TAB on her Sprite and listened to the ringing of the phone. It was a lulling sound, and she had nowhere to go. She let it ring on and on.

"What? Hello!" Rozlynn's irritation was unmistakable.

"Oh. Rozlynn. Sorry, did I disturb you, dear?"

"Who is this?"

"It's Selia. Selia Meyer. Are you busy?"

Selia took the heavy silence as a sign of encouragement. She'd answered; she hadn't hung up. They were on their way to a conversation.

"Selia, I'm not in the mood to talk right now. Why don't I call you back sometime?"

"I don't mind. I know how it is, the blasted phone always taking you away from nothing. It's exhausting holding that heavy thing to your ear, isn't it?"

Rozlynn's grunt hinted at begrudging amusement. At her end, Selia smiled.

"Tell me, how are you doing, dear?" Selia didn't have to fake the concern. She wasn't about to turn her great-grandbaby over to someone who couldn't handle the task.

"You want the truth or the party line?"

"Party line? You talk to others?"

"Okay, the truth. I can't see much reason for getting up in the morning so I don't. My husband pretends he's all right, but he's in the shitter too. Only he's doing it the man way. Working thirty hours a

day, drinking himself to sleep at night. Not me. I don't even pretend."
She snorted, added, "Glad you asked?"

"As a matter of fact, I am glad. Way I figure it, you can put a new
baby in bed with you for a nap so long as you're there anyway." She
heard the intake of Rozlynn's breath.

"You're still thinking about that craziness?" A long pause, then
quietly, "Did you actually ask your granddaughter? And she agreed?"

"Almost. You know how kids are. Oh, sorry. But you do. And
this one's no different than the rest. She'll come around. Some things
a grandmother just knows."

She listened to Rozlynn's silence. Selia liked the phone, liked the
guessing that went along with not being able to see someone's face.
She'd had a blind friend years ago; he was the most intuitive person
she ever met. Taught her how to see without eyes.

"Rozlynn? You there?" Selia finally asked.

"So what makes you so sure about your granddaughter?"

Selia heard the sound of tentative hope. She felt it herself, the
glimmer of change, like the sliver of a new moon in a pitch-dark sky.
"I can be a tad pushy when I know I'm right."

Rozlynn laughed. "So I've noticed."

"There's your answer. Is it the one you want? And what about
your husband?"

"I've never told him about any of this."

"Well, that's no problem."

"Among the many, *many* things he'd say is we're too old. I'll be
forty-three at my next birthday."

"Perfect. Just old enough for wisdom and young enough for
energy."

Selia waited as Rozlynn made no comment. The woman was a
harder read than most. She felt a pang of missing Harriet that hurt
like gas.

"I never asked you. How far along is she?"

"Nearing three months. And think how fast other women's
pregnancies go."

"Hold a minute, will you?" Rozlynn clanked the phone down,
not waiting for an answer. Selia put her end on speaker and walked
over to the refrigerator. She hadn't decided what she'd make tonight.
They'd had meatloaf last week and again last night. She opened the

foil. It was barely touched; only Carly's new friend had taken some, and Len. May as well serve it again tonight. Nothing wrong with a good meal of leftovers; personally, she thought it was better on the second night. Carly better start eating it too. The baby needed protein.

The sound of a scratch, a burst of air, an inhalation, filled the kitchen from the small speaker on the counter. Selia picked up the phone, hit the speaker off and cradled the receiver against her shoulder. "You're still smoking?"

"So?" Rozlynn's voice sounded more contrite than challenging.

"You won't smoke around the baby?"

Selia could hear the deep dragging in of a breath, followed by a long exhale. She pictured Rozlynn, hair uncombed, sitting among old newspapers and dirty dishes, a cigarette dangling from her pudgy fingers. She shuddered.

"There doesn't seem to be a reason not to smoke." Rozlynn's voice lacked its usual hard edge.

"You never really answered me, you know," Selia said gently. "Are things getting even a bit easier?"

"It's getting harder. I told you. I keep waiting for her to come home and she doesn't."

Selia leaned into the phone. "I still hear my husband's voice sometimes. And he's been gone almost as long as we were married."

Rozlynn drew a raggedy breath. "You hear his voice?" The question was filled with palpable envy. "I've lost that already. All I have are pictures. And they're so flat."

"Have any tapes?"

"We're probably the only fucking family in America who never videotaped their kid. By the time we could afford a video camera Elise was a teenager. She seemed too old." The whistling inhalation of drawing on a cigarette followed by a prolonged exhale. "The day before the accident, Elise called and left a message on voicemail. I begged the phone company to save it for me, but apparently they can't—or won't. That first week I called my messages over and over. I knew my girl's voice better than my own." Again, the sound of a mouthful of smoke.

For the first time in years Selia wanted a cigarette so badly she could taste it, could feel the smooth acrid smoke in her upper jaw and back of her throat, throwing her back to the two decades in which she'd been a chain quitter. She stretched the phone cord and reached into the refrigerator, pulling out a container of week-old lasagna.

"What are you eating?" Rozlynn asked.

"Lasagna."

"Sounds crunchy."

"It's cold."

"Better watch out. I've gained nearly thirty pounds since the funeral, most of it on cold leftovers that weren't any good to begin with."

Selia looked at her sticky fingers, thick with crumbly cheese and bits of congealed tomato. "That's nothing. I think I gained forty and lost fifty in the first year after my husband died."

"Hey, it's only been five months." There was a gay desperation to Rozlynn's voice. After a pause she asked, "*Does* it ever get better?"

"Oh, Rozlynn. Yeah, it does. Of course losing a child has got to be worse. But all those horrible clichés are true. You just keep surviving each hour and eventually enough time passes and one day you wake up and say, 'Okay, today maybe I can discover a reason to live.' And that's when you find the rubber in you to bounce back."

"What's the point?"

"What's the choice?"

The long silence needed no words. They both knew the choice, the spiraling grayness, the temptation to just give up.

"Do you talk to the sky?"

Rozlynn answered slowly. "No. It would be useless. I'd never be able to hear her." Her voice caught at the end, the first hint of tears. How many women cried when they wanted to scream? A few moments passed. Selia could hear sniffling then the sound of the back of a hand wiping a nose.

"The absolute worst time is the moment I wake up, when I *remember*."

"I'm going to get you that baby. I didn't know your daughter, but I believe it's what she would have wanted for you."

"I didn't know her either. Do any mothers and daughters?"

Selia took a long sip of the Sprite. It had grown warm and it tasted thick and too sweet. "Maybe this will be a boy."

Rozlynn laughed. "Selia, if I don't watch myself, I could learn to like you."

"Hey, we're *mishpocheh*. I'm your kid's great-grandma."

"This is completely nuts and—I haven't said yes."

Selia felt a shiver of power go through her. Rozlynn hadn't said no.

31

CARLY

THE ROOM WAS DECORATED in swirls of teal, cream and mauve, which her mom would call "comfort" colors. Carly found the décor annoying as hell. What was the point in trying to hide what you were? She would have covered the room in blood red and black.

"You brought the cash, right?"

"Yeah. Here's a joke, I earned it from babysitting." Carly reached into the pocket of her unsnapped jeans, feeling for the wad of tens and twenties.

Markieta gave a sheepish shrug. "I'd been saving birthday present money hoping to get my own cell phone. Not like I have many friends to call anyway."

"Well, you can call me from any phone, anytime you want." At Markieta's grimace, Carly remembered their phone had been cut off. "I'm sorry. I mean—"

"Don't get all stupid on me. I know what you mean. It's good."

They sat for a few moments staring straight ahead, suddenly shy with one another. Markieta snickered and with her chin motioned toward the corner where a teenage boy sat ramrod straight between two stern looking, middle-aged women, presumably the unhappy mothers of the boy and his girlfriend. "How much do you think he'd pay to have kept his thingy in his pants?" Markieta whispered.

"About as much as Jason," Carly quipped and at Markieta's startled glance she laughed outright.

"Sharon Jones, is there a Sharon Jones?" The nurse's voice sounded tired, as if she'd overseen one too many abortions. Carly felt her stomach tighten and her heart lurch as no one got up. She grabbed Markieta's hand with her own icy one and waited for her name. Just then a young girl dashed into the room followed by an older woman and they hurried to the front, spoke quietly to the nurse, and went through the doors.

Carly leaned back into her seat, feeling her spine go soft with temporary relief. She rifled through a two-month-old *People* magazine, flipping past photos she didn't see, stopping about halfway and turning to Markieta. "Can I ask you something kind of personal?"

"What size bra I wear?"

"No!" Carly stuck her chest out. "But whatever it is, I bet it's not as big as mine right now."

Markieta grinned and gave a small shake of her head. So Carly plunged. "Do you live with your mom too or just your auntie? And, I mean, do you have a dad?"

The shift was slight but obvious as Markieta pulled her body tighter and scooted a bit away in her seat. "Of course I have a dad. What do you think? My mama went to the sperm bank?"

Her tone carried forced neutrality, reminding Carly of the Markieta she'd known, or rather not known, in the past. But when Carly looked at her she saw a friend, so rather than apologize she pushed a little. "You don't have to answer. I just want to get to know you better."

"Naw, I don't see him. Deadbeat guy, I guess. I never did see him. And my mom kinda comes and goes. But my auntie is cool, better than a mom." She seemed to be studying Carly's face. "How about your whole family?"

Carly realized it was both a simple and a complicated answer, as she supposed all family answers were. But before she could decide whether to break her mom's confidence and tell Markieta about Elise the double doors opened and this time the nurse said: "Carly Berger. Is Carly Berger here?"

She stood quickly, saw black popping spots, and grabbed the chair, suddenly faint. Markieta hopped up and clasped both of Carly's arms to hold her steady. "You can do this. Just remember to let your mind go totally blank. And in a couple of minutes it's over. I'll be out here waiting for you."

"Carly Berger?" The nurse sounded annoyed this time, like *she* was the one having a bad day. Maybe she'd been harassed this morning by a pro-lifer picketing the front of the building, one of those horrible people holding a sign like, "YOUR MOTHER IS YOUR GRAVE." They'd tried to stop Carly, but Markieta had shoved one of them aside and pulled Carly in.

"Step this way. We have a short movie, which will explain the procedure. We require a counseling session, since you're only, let's see, how old," the nurse raised the top page on her clipboard, "Seventeen. Then, if you still wish, we'll take you down the hall to the procedure room. The entire process takes about one hour. Your friend may come along for the film."

Carly glanced at Markieta, who was now thumbing through the same *People* magazine. She felt a sharp tug down *there*, the stretching of ligaments, she'd read. "No. I'll go alone."

Carly kept her head down, studying the low nap of the carpeting. She stopped in front of a picture of a horse grazing in an open field, and could feel her throat choking with envy for its freedom. Next, she was in the video room, a closet-sized room filled with brochures and a small television. Markieta had warned her about the film, about its graphic content, a zoomed-in view of the bloody tissue being sucked out, the pale thighs spread and covered by a dark green cloth, the masked doctor, and somber nurse. The only thing missing was the final scene, the snuffed-out life flung into a plastic-coated trash barrel. She watched every detail, leaning as close to the screen as she could. When it was over, Carly sat back and managed an acknowledgment to proceed down the hall.

Somehow she was now sitting in a hard-backed chair, her hands clasped together in her swelling lap. As though through an echo chamber she heard snatches of sentences ... "there are other options, have you thought this through, do your parents know, how do you imagine you'll feel later ..." snippets of what might have been a dialogue if she had been able to speak. A piece of paper was shoved across the desk, black letters swimming together, teeny tiny letters that would grow into an ending. Her hand was gripping a pen, moving across the page. A name, looking vaguely like her own, was somehow sitting atop a thin black line.

Everything seemed simultaneously sharp and blurred, the antiseptic-laced odor, the sudden bright blue-white lights, floor tile the color of slushy snow. On her back, her butt freezing against the stiff crinkled paper, Carly felt something warm and wet on her cheek and wondered if it was a tear. But she couldn't seem to lift her hands from the bed, where they lay splayed flat.

"Carly, are you okay?" The nurse's hand was warm on Carly's shoulder, her large bosom a shelf that hung over Carly's face. At least this one was consoling, a fellow woman who appeared to understand what Carly was feeling. Carly must have shaken her head yes, *she was okay*, because she heard a voice from over and behind the surgical drape, between her thighs. She glanced at the four-leaf clover on her ankle, then squeezed her eyes shut.

Last night, her Grandma hadn't known she was awake. Carly heard everything, felt every loving stroke as Selia brushed back her hair. *It will be so wonderful, Carly Jane. This baby will heal us all. Your mother will be grateful and Mrs. Horowitz, oh Carly, this time she'll be a great mother and the rest of your life you'll know you've done right. You and me.* Carly had lain still, feigning the sleep of the innocent.

"This will feel cold, there, now that wasn't so bad, was it?"

No, not bad if you liked steel pliers pulling apart your insides. She tried to squeeze her legs together; the straps tugged tight against the skin of her ankles, the stirrups more than a horse width apart.

It's a miracle, Carly Jane. The giving of life to erase the taking of another. God does work in mysterious ways. Selia's voice chanting like a mantra into her ear. The room vacant and cold when she'd gone.

Carly had stayed awake for a long time afterward. Images floating in her head: The pitiful way Jason kept looking at her, begging to tell him what was wrong. Becca pulling back because she knew Carly was keeping a secret. Her dad eyeing her as though he wanted to ask, but was afraid of the answer. Elise stumbling away from Carly, drunk, stoned, mocking, still alive. She must have slept because the ringing of the phone woke her. A call from Markieta. At the bus stop. Ready to be picked up and to come along. Plans in place.

Did you do this on purpose? Who do we both know with tattoos all over her body?

A mistake. That's all it was. No big deal. In five minutes it would be over. Her grandmother would have to deal with it. So would her mom and so would Elise's mom. It was Carly's life. Her life.

"You'll feel a pinching. It may be intense but it should last only a few moments. Are you okay?"

Oh, you're not gonna be okay for a long time. The weariness on the old face of that young mother, the way she had yanked her child's arm out of frustration and exhaustion.

"Try to relax, Carly."

But it was kind of awesome to think she had a baby inside her.

When it's over, it's over. That baby is gone, girl, gone.

Suddenly a loud whooshing noise in the room, the machine humming, adjustments being made.

Her grandma's face as she looked at baby Jimmy.

There's no going back and saying, oh shit, I changed my mind. You weren't thinking of killing it?

"We're going to start now." Fingers on her skin. A tiny pinch on the outside, the beginning of a thread weaving up and around into her—

I have an answer that will work for everybody.

"Stop!" Her shriek ripping against her ears. The intake of startled breaths. The slithering out of the steel thread. Everything spinning as she bolts up, yanks out her feet and stumbles to the floor, gripping her round stomach.

"Carly, wait. Please." A hand trying to grab her arm but she slides by, out past the lights and the tile and down the carpeted hall and into the room—that room—filled with girls and women and sorry boys and so many sad eyes. "Carly?" Markieta's voice.

She can't stop. Into the elevator, plunging down, the doors open, she's walking, getting astonished looks. All those people, their arms linked together and their signs, coming toward her. And now, a slender body is wrapping her into a strong-armed hug, and Markieta is rubbing her back and patting her hair and whispering, "It's cool, girl, it's cool."

32

TERI

SHE GLANCED AT HER WATCH, just enough time for a cup of coffee before the next class. The teacher's lounge was crowded as usual. Overflowing with files and discarded books, the lounge evoked an air of purpose and panic, of too many bodies in too small a space.

Teri smiled at a number of teachers, scanning the room for DeDe. She hadn't seen her for several days, and had already decided if DeDe didn't show today, she'd call her tonight at home. So far, they'd limited their contact to school, but Teri sensed the potential for a friendship that could go deeper than just as co-workers.

She gulped the rest of the coffee, lukewarm and gritty, as DeDe walked in. "Hey! Where you been hiding?"

DeDe's smile didn't quite reach her eyes. "Just some stuff going on. How are you doing?" Without waiting for an answer, she went to her mailbox slot, removed some papers, and began to walk out. Teri scurried to catch up.

"Were you sick?"

"I've been here. Just busy." Her voice was clipped and for an unveiled moment, Teri saw a flash of anger in DeDe's eyes—or was it disgust?

"Is something wrong?"

DeDe continued toward her classroom.

Shifting topics, Teri asked, "You know Rochelle Monroe? Well, I think she's pregnant. She keeps writing about it and claiming her stories are fiction. Should I directly ask her? Tell the social worker?"

She hesitated, thinking. "Or I guess I could call her mom, but it probably won't do any good."

"Why do you say that?"

"Well, I mean it doesn't exactly seem like Rochelle's mom is tuned in to her daughter."

"And exactly how does a daughter with a *tuned-in mom* seem?"

"You know what I mean," Teri said.

"Yeah, I think I do. The question is," DeDe said, turning on her heel and closing the classroom door between them, "do you?"

Teri's feet scuffed the floor as she trudged back to her own room. Her neck and chest were itchy from sweat. It was an unseasonably hot May day, the air heavy and sticky, hearkening the onset of St. Louis summer. She couldn't imagine how the eighty-year-old, all-brick, unairconditioned school would feel a month from now.

"Yo, Mrs. Berger. I was wondering if you'd look at ..." Anthony reached into his backpack, but before retrieving anything a group of students shoved him aside as they sauntered into the classroom.

"So I told him, 'kiss my ass' and he leaned down and smacked his lips against—"

"Your big fat booty."

"My booty ain't fat, you pig."

"Aw, sheeeet, we writing *again*?"

Teri clapped her hands together so sharply her palms stung. "Everybody sit and get out your journals. We're going to have quiet time today, just writing. The prompt is on the board. You know what to do." She ignored their groans and sank into her chair. She must have looked as dispirited as she felt because they settled down quickly and for the most part began to write.

Absently, Teri flipped though the last hour's stories. She came to Rochelle's paper and read again, "I'm pregnant and I need help." The story was poorly written but poignant. A teenage girl afraid to tell her mom she was having a baby and didn't know which guy was the father. In the end, she decides she can make it on her own after all. The character just happened to be in eighth grade and her name just happened to start with the letter R.

Teri puzzled again over the conversation with DeDe. Several times, they'd conferred when students' writing indicated possible abuse, neglect, or other serious issues. So why the negative attitude today?

The hour dragged and Teri found herself glancing repeatedly at the clock until the bell rang and the students piled out, noisily and with palpable relief to be away from her churlish mood.

She walked aimlessly down the hallway, past DeDe's room, and then wheeled around. She tapped on the glass pane and, at DeDe's wave, stuck her head in. "Can you talk?"

DeDe offered a curt nod.

"Please tell me what's going on. Have I offended you or something?"

"Have you even met my niece?"

"Huh?" Teri asked.

"She's slept over at your house. Did you know?"

Teri strained her memory, but the only faces that appeared in her mind were Jason's and Becca's. Though, come to think of it, she hadn't seen them in a while. She shrugged somewhat sheepishly, recalling DeDe's prior reference to her niece's friendship with Carly.

"With all the traveling we're doing and the extra hours I'm putting in—anyway, you know how kids are—friends one minute and not the next." When DeDe didn't respond, Teri searched her face for clues. "Well, it's good they're friends, yes?"

"You really don't know, do you? When Markieta told me your girl Carly said her mom hadn't noticed anything, I told her she must be wrong. That's the kind of mom my sister is, but I never figured it for you. I know you care tons about all these kids here. Hell, you're, as you say, *tuned into* Rochelle Monroe, for God's sake. But what about ..."

Her voice trailed off and again she turned her back to Teri as she mumbled, "Look it's none of my business. I guess I'm just disappointed in you and I'm having a hard time pretending otherwise."

"What the hell are you talking about?" Teri blurted.

Instead of answering, DeDe pointedly began shuffling through a pile of papers, keeping her eyes averted.

After a few seconds of edgy silence, Teri walked out and headed to her car. She was off the school grounds and past the first stop sign before she realized she'd forgotten to shift into hyper-alert. She hit the auto lock button and accelerated, her shoulders and neck stiff with tension. She did a slow slide through the next stop sign, and one block down, came to the last stop before the highway. Then she heard a knock.

A bang really.

Teri's heart lurched as she looked up into the coal eyes of a teenage boy. He appeared so familiar that at first she assumed he was one of her students saying hi. His rapping became more insistent. Teri was instantly alert and dulled, watching in what suddenly felt inevitable. A pink mouth moved in a kind of dance, white foamy spittle stretched between his lips.

"Open the fucking car."

He pressed his face against the window; his eyes swept down and burned against her pale bare thighs, exposed when the clenched seat belt pulled her khaki skirt high. They reached together, Teri for the mace, he into his waist where she spotted the glint of silver metal. The moment lasted an anguished eternity, until, without realizing her brain had sent the signal, Teri's foot gunned the accelerator. She leaned on the horn and flew through the red light, across the intersection, missing by inches the crash of an oncoming truck. She crouched down and fearfully peeked into her rearview mirror. He was ambling through the street, weaving among the passing cars.

She couldn't stop shaking as she sped west along Highway 70 by rote, registering landmarks: the city limit, inner beltway, and airport, swerving as a sports car zoomed past narrowly missing her. Her whole body felt exposed, as if someone had removed the flesh and bones and left just the nerves and blood. Then somehow, she was in her own driveway. She slumped against the car door in trembling relief, recognizing it was pure instinct that propelled her through the red light, and pure luck she'd not been t-boned or killed. She reached into her glove box to push the button of the electric garage door. As she watched it rise and reveal Carly's roller blades and Jimmy's ten-speed bike, for the first in a very, very long time, she was aware of being *home*. Of being their *mom*. Of being *safe*. She lifted the visor and caught a glimpse of her eyes, the fright and the relief evident.

And in that instant, as she recognized herself in the mirror, as a moan escaped her lips, and as she remembered the blazing judgment on DeDe's face—she knew.

She raced up the stairs, taking them two at a time. "Carly," she shouted, knocking on the closed and locked bedroom door. "Let me in. We need to talk."

"Go away."

Teri banged repeatedly.

"Leave me alone. I'm sleeping."

"It's four in the afternoon. Now open this door."

"Teri, is that you?" Selia's voice carried from downstairs. "What are you doing home so early?"

She slumped against her daughter's door, her voice dropping, pleading, "Sweetheart, let me in. Please."

"FUCK YOU! Why should I?"

Teri bounced back as though stung. Feeling a surge of white-hot anger, she kicked the door as hard as she could. "You little bit—" Horrified, she bit back the word, nearly drawing blood as her teeth sunk into her tongue.

She stumbled down the hall, fell flat against her bed. She sensed when Selia entered the room. "You need to cut her some slack, Teri. She's going through a lot right now."

Teri sat up and looked at her mother. "You know?"

"Yes." Selia moved to the foot of the bed, a light peach dishtowel draped over her shoulder.

"Oh, Mom. I've really screwed up this time. How could I have been so blind?"

Selia nestled beside Teri and put an arm around her shoulders. Teri let herself sink against her mother's slender warmth. "I realize it shouldn't matter, but did Carly tell you?" Teri couldn't keep the hurt out of her voice.

"She didn't have to."

"What's she going to do?"

Selia's face brightened. Immediately, Teri went on guard. "Mother, what are you up to?"

A beatific smile stretched Selia's lips thin against her oversized teeth and Teri had a sudden image of a beast about to pounce. "God damn it. My daughter won't talk to me. My mother won't talk to me. What the hell is going on?"

"My dear, this really isn't about you."

"But I suppose it is about you?"

"Well," Selia adjusted her face to assume the blankness of false humility. "Let's just say I'm helping out."

"How dare you?"

Selia leaned in close, so close their noses nearly brushed. "I dare because I'm not the one who is so caught up in herself that she pays no mind to anyone else."

Teri felt her mouth fall agape. "Did *you* really say that? You're the most self-righteous, self-centered mother I know."

"Perhaps so, but at least I'm here, truly here, for them."

"It's the twenty-first century. I'm allowed to have a career."

"Of course you can work! But you've lost sight of your family." Selia stood abruptly, tossing back her shoulders and dishtowel to make a dramatic exit, then couldn't seem to stop herself as she paused in the doorway. "They need you, Teri—and you're not here."

Teri heard the creaking of the stairs and moments later the banging of pots in the kitchen as Selia prepared to cook something no one but she liked. She stared down at her palms, at her long life lines, remembering a comment Bud had made early on: "These students will suck you dry if you let them. But save something for your own family. It's not good work if it doesn't begin at home." Down the hall, she thought she heard Carly weeping, but perhaps it was air whistling through the vents. She'd forgotten the sounds of afternoon in her own home. She felt her body suffuse with shame and regret as she squeezed her eyes shut and grabbed her wrists, handcuffing them to her chest.

33

LEN

LEN CLOSED THE BLINDS to slits, trying to block out the glare of sunlight. His head was pounding with an ache that started behind his eyelids and traveled up to the roots of his scalp. A new client was scheduled next, Sue Smith, followed by a session with Gretchen. He needed to be sharp.

Len straightened his tie and rose to open the door to the waiting area. With any luck, the client would do most of the talking. He thought he could probably manage small nods.

As she walked through the doorway and settled onto the center of the couch, Len had a sense of having previously seen Sue Smith, though her features, while unattractive, were otherwise unremarkable or familiar. A round and pasty face, stringy, chestnut hair that was plastered to her scalp. Her slacks were pulled tightly around a bulging abdomen and her blouse gaped open between buttons.

"You're looking at me like you know me from somewhere. Do you, Dr. Berger?" Her voice had the rough huskiness of a smoker.

He pulled on his chin, struggled to remember. "I'm not sure. Have we met?"

"Your wife killed my daughter."

He shot up in his seat. "Rozlynn Horowitz."

"Sorry about the fake name. I didn't think you'd meet with me otherwise."

The headache was completely gone and in its place was the kind of vacuumed, white shock he'd heard clients describe but had never himself experienced.

"Do I really look *that* different?"

"Well ... I think I've only seen you—once. And we were all in a daze that day." He could picture her clearly, poised, slender, and expressionless. She was one of the few people who didn't cry at the funeral. The only sign of emotion had come from her fingers, which continually twisted together in her lap. Teri had not cried either. She'd chewed her bottom lip until it actually drew blood, and then spent the bulk of the service making quiet sucking noises.

"I didn't come here to make you uncomfortable. I need to talk and I thought your family owed me that, at least." She opened her purse with rapid, jerky movements, withdrew a cigarette, brought it up to her lips, asked, "Mind?"

He nodded yes, he minded.

"You do?"

He pointed toward the "Thanks for not smoking" sign above his desk.

She stuck the cigarette behind her ear, causing a piece of limp hair to fall forward. "When Elise was thirteen years old, I came home one afternoon and found her in bed with an eighteen-year-old neighbor boy. I threw him out, grounded her for weeks. Later, the same year, I was doing the wash and found a roach clip in her jeans pocket. You know what that is? Well, I didn't. Not at the time. I confronted her and she didn't even try to lie. So, no more parties, no more phone, no more TV. Was I too strict? Who knows? Probably. How do you ever know?" She paused, seeking affirmation. He offered it by lowering his chin and raising his palms. Rozlynn slouched back, uncrossed her legs, and seemed to let go of something.

"Things went from bad to worse, or so it seemed. At fourteen, I found birth control pills in her vanity drawer. I guess I should've been grateful she was smart enough to take them. She just left them there, daring me. At fifteen, I found hash right on top of her sock drawer. That was one thing about Elise, she seemed to always want to be caught. I'm no dummy. I didn't go to college, but I read plenty and I knew all about cries for help. So we sent her to therapy, put her in rehab—then again and again."

His eyes strayed to where her legs had parted and he noticed a tear along the seam of her pants, the material stretched thin. He looked away.

"I went back to work. Partly to pay for the therapy, although I told everyone it was for Elise's college fund, but mostly it was just to get away from her. Be careful what you wish for, right?" She laughed bitterly. "Her father stuck by her the whole time. Good thing, because I couldn't stand to be near her. And then all of a sudden, about age eighteen, right before she graduated high school, she woke up one day and was the old Elise. She started hanging around the house and she even pulled her grades up. I don't know what brought about the switch, but I wasn't asking any questions. I was just grateful to have her back. She worked at McDonald's for a while, and got really skinny, scary skinny. I thought, oh boy, here we go again. But at age nineteen she took her savings and enrolled at Mizzou."

Rozlynn's eyes filled with tears. She wiped her nose with the back of her hand. Len offered the tissue box. For the first time, she seemed almost embarrassed. "I'm sorry. I don't usually cry about this. It's just—I was so full of hope. I used to wake up and whistle. Whistle! I didn't know I could ever feel so light again as I did the first year Elise went to college.

"She came back for the summer and started bugging me about getting a dog or cat. She even brought a couple home, full of God knows what diseases. I made her return them to the shelter. She threw a fit, accused me of killing them myself by sending the animals back. Right after that, I noticed our liquor bottles disappearing. Next it was my … um … my Xanax." Len offered a shrug of non-judgment and Rozlynn continued, "I found the bottle in her jeans pocket when I was doing her laundry. Why didn't she just put a sign out, 'I'm fucking up, Mom.' Anyway, when you've got a kid who is using, you take it one crisis at a time. We threw her out. She came back. We tried love, we tried punishment, we tried giving up on her. We went to therapy. She went to more therapy. Everyone but the goddamned roaches went to therapy. And I wanna tell you something, Dr. Berger. What you folks do ain't worth the cost of a dollar. Thanksgiving we had our biggest fight yet. She had a baggie of coke. I said terrible things. She said worse. I grabbed her cell phone and wouldn't give it back. I threw her out. Heard her take the car and knew it was on empty, and her with no phone. Know what? At that moment I was so beyond disgusted I didn't even care. I told her I never wanted to see her again, called her a terrible name. And …" She pulled the cigarette from behind her ear and stuck it in her mouth, took it out, rolled it between her palms. Bits of tobacco fell to her lap and onto the couch. "I never did … see her again. Not alive."

"Oh," he groaned. He closed his eyes and tried to clear his head, to imagine a small lightless box, but all he saw was the split in Rozlynn's pants seam. When he opened his eyes, she was halfway across the room. "Wait," he motioned her back. "Why are you leaving?"

Her forehead creased as though she herself didn't know. "I read an article that said if you talk about the most horrible things that happened, you can begin to heal. I thought this might help."

His eyes stung with tears. "Has it?"

She shook her head slowly back and forth. "No. You see, the worst thing isn't just that Elise died. It isn't even that it could have been prevented. I probably had her phone in my hand as she stood there stranded. It's that I can never tell her I didn't mean it. People might wonder if a mother can love a daughter like Elise. I hated her, but I never quit loving her. I don't know if she knew." Rozlynn turned from Len and walked to the door. She stood there, in the open doorway, her gaze blank but her face twisted in transparent agony. "Oh, and tell your mother, I guess she's your mother in law, never to contact us again. What she's proposed is not only absurd, it's insulting and terribly hurtful. She seems to think I was considering it but … well, just tell her to leave us alone." She blinked, met his eyes, her face softening somewhat. "Clearly she meant well. Tell her thanks for that."

Dazed, Len peered out the window. The dogwood tree was in full bloom with vibrant, pink flowers soaking up the sunlight. It was a dogwood that had caught his eyes the day he visited Teri at the Drury Inn. *You seem to want to snap your fingers and somehow put it all behind us. Is that what you tell your clients?* she had accused as he studied the new buds, envying their ability to cocoon themselves.

Len put his head down on his arms and cried with a pain he hadn't felt since his dad died. For several minutes, he allowed his head to rest in his palms while he tried to calm himself. The door opened and closed in the waiting room, followed by the impatient sound of a stomped foot. One more hour was all he had to get through … just one more hour.

An aura of melancholy seemed to drift off Gretchen's skin as she shuffled, shoulders slumping, past him and to the couch. He sat directly across from her and folded his hands together. "How are you?"

Gretchen looked up and Len felt his stomach lurch. Her face had grown hollow, sunken into herself. Her eyes were red, the skin underneath puffy and dark. When she tried to smile, her lips curled upward, revealing teeth that in the two weeks since he'd seen her, had taken on the gray cast of a corpse.

She shook her head from side to side, then let it drop, chin to chest. He noticed a bald spot next to her part.

"Gretchen?" he prodded gently.

She spoke from her chin, the words muffled and thick. "He's still gone."

"Tell me."

Her arms had become stick-like, with elbows jutting against taut thin skin. He experienced an immediate sense of alarm. In all his years as a psychologist, he'd had to hospitalize only a handful of patients; each time the situation had been painful and draining.

He asked again, more forcefully this time. "Gretchen?"

"I don't think he's ever coming back."

"Your brother?"

She snapped her head up. "Of course my brother. Who else would I be talking about?"

"You canceled last week. Tell me what happened."

Her body stiffened. "It's been three weeks and we've heard nothing. His friends don't know where he is. My mother's a lunatic. Like it's my fucking fault. She's the one who drove him away. She told him to get the fuck out and he has. Prick. How dare he leave me alone with her?" She jumped up and began to pace, from window to couch and back, her steps hard and loud.

Len could feel his own breath quicken. Her pacing was making him dizzy. He wanted to shout, Stop, but he clamped his lips tightly together, hoping her venom would give him strength.

"Why is everyone my responsibility? My mom waits for me to make her happy. I can't do it. I can't bring him back. He left me too." She stopped suddenly and crinkled to the floor, a puddle on his carpet. She began to weep, her shoulders shuddering.

He bowed his head low, trying to blot from his mind the sets of eyes that continued to peer into his for wisdom.

"Dr. Berger?"

She looked all of a sudden like Elise, like the last memory he held of Elise, as a skinny almost waif-like teen, standing outside of the high school as he waited in his car for Carly to bounce down the stairs from freshman basketball practice. Though he barely knew Elise, he'd sensed her angst and anger, even from across the schoolyard. He could remember the passing observation that she must need help. Then Carly had opened the door, full of energy and the fresh smell of sweat, and they'd driven away.

As this woman on the floor continued to speak, he couldn't distinguish her face anymore. He could feel the collapsing begin in his neck and travel the length of his spine. He couldn't do it. Not for one more person, especially not for this woman—this wounded damaged woman who took from him more than he had left to give. He checked his watch and noted the time with relief. Shakily he stood. Slowly, he put forward one foot then the other. As he passed Gretchen, he reached out and placed his flat palm upon her thinning scalp. "I'm sorry; our time is up." He managed to wait until she left, then opened the side door connecting his office to Marilyn's. She turned from the client sitting on her couch.

"Len?"

"Mare, please cancel tomorrow's appointments for me."

Somehow he made it home. Parked his car next to Teri's. He stumbled past Selia, trudged up the stairs leaning into the wall for support, down the hall beyond Carly's closed door, and toward his own closed bedroom.

Teri was in bed, fingers clamped to her wrists, her eyes shut tight. She had pulled the curtains closed but rays of sun snuck in, dressing her body in prison-like bars of light. With a few snapping tugs, he stripped down to his boxers and climbed into bed, curving spoon-like to her backside. She wiggled closer. He draped an arm over her chest. "Len," she said, "we need to talk."

34

JIMMY

SEVERAL WEEKS AGO, as a surprise, Jimmy's grandma bought six new fish for his aquarium: three angels, two dwarf fish, and a bottom feeder. Within a few days, the angels ate the dwarf fish and the bottom feeder died. By the next week, the smallest angel fought and killed the other two. Grandma Selia had clapped when Jimmy showed her the sole surviving fish. "Name that one for me," she'd said. The next day she brought home a population of supposedly hearty fish, though he was just waiting for the angel to kill them too.

As he crossed the hall to fill the bucket with new water, he could hear his sister crying in her room. His mom and dad had been in their room with the door shut for hours. It was nearly six thirty and only his grandma seemed aware a normal family should be thinking about dinner. She was making lots of noises downstairs, singing, and every once in a while calling out something even though no one bothered to answer.

He stepped back into his room and refilled the tank to the top. He swished his hand counterclockwise in the warm water, watching as the tigers and rainbow fish swam through his fingers, around and back again. Supposedly fish couldn't be trained, but that wasn't true. As his Grandma had taught him, it all depended on who was doing the training.

"You need me to set the table?" he shouted as he stomped down the steps, hoping he might annoy someone enough to at least get them to open a bedroom door.

"That you, Jimmy?" Grandma Selia gave him one of her huge-toothed smiles, the ones she saved for when she wanted a favor. "Be a doll. Run back up and tell your folks dinner's ready. It's a surprise too."

Jimmy bit his lips so she wouldn't see his grin. His dad called all of Grandma Selia's dinners *a surprise*. "Even once we're done, we're not sure what we've eaten." He stood outside his parents' door. They were talking, but he couldn't hear actual words. He tiptoed away. His sister's room was now silent. This time he went down the stairs as quietly as he could.

His grandma placed two plates on the table and set a huge casserole down, overflowing with bubbling liquid. "What is it, Grandma?"

"A new version of tuna casserole with peas and cheese. It calls for cream of mushroom soup, but we didn't have any so I added cream of asparagus. For a little extra protein I threw in bite-sized pieces of leftover chicken, and your sister better quit being a vegetarian. Let's face it, we all need more protein these days." She lowered her nose to the dish and inhaled. "Hmm. Smells great."

His stomach knotted up like it did when he forgot to study for a test. If Carly and his parents didn't come down, was he supposed to eat it all? He picked up his fork, swallowed a mouthful of saliva in preparation and then the doorbell rang.

Jimmy raced across the room and swung the door open. "Jason! I've missed you."

"Hey there, Cheese Cube." Jason high-fived with one arm and punched him in the shoulder with the other. "Your favorite sister around?" He said it jokingly, but Jimmy could hear something wobbly in his voice.

"Have you eaten, Jason? We have plenty," Selia offered.

Jason shifted from leg to leg, a tight, worried look on his face. "I'm not hungry, ma'am. Thanks." Jimmy pointed his chin toward the stairs.

The tuna casserole was surprisingly tasty except for the occasional chunks of dried chicken, which nearly made him gag. His grandma kept jumping up and standing at the bottom of the stairs, leaning into the empty space trying to hear conversations. Finally she sat, put her elbows on the table and asked, "Do you know what's going on?"

"No. Do you?"

She heaped a huge second helping on top of his first and winked. "Eat. You're too skinny. The girls like a little something to hug."

"Grandma."

She winked again. He wondered if maybe she had a twitch or something.

"You know what a marionette is?"

"Something with a string puppet?"

"They're up there, all of them, trying to untangle strings. They could save a lot of time if they'd just listen to me." She puffed out her chest. "But I suppose they need to percolate first. Like a good cup of coffee. Speaking of which," she stood suddenly, "I bet your folks will be ready for a nice strong cup when they come down."

Jimmy watched as she took the coffee beans out of the freezer. She'd bought a new coffee maker for them right after coming to stay, one that seemed to take a lot more steps and way more time than the one his mom and dad used. She had to grind the beans, boil the water separately, and stand while she poured through a paper cone an inch of water at a time. His dad said the coffee always had grounds in it, and usually was too weak or too strong, but rarely drinkable. Sometimes his dad would take a sip and smile at Jimmy, coffee granules dotting his teeth.

Jimmy heard footsteps coming and felt himself tense up.

"Hi, Jimmy. You're eating dinner?" His dad walked over and planted a kiss on his cheek. Turning his back so Grandma Selia couldn't see, he whispered, "What is it?"

Jimmy offered a forkful, making sure a hunk of dried chicken dangled from the prongs. His dad grabbed his neck with both hands like he was choking.

"Leonard, I'm about to make some coffee. And how about eating now too?" Before his dad could answer, the phone rang and his grandma grabbed it.

"Harriet. Oh my God, it's so good to hear your voice. Hold on, doll, let me switch to the other room."

She scurried out and his dad sat down, looking exhausted and sad. He motioned for Jimmy. "You too old to sit on your dad's lap?"

It had been a long time. Jimmy could feel that he didn't really fit anymore, his legs too long, his back too high, his head had nowhere comfortable to go. But his dad hugged him and Jimmy melded into the right shape. They sat close for a few moments, just the two of them in the quiet kitchen. Jimmy knew he better ask before he lost his nerve. "Are you and Mom getting a divorce?"

"No, no, nothing like that."

"Well, is Carly … is she dying?"

"No, I promise."

"So …" he moved so his body was barely touching his dad's. "Did I do something wrong? I still … um … have accidents sometimes."

"Cheese." His father yanked him back into his lap, squeezing so tight it almost hurt. He felt something wet on his neck. When his dad finally loosened his grip, Jimmy saw tears were running down his dad's cheeks and he wasn't trying to wipe them away.

"Listen to me, son. A lot is going on, but you need to understand two very, very important things. Are you listening carefully?"

Jimmy stared right at him, daring not to blink, afraid to even nod in case his dad thought he'd quit paying attention.

"Number one, none of this, I repeat, none of this, is your fault. Not even a little bit. Number two, I am sure everything is being worked out. I'm telling you the truth here. You understand?"

This time Jimmy did nod; in fact, once he started, he couldn't seem to stop as his dad again tightened his arms. They stayed like that for a while, until his mom came in. She sniffed the casserole, raised her eyebrows, and walked out. His dad pushed him off gently and stood. "Well, there's my cue. Now, remember what I've told you." He started up the stairs just as Grandma Selia came back in.

He stopped mid-step. "Selia, I got an unexpected visit today from Rozlynn Horowitz."

Her face twisted into a series of different shapes and flushed several shades of red.

"She said to tell you, let's see, it was, 'Tell her to never contact us again.'" He stared at Selia. "I think you and I need to have a talk later." He turned away before she could answer.

She stood straight up, her back erect, which actually made her seem shorter. Jimmy wondered if that's how he looked when he tried to stand taller than he was.

"I tell you, Jimmy. There just isn't enough of me to go around. Harriet needs me. Mrs. Horowitz needs me." She tilted her head toward the second story. "Each of them needs me. But right now, the coffee needs me most."

He went upstairs to get his shoes. Every door but his was closed. As he walked by Carly's room, he heard Jason say, "I can't believe you didn't tell me sooner." Jimmy held his breath as he put his ear up against the wood.

"I just couldn't." She was crying, as usual.

"It's my baby too."

Jimmy sprang back. Baby? That's what was going on? Carly was having a baby? He raced down the steps two at a time and hurried out, not bothering to tell anyone he was leaving, as though they'd care or notice.

Sometimes he counted the sidewalk cracks to Alan's and sometimes he tried walking the block backwards, but today he just ran, head down, to get there as quickly as he could. Even though things weren't the same as they used to be, it was still a relief to be friends again, to have a normal house to go to. Sure enough, the smell of cookies baking in the oven hit his nose the moment he opened the door. Mrs. Rubin hugged him and within a minute he was wolfing down warm tollhouse cookies and ice-cold milk.

Alan came into the room shouting, "News flash, news flash!"

"What?" Mrs. Rubin asked before Jimmy could say anything.

"Amanda Sparks told me—"

"Yes?"

"That—"

Jimmy grabbed another cookie. He could feel his heart beating faster and was grateful Mrs. Rubin talked so he didn't have to.

"Tell us."

"That she wants to kiss Jimmy Cheese Berger *on the lips*. If he'll let her."

Mrs. Rubin grabbed one of Jimmy's hands and one of Alan's, clapping them together. "This is so thrilling."

Jimmy knew he should be excited too. Ever since that letter from Katie, a hundred years ago, Amanda had acted like she didn't even know him. And now, she was thinking about kissing him *on the lips*? He pretended to be excited about Amanda, only he could tell he wasn't fooling anyone. Carly was having a baby?

Mrs. Rubin wiped her hands on the half apron she wore whenever she was baking, which was almost every day. "Well," she said, "you're probably scared too. It's natural." She waved both arms in the air as if cheering on a team. "I'll leave you boys to figure it all out. You don't need an old lady hanging around."

"Mom, you're not old."

"No, Mrs. Rubin. Not at all." But his voice sounded fake, sounded a lot like the way most of his family now talked.

He hung around for a while, even called Amanda while Alan listened on the other end, and when no one answered at her house, Jimmy mumbled something about needing to get back home for a family dinner.

"You okay, Cheese? You're acting weird again. Your mom didn't have another accident, did she?"

He tried to shrug, as if the biggest worry he had was how to keep his lips soft for the big kiss.

It was muggy outside from a brief afternoon storm. As he walked by the middle neighbor's house, an in-ground sprinkler suddenly popped on. Jimmy stood and watched for several moments. He remembered this time last year. It was nearly the end of fourth grade and his class had been given an assignment. They were supposed to color in a picture of Flat Stanley and mail it to their grandparent or to a favorite aunt or uncle who lived in another part of the country or world. Jimmy had been at Alan's house as he and his mom sat around trying to decide which of their gazillion, wonderful, out-of-town relatives Alan could approach. Jimmy had been quiet, knowing his Grandma Selia was the only one he could send it to; but he couldn't do that because his grandma and mom didn't talk to each other anymore. On the way home, the same neighbor's sprinkler system had come on and Jimmy had sort of accidentally on purpose let his Flat Stanley float into the water until it was so wet he couldn't possibly mail it anywhere.

He entered the kitchen, unsure what he'd find. Grandma Selia was on the phone again with her friend Harriet. Jimmy watched her for a few moments and then tumbled into her arms, nearly knocking her down. Without a break in conversation, she switched the phone to her left hand, grabbed him close with her right arm, and kept talking while she hugged his body to hers. He could feel her chest vibrate as she threw her head back and laughed a booming laugh, blocking out all the sounds of sadness upstairs.

35

TERI

TERI HAD NOT FELT SUCH TREPIDATION since standing outside the home of Rozlynn Horowitz. She pressed the button and waited to be buzzed in, the days when a synagogue could safely stay unlocked now gone.

Except to drive carpools or meet with Jimmy's Hebrew School teacher, Teri mostly avoided synagogues, a carry-over from both of her parents. Selia loved her Yiddish phrases and Charles had enjoyed the Jewish holidays, but as a family, they'd rarely gone to services. As an adult, it was more than just the God talk Teri found alienating; the whole idea of organized religion seemed bizarre. Soundless lips shaping private pleas in a public setting. Rabbis, with deep booming voices, telling congregants when to stand, when to sit, and when to pray as though they were the conduit to God.

Not once, since the accident, had Teri sought religious solace. But this rabbi now opening the synagogue door had context. He had buried Elise.

He motioned for her to sit in the leather chair opposite his desk. "Do we have an appointment?"

"No, sorry. Do you have a few minutes to talk?"

He glanced at his watch and nodded. "How can I help you, Mrs …?" His eyes were kind and inviting, silvery gray with long lashes, nearly the identical shade as his beard and hair.

She realized she was staring. "I'm Teri Berger."

"And I'm Rabbi Ben Feldman. Have we ever met?"

"I was at Elise Horowitz's funeral."

"Ahh," his eyes clouded. "Tragic situation." He tugged on his beard, transporting her back to that icy wind and partially frozen ground, to the father's wailing, the mother's stunned stoicism, to the reason she was here.

"May I tell you something?"

"Of course."

"My daughter is pregnant."

"Okay...."

"She's in high school."

"I see."

She pressed, "I guess I'm wondering if there are any Jewish teachings that might help me."

"The Torah provides us with infinite wisdom except I'm not sure what you're asking for." He straightened the yarmulke on his head. "Were you raised Jewish?"

"We ate a lot of *kugel*."

"A gastronomical Jew. And today you seek wisdom from a rabbi."

His tone was teasing and Teri felt the tightness in her chest begin to loosen. "Rabbi Feldman, what do we owe the dead?"

"We only owe the living." He stood, surprising Teri again with his imposing height and broad shoulders. She'd never quite shaken the old-world image that a rabbi ought to be stooped over. He walked around the desk and sat in the chair next to hers.

For twenty years, Teri had lived with a therapist and she'd never understood the temptation or the need to talk intimately with a stranger. But there was something so freeing in the kind, gray eyes, a sense of absolution, a word Teri had never before considered yet now found essential.

She inhaled, and on the exhale blurted, "I'm the one who killed Elise."

He sat up straight. "The driver?"

"Yes."

The window air conditioning unit rumbled and kicked on. A full blast filled the room with a whoosh of cool air, momentarily interrupting her courage. After a few beats of silence, she continued, "I don't know if you knew this, but Elise was, well, apparently she abused drugs."

He didn't respond.

"She used to babysit for our kids." Teri gave a rueful shrug at his surprised gasp. "Bizarre coincidence, huh? In fact, it's how I knew her. I'd heard she went through rehab and was doing pretty well. But I was angry when I put it together that she'd been stoned while taking care of our kids. Anyway, I ran into her—" She coughed, "Poor choice of words. I saw her at a coffee shop several months before the accident. She was alone and when I went to say hello, she rolled her eyes. So I blasted her. I told her I should have had her arrested, that I wished I'd never allowed her into our house." Teri held her hands out, a futile, ghostly apology. "Apparently, she started using drugs again right around that time."

He clucked as though it was a story he heard too often.

"From what I understand, Elise and her mom fought about drugs the day she rushed out of the house and stalled her car and— Maybe none of this would have happened if, you know … It's like I killed her twice."

The rabbi pressed Teri's palms together prayer style. "It must be terrible to be so powerful."

She yanked her hands back. "Are you mocking me?"

"No, Mrs. Berger. But I believe you have come here for a pardon. As Jews, it is not for a rabbi to forgive you for what you have done or even what you fear you may have done."

She averted her eyes from his and for the first time noticed the Jewish symbols scattered around the office: the six-pointed Star of David hanging in the window, the velvet-clad Torah on the nearby table, the Hebrew *ketubah* marriage certificate behind his desk, and she found surprising comfort in their familiarity.

"There's still more. Something I've never told anybody, not even my husband. Something so horrible…." She could stop here, probably *should* stop here—never utter the words aloud. But wasn't this the real reason she had come? So in spite of her better judgment, the story tumbled out. "When my daughter, Carly, was just six and my son was an infant, I starting going with the kids to matinee movies. Carly had become clingy and jealous of the baby and I needed a breather. At first we went into the same theater, but even there Carly would yank on my arm, constantly interrupting the movie. So one day I took her into a different movie in the adjoining theater, bribed her with a box of candy, and told her we would be next door and I would come find her at the end of our films. Because Carly didn't seem to mind, we did it again several days later and again the following week.

"I knew it was wrong, and every time I'd see her, hours later, her little body scrunched down in the seat, unharmed, I'd promise myself it was the last time. Except days later, I'd do it again. One day Carly wasn't in the theater at the end of my show. At first, I wasn't alarmed, but after searching the bathroom, the popcorn counter, and other theaters without finding her, I panicked. I was just short of calling for help when I finally found her sitting in the front row on the floor of a theater at the far end of the building, trembling and sobbing."

He was still watching her, his expression carefully neutral. She bowed her head and muttered, "Believe me, that was the last time. But when I think about what could have happened …." She smothered a sob and trained her eyes on the Torah, fighting for control. "Rabbi, I was spared even when I was totally undeserving. But some mothers don't get a second or third chance. Why," she choked, then whispered, "was I?"

He took his time before he responded, seeming to carefully weigh his words. "Mrs. Berger, many years ago, before going to rabbinical school, I fancied myself a mathematician. Don't look so surprised, rabbis are people too you know." At her appreciative grin, he went on. "There's a wonderful mathematical concept, broken symmetries, which reminds us that life is a mixture of the predictable and the random. We have all heard the platitude about a rock that falls through the smooth surface of a lake. It breaks the symmetry. A new point is formed and multiple ripples occur. Whether from a mortal or divine perspective, whichever you might believe, it is certain that rocks will be thrown into the lake. It's the ripples that are uncertain."

He stood and walked to the bookshelves, where he retrieved a black, leather book, fringed along the spine from overuse. "You have asked for a teaching. As you probably know, every year on Yom Kippur congregations around the world confess aloud their transgressions. Let me share one passage." He turned immediately to the page he sought and in a voice that at once deepened, read. *"For transgressions against God, the Day of Atonement atones; but for transgressions of one human being against another, the Day of Atonement does not atone until they have made peace with one another."* He closed the book, keeping his index finger in place.

"Elise is dead. And her mother, Rozlynn, doesn't want my peace."

"I'm curious. Why did you tell me your daughter is pregnant?"

Teri flushed. "I don't know."

He tilted his head, his eyes probing.

"Okay, I do know," she answered. "I wonder ... See, my mother is scheming something, and I'm not sure, but I've pieced together enough to think she believes we ought to—This is going to sound crazy."

He moved across the room and sat once more in the chair immediately next to Teri.

"If my daughter has the baby and we give it to Rozlynn Horowitz—"

He shook his head several times, this time pulling with some force on his beard. "What does your daughter think about this?"

"I have no idea."

"Mrs. Berger, I believe forgiveness is meaningless without *tshuvah*, an honest and true change for the better." He leaned in close, opened the prayer book, and quietly read again. "... *'but for transgressions of one human being against another, the Day of Atonement does not atone until they have made peace with one another.'* I wonder, Mrs. Berger, exactly with whom do you need to make peace?"

TERI AWOKE TO THE INSISTENT HONKING of a car outside their bedroom window. She peeked through the blinds just as the Rubins' oversized black van pulled into her driveway.

She hurried to Jimmy's room, and seeing an empty bed, rushed down the stairs. Jimmy was frantically zipping his backpack, toothbrush sticking out of his mouth.

"Hey, good morning."

His expression registered surprise. "Mom, you're still home?"

She nodded and reached into the pantry to retrieve a granola bar. "Want one or two?" she asked, handing him three.

The van's honk sounded again. Teri grasped Jimmy's arm. "How about if we go out to lunch or something this weekend? Just the two of us."

He flushed with pleasure. "Awesome," his voice squeaking high on the last syllable.

Teri watched him walk out, all arms, legs and lean torso, and felt the clutch of time's passage. She stood for long moments, staring into her nearly finished kitchen, at the new ash-wood cabinets, sage-colored backsplash, granite countertop—the "heart-of-every-home"—waiting for Carly to appear.

36

CARLY

"MOM, WHAT ARE YOU DOING HOME?"
"Have you made a decision? Is today the day?"

Carly hesitated, that moment when any answer was still possible. She looked down. Her ankles swelled over her flip-flops. They were gross. She was gross.

Her mom lifted Carly's chin so their eyes met. "Please don't lie to me. You don't have to tell me what you don't want me to know, but don't lie."

Carly swallowed hard under her gaze, feeling exposed. She gathered her books on the counter, shoved them into her backpack, willing herself not to cry.

"Come on," Teri said, cuffing Carly on the back. "I'm here for you. Unless, someone else was taking you?"

"Um, yeah. My friend Markieta. I better call her." She picked up the portable phone and walked into the den. Markieta answered on the first ring.

"I was just leaving for the bus. You change your mind again?"

"My mom wants to take me."

"Well, that's good, right?"

"I guess." She felt her throat closing up. "I'm so scared."

"I told you, just shut your eyes and think about other things. It's over so fast you can't believe it."

They didn't say a word until they were on the highway heading east when her mom asked, "Just curious, why did you tell your grandmother of all people?"

"She told me."

Teri laughed. "I bet she did."

Carly felt herself bristle. She wanted to defend Selia, wanted to say, "At least she's been concerned about me," but Carly knew if she made her mom angry, she might turn around and head home.

Teri fidgeted with the radio, changing from station to station. Impatiently, she pressed the button off. "Okay, answer me this—"

"Who is the father?"

"I assume Jason, right? And if not, I'm not sure I want to know." Carly raised her eyebrows teasingly, then nodded yes.

"What's he say about this?

"He's pretty freaked out. I think—" She paused. "I think I need to break up with him when this is over."

"Oh, sweetie, I'm sorry." She clasped Carly's hand. Both palms were sweaty with fingertips like ice. Carly had never noticed before, they had the exact same hands, same shape, same length. It comforted her somehow and she squeezed back.

"Actually, what I was going to ask is how far along are you?"

Under her breath, Carly said, "Ten weeks."

Teri gasped. She flipped the radio back on, immediately filling the car with chatter. Then she turned to Carly, keeping one hand loosely on the wheel. "It has a beating heart … and arms and legs and fingers and toes."

"Mo-om," Carly's voice caught and came out a sob. "Why did you say that?"

Teri exited onto a side street. She put the car in park, but didn't turn it off. She reached for Carly, who immediately shifted her body as far away as the bucket seat would allow.

"Don't touch me. Why did you say that?"

"Because it is important for you, whatever you decide, to know you do have a choice."

"Quit talking about it."

"I wish you had come to me."

"You would have just gotten all upset and that would make it even worse. Plus …" She hesitated.

"Plus?"

"You're never around anymore."

"I know I've made big mistakes." Teri's voice sounded weird, reminding Carly of the early months after the accident when she never knew what to expect.

"Can we please—?"

Teri held her hand up. "I feel as if I've turned into the kind of mother I never should have been." Her eyes were glazed and shiny. "But no matter what, I always love you. Nothing will ever change that."

Carly had no idea how to respond. She knew her mom was trying to make her feel better or at least explain something, but all she could think about was whether those protesters would be in front of the building again today. Would they recognize her? Ram their picket signs into her?

"I want to tell you something."

She felt her heart quicken. Now what?

"When I was your age, something awful happened to me. I was working part time for a laundry and dry cleaners. The owner, Verne, made all the high school girls wear an unbelievably short mini-skirt uniform. He was about fifty years old and he thought he was so good looking, even made a joke of calling himself a *ladies' man*, though all of us found him repulsive with his tight shirts and this thick gold chain he wore around his neck.

"One Saturday I was alone in the laundry and Verne came strolling in, rubbing his neck with a hand vibrator. He asked me to get a laundered coat down from the pulley, which meant I had to step onto a ladder as he stood right under me." Teri stopped, stared into space for several long moments, as if transported to another time. She visibly shuddered then continued in a flat voice. "I knew it was creepy and I was alone; but Carly, it was another time and girls didn't know about sexual harassment. So I climbed the ladder and with my back to him I reached for the coat just as I felt a vibration on my calf."

"What the …!"

"Yeah, right? Anyway, I stood there on that ladder in my short, short skirt as he rubbed first one calf and then the other. He asked me if it felt good and I just went mute, totally panicked and stunned." She twisted her wedding band, shoved it past her knuckle and slid it back on. "Fortunately, it ended there. I climbed down; he patted my shoulder and went back into his office in another part of the building. But all these years later, I still remember the feeling of helplessness and the way he smelled standing behind me—like hair grease and the English Leather. To this day I get nauseous when I smell someone wearing it."

Teri turned forward, put the car in drive but continued to keep her foot on the brake. "So why am I telling you this now? Because you are so much more knowledgeable and smarter than I was at your age. You can use your strength and awareness to make the right choices in situations where I didn't even know I had a choice."

This time as she reached across the car and enclosed Carly into a tight hug, Carly squeezed back, wishing she had the words to make her mom feel better.

Traffic was beginning to pick up. They drove in silence for several miles. Carly watched the trees and roofs of houses pass. She heaved a sigh that made her breasts ache. As they pulled into the parking lot, she grabbed her mom's arm. "What if this is the wrong decision?"

Teri seemed to think carefully before speaking. "You believe this is the best answer for this situation?" At Carly's nod, she said, "You make peace with it."

"Would you have had the baby?"

"I don't know. Probably not if I were your age. But …" her voice dropped off and she waved her arm. "It's just hard for me to think about *choosing* to … I mean, well, you know. There's been so much unhappiness and guilt. At this point, at this age in my life, I don't know…"

Carly slumped against the seat, feeling as if she might black out. "Mom, do you think I'm doing … like what happened … Is this like one of us killing … is this like Elise?"

"No!" She clasped Carly's hands. "I wasn't trying to imply anything like that. It's just what I said, Car. Just sad."

"What about Daddy?"

"I'm not sure what he needs right now."

"I mean, is he really upset with me? He wouldn't even look at me yesterday."

Her mom was quiet for such a long time Carly nearly screamed, "Tell me!" Teri answered in her gloomiest voice yet. "Sweetie, you have to understand how difficult this is for Dad—for both of us—but especially for Dad, to think about you and Jason … You're his little girl, Carly."

That first time with Jason, in his brother's empty apartment, had been so awful. And even the times since, there was the sense she was doing something she didn't really want to do. And now, her Dad probably thought she was the biggest slut in America. She felt her face flush with shame. Carly wanted to explain, but what came out of her mouth instead was, "Would it help if I have the baby?"

The answer was immediate. "I don't think that is what upsets him. But this is *your* life, Carly. You get one go around and you've got to figure how to make it work for *you*. That much I have learned."

Carly kneaded her stomach, letting her fingertips dance over the edges of her belly, imagining arms, legs, and a beating heart. Her mom on a ladder in a short skirt with a horrible man's hands on her calves. She looked up. Her mom seemed sad, but strong. "Okay, let's go."

⁓

THE ROOM'S CHILL was not unexpected this time, but still unpleasant. Carly couldn't stop the shaking and the nurse had to actually help place her heels into the stirrups because she kept missing.

The white-hot lightning, the cramping, the pinching, and Carly moaned aloud, feeling a sharp pain throughout her lower back. She heard the sound of a vacuum, remembered Markieta's warning, tried to close her ears and shut her eyes. "Uh, oh," she groaned and turned her head in time to heave out a yellow stream of thin sour vomit onto the side of the bed and into her hair. The sucking noise seemed to end as quickly as it had begun. There was sudden and complete silence in the room. A masked face loomed above her own. Tired brown eyes surrounded by small wrinkles. "It's over. When you feel ready, you may sit up."

She reached her hands to touch her stomach, but the drape was still covering her body. She could hear a lot of movement, instruments being carted away, footsteps already moving on, readying for the next procedure.

When she opened her eyes again, she was startled to see her mother, her face drawn tight. "Let's go home."

The house was empty when they arrived. "Where's Jimmy?" she asked, surprised to find her throat dry and sore. A vile taste filled her mouth and she remembered the vomit.

"At school."

"Oh, yeah, it's only Thursday. What about Dad?" Carly was exhausted suddenly, almost too tired to stand.

"He had to go to the office. To get some files. You want to go to bed?"

She nodded gratefully.

"You need help?"

Carly stopped at the bottom stair and looked up. She slumped against the wall. Immediately, Teri was by her side. Carly couldn't remember the last time her mom had tucked her in but it felt wonderful. She pulled the covers up to Carly's chin, closed the blinds and pushed the hair off her forehead.

"Mom?"

"Yes, dear?"

"How come you didn't tell Grandma about the laundromat boss?"

She leaned into the door jamb, her expression thoughtful. "I guess for the same reason you didn't come to me. Mother-daughter stuff."

"Oh."

"Plus," with a smile, "can you even imagine what my mother would have done to that man?" She giggled, a teenage-sounding silly giggle. "Boy, did I miss my chance. I totally should have sicced Selia on him."

"Well, thanks for telling me." Carly's voice choked, "And thanks for today."

The moment she heard the door close and her mom's footsteps on the stairs the flood of tears began. She kept hearing the terrible sucking sound of her baby being vacuumed away like yesterday's crumbs. She cried louder, trying to drown out the noise. Finally the tears slowed and stopped. She glanced at the desk chair where she'd crumpled her favorite pair of jeans. They hadn't zipped for two weeks. At least she could wear them soon. She rolled over onto her stomach. Her boobs were still swollen and sore and her sheet smelled gross from her pukey hair. She needed to shower. She'd have to call Jason and Markieta. And finally tell Becca. But first she was going to sleep.

❧

CARLY AWOKE ABRUPTLY to shouting below. She strained to hear. Selia and her mother. A loud clomping on the stairs and her door was swung open, bright hallway light flooding the darkness.

"How *dare* you!" Her grandmother's compact body was wired with anger. "How could you be so foolish?" She stood menacingly over the bed, her eyes bulging and her mouth twisted. "That baby wasn't yours. It belonged to Rozlynn."

"Mother, this isn't your concern," Teri shouted, rushing into the room.

They stood glowering at one another. Carly watched, her heart hammering against her chest, feeling the cramping down below. Suddenly, Selia's whole body seemed to crumble and she dropped onto the nearby chair. "Oh, Carly, why?" she whimpered. "We could have made everything good for everybody."

Teri reached her arm out, falling inches short of touching Selia. "No, Mom. This baby wouldn't have brought back Elise. What made you think it would?"

Her grandma's grimace was ugly as she shook her head back and forth. "That's your problem, Teri. It's always been your problem. You don't see the answers even when they're staring at you."

"Did you honestly imagine you could just give Carly's baby to Rozlynn? Like a trade-in? And even if you could, why on earth would you consider placing our baby with that horrible woman? Jesus, they live so close to here. We'd potentially see her every time we went anywhere." By this point, her mom was actually sweating with round wet stains on the front of her blouse. "And what about Carly? How could this possibly have been a good solution for Carly?"

Using the arms of the chair for support, Selia pulled herself up and crossed the room to the bed. She lifted the end of the sheet and shoved it to the side, traced her finger across Carly's ankle, outlining each of the four small leaves. "You know, you can't be buried in a religious Jewish cemetery because of this tattoo." Selia gave one of her all-teeth, all-knowing smiles that wasn't really a smile.

"Enough!" Teri exploded. "Enough of your comments and your intrusion into everything in our lives. I am Carly's mother, not you. If anyone is going to help her make decisions, it will be me."

A look of confusion briefly flitted across Selia's face, then she straightened up, her spine visibly stiffening. "Humph! After all I've done. Well ... I can see it's time for me to leave."

"You're right. It is," Teri said.

They glared at one another, both faces hardened into a righteousness that turned their profiles into one and the same. Selia looked away first.

"I'll go pack my bags." She paused at the door, and when no one stopped her, walked out of the room.

Teri collapsed onto Carly's bed. "Ouch," she said, "that didn't go well."

Carly sank deeper into her pillow, stunned into silence.

"I'm sorry, honey. I didn't mean to upset you. Or to chase your grandma away from you. But for once she's right about something—it is time for her to leave. We need to get our own little family back on track."

Carly felt a gush of fresh blood pour out of her, even as she laid still. She grasped her mom's hand, fisting it against her chest.

"Honey, this will all get better … I promise."

Carly's thoughts flashed to the night Selia promised to come up with a solution, the moment when her grandma placed her cheek on Carly's stomach and they both felt a third presence in the room. For the first time it hit: she really wasn't pregnant anymore.

"Does Grandma hate me?"

"She might … for this minute. But she'll get over it. After all, you're her Carly Jane." Something indefinable flickered in her mom's eyes. She stood to leave, but stopped in the doorway. "You want her to forgive you, eat her meatloaf."

"Oh, Mom, I wasn't *that* bad."

Teri threw her head back and laughed, again looking like Selia, though the laugh sounded more like a stifled cry. "I better go have a talk with your grandma. Holler if you need anything."

Carly lay back against her pillows, listening to the sounds of drawers opening and multiple suitcases dropping to the floor. It had been two months since her grandma and all those near-empty suitcases arrived at their doorstep. She could hardly remember a time when Selia hadn't been staying with them, or a time before the baby, or when her mom didn't work a gazillion hours. Or the day before Thanksgiving. That one seemed a hundred years ago. She was so mad at her mom that morning for not letting her take the car to school. If only she'd pushed harder.

She was still a virgin then.

Jason had begged her last night to let him come along, but she'd refused. He'd cried, which of course made her cry. Her mom and dad had been crying for days. Other families weren't like that. Becca's mom and dad had their act totally together and even Jason's divorced parents seemed normal compared to the Bergers. Only Markieta's family was more screwed up. Just in the time they'd been friends, Markieta and her aunt had moved twice. *I haven't got room in my life for sorry.*

Carly pulled her underpants down several inches and looked. Thick blood covered the pad, bright red, much brighter than the period blood she sloughed off, more like the red of fresh injury. She was never going to have sex again until she was married, which for sure meant the end of Jason. Becca told her *Cosmo* said once you slept with a guy, you couldn't turn the clock back, no daylight savings time on sex. She switched on the lava lamp. Now it was done. Over. As Selia said, time to move on. She pressed her palms against her stomach, tender but already softer. Almost as if nothing had ever happened. But something *had* happened. She sat up, hit by a sudden overwhelming panic. This is what Markieta had tried to tell her. This is what her mom was trying to say.

The baby was *gone.*

"Oh no," she whimpered. She grabbed the pillow and buried her face, breathing in the musty smell from the recent weeks of night sweats. She felt the tears closing her throat, and struggled to tamp them down. Tears would change nothing.

Reaching out a blind hand, she turned the lava lamp off.

In three weeks, she'd go to junior/senior prom with Jason. Well, maybe. In two weeks, she would take her SAT tests. Her grandma wanted her to go to the University of Florida. She was thinking it would be better to go to school somewhere on the east coast, some place where no one ever knew Elise—maybe New York. Most people didn't even drive cars in New York.

37

ROZLYNN

SHE ROLLED OVER FROM HER FRONT to her back and peeked from under the blanket. The room was dimly lit, must be cloudy out, probably already mid-afternoon. Another wasted day in bed. Not that it mattered. She didn't care. George didn't seem to care. Certainly no one else gave a fuck.

But ever since going to Dr. Berger several days ago, she'd been haunted by the sense that if she didn't start trying to "move on" she never would. Just linking the words together in her mind brought forth the image of crazy-ass Selia with her orange hair, scary teeth, and her insane idea. With a start, Rozlynn realized: Selia gave a fuck.

With that realization, even knowing that Selia was bat-shit crazy, for the first time she allowed herself to wonder: How *would* it have felt to hold another infant in her arms? To get another chance? No! The woman was nuts and her plan even more so.

But now what? Would the girl have an abortion? Or would she have the baby and leave it in Teri Berger's care? Would she herself one day be pushing a cart full of groceries at Dierbergs and run into Teri Berger, walking hand in hand with the toddler Selia had wanted her to raise? Good God, what a thought.

"Yeah, yeah," she muttered, swinging her legs over the side of the bed and slowly standing to a full stretch. Her neck was stiff from lying down. She lifted her shirt; the rash under her arm was becoming painful. How long had it been since she'd last showered?

Later. For sure before George came home.

She shuffled into the kitchen, pulled down an empty bowl, retrieved the Raisin Bran and stood in front of the refrigerator. Some days she spent so much time absorbing each image of Elise she could shut her eyes and see the photos more clearly than when her eyes were open.

"Oh, Elise." Placing a fingertip to her lips, she touched it to each of the many ages of her daughter until she reached the last photo, the one showing Elise did die pretty.

Outside, the rumble of a large truck could be heard several doors down. She glanced around the kitchen and then with a burst of energy, that seemed to come from somewhere else, she grabbed a clear plastic bag and began shoving piles of newspapers into it until the bag was teeming over. She filled a second bag, and a third one. Both arms loaded, she half-carried, half-dragged the trash down the hall and hauled the bags to the curb, just as the recycling truck screeched to a halt in front of her house.

"Afternoon, ma'am," a short, stocky man said, jumping down from the driver's side. With one arm, he hurled all three bags onto the truck before climbing back in and pulling away, leaving behind a waft of black exhaust fumes.

Rozlynn watched the truck as it went from house to house, as the man, with seeming effortlessness, hefted used-up trash to be taken away. When the truck turned the corner, Rozlynn realized she actually felt a little bit lighter, felt the relief of having literally discarded a heavy weight. She closed her eyes and tilted her face up, standing still for what might have been seconds, or minutes. At some point since the accident, she had ceased to recognize the passage of time, having come to the universal reality that sixty seconds are a minute, sixty minutes are an hour, twenty-four hours are a day. Even when the prospect of an entire day felt interminable, even when getting through each hour was brutal, it was the same sixty-second minute.

With eyes still closed, she sensed the sun peeking through the clouds. "Find the rubber," Selia had said.

Tentatively, she whispered, "Elise? Can you hear me?" The words echoed in her ears, so she said them again. "Elise! Do you hear me?" Her voice cracked and her eyes teared, but she didn't fall down. And she didn't die with anger or regret. So she said it once more, louder, even daring to smile through the lump in her throat, "If you can hear me, Elise, I love you!"

The clouds traveled across the sun, turning the air cooler and the light dimmer. She walked into the house and shut the door. Without the stacks of newspaper, the kitchen table seemed larger, the room less cluttered. She opened the morning paper and began flipping the pages, not paying much attention, not particularly interested, until she got to the classified ads, until her finger trailed down to the section, "Puppies for sale." She skimmed the ads, then closed the paper and dropped it into a new recycling bag. Puppies were so much damn work.

The freezer was overstuffed with microwave dinners, but way in the back was a package of chicken thighs and drumsticks. She pulled off the plastic wrap, dumped the frozen lump into a casserole, covered it with a paper towel and placed the dish in the microwave on defrost. She reached for the pack of cigarettes and matches on the top of the refrigerator. As she tapped one out, her mindless gaze settled again on the photos, this time of eight-year-old Elise in a dance recital costume looking like she owned the world. There *had* been happy times. Tears stung her eyes. Would it ever get easier? Ever?

Rozlynn sank into a chair, willing herself not to crawl back to bed. Her hands trembled as she lit the cigarette. The first draw and exhalation quieted the shaking. The microwave beeped but she continued to sit. She smoked a second cigarette, and a third. Part of her was waiting for George to get angry about the stench in the house. Before Elise died, she'd only smoked outside.

She dared to look. It was not quite four. Chances were George would work late and she wasn't hungry. She left the chicken in the microwave and shuffled down the hall, depleted. On the bed stand was the junk mail envelope on which Selia had written her cell phone number the day of her visit. She'd stared at the grease-stained envelope so many damned times without ever focusing enough to memorize the number. At some point, she needed to trash the thing.

Puppies shit and pissed in the house, chewed furniture legs, destroyed the carpeting, barked too much, needed constant attention, had to be walked. It took three years for most of them to even settle down. It was why she'd never wanted a dog. Why she'd disregarded Elise's pleas for a puppy. As she'd admitted to both Selia and Dr. Berger, it was perhaps one of her most painful regrets. A dog might have soothed Elise. Or a cat.

One ad mentioned an eight-month-old rescue Aussie. Might be reasonable to just take a look. No. What was she thinking? She'd go to the shelter where Elise volunteered—and save a life.

38

TERI

THE TERMINAL WAS TEEMING with people, but Teri easily spotted the flaming orange hair. She waited on the other side of the rope and watched as Selia purchased her ticket at the counter. The process seemed to take longer than it should have; and by the time Selia was putting her charge card back into her wallet, the airline rep had grown red-faced and visible pockets of sweat dotted his uniform shirt.

Teri shook her head in bemused horror as her mom walked forward, waving her ticket. "Don't tell me. He gave you a first-class ticket for half the usual price?"

Selia grinned with smug pleasure. "Not quite. But I did get a bit of a discount."

"You have about twenty minutes to spare. Let's grab a cup of coffee."

Teri stood in line while Selia squeezed through the crowded area to secure a small table in the front of the Starbucks shop. She watched as her mother swept the crumbs onto the floor and wiped the table with a fistful of napkins. It might have been her stooped posture or the unyielding nature of the plastic chair, but Selia looked so shrunken, so suddenly old, that Teri felt a rush of dismay. The emotion deepened as a blank, confused expression momentarily flattened the features on her mother's face.

"Here, Mom," she said, placing the two cups of coffee down while taking deliberate and obvious care to clutch her purse close to her chest.

Selia uttered a curt "humph" and looked away, holding her body tight.

"It was your idea to leave immediately, you know," Teri said.

Selia tilted her head. "Do you think there are actually daughters who appreciate when their mothers try to help?"

Teri sipped her coffee for several moments, trying to sort through the many responses, ultimately settling on simple appeal. "Mom, can we try to stop this zero-sum game we both play? Some mothers and daughters know how to just *be*."

"Name one."

"Well ..." Teri waved her arm, mocking herself for both of their benefits. "Okay, but they must be out there somewhere."

Selia grunted as she picked up her coffee and took a long drink. She offered a crooked smile and Teri felt her shoulders relax. They watched as streams of people entered the airport and queued into the ticket lines, everyone with his or her own destination, his or her own story. It had been years since Teri had flown anywhere for pleasure. Before the accident, she was afraid of flying, assuming every flight was a potential crash. She no longer assumed anything. It freed her to travel, she realized suddenly.

"You and Leonard ought to try to get away. It would be good for you to take a trip somewhere together. We can go right now and buy two tickets for somewhere fun. Surprise Leonard."

Teri was not even startled. Long ago she'd become resigned to Selia taking up residency inside her head. "This is hardly the time for Len and me to go on vacation."

"Just once, Teri, can't you follow my advice without arguing?"

"Just once, Mom, can you not be so pushy?"

"Someone's got to fix things. Luckily for all of you, I let bygones be bygones or you'd still be eating out of boxes."

Teri rolled her eyes. Selia's incorrigible nature was almost amusing when she was about to become long distance.

Unexpectedly, Selia patted Teri's hand and in an abrupt shift, gently said, "Tell me how you're doing. I mean really doing."

"I'm fine," she muttered.

Selia stared until Teri reluctantly raised her head. "You don't have to tell me the truth, but don't lie to me."

"I don't know the answer." Her eyes settled on a balding, gray-haired man one table over whose head was buried into the blonde curls of a small girl sitting on his lap. "I used to wait to get over the accident, to return to how things were. But I'm beginning to realize *before* will never exist again."

"Certainly not for Rozlynn *now.*"

Teri inhaled a lungful of bitter air and exhaled slowly and fully. "We can't fix it, Mom. Not even you. I have to learn how to live with this. For the rest of my life."

Selia peered intently at Teri as though studying a not-quite-familiar face. "I can't possibly know the hell you've gone through. But you should never know, as a mother, what it's like to see your own daughter in so much pain."

Teri felt herself bristle; even this, Selia had to make about herself. Then she looked and saw anguish in her mother's red-rimmed eyes. Complicated love, Rozlynn called it.

"Teri, I want what every mother wants for her child. I want you to live a glorious life."

Teri smiled ruefully. "So long as I live it your way?"

"Speaking of which, are you going to quit that horrible job?"

"I love my work." She caught her breath at the sudden memory of the face looming against her window, his eyes raping her, his hand reaching for a gun. She shuddered. "I'm going to try to balance everything better. But I need this, Mom. Can you understand? When I'm with those kids I can almost forget, and even forgive myself a little."

"What about Leonard?"

"I don't know. I'm scared. He seems so lost suddenly. And he's really mad at me."

Selia leaned in close. "Fight for him, for both of you. You're worth it."

The old man and young girl were now sitting apart, but their shoulders continued to touch.

Selia reached into her purse, grabbed Teri's hand, placed something hard and round against her palm, and squeezed her fingers together. Teri unfolded her fist.

"Is this Daddy's?" She felt almost light headed as she stared in wonder and memory. She clasped her hand around the watch, felt its solid warmth, and brought it up to her lips. She could hear the steady ticking. "Oh no. Did you take this back from Henry?"

"Just let me worry about the details."

"Thank you." Teri said, trying to talk around the thick lump in her throat. "But I don't really need this anymore."

"Jimmy does."

Teri wrapped the watch in a tissue and placed it in a zipped pocket of her purse, stalling as she struggled to collect her emotions. The purse felt heavier in her lap, weighted and more stable. Selia gave her the space she needed, quiet moments in which the unsaid was clearer than most of their conversations.

Finally, Teri could speak again. "I think I'll get Len and the kids to help me paint the kitchen walls this weekend. Got any suggestions for a color?"

"I would have been happy to provide input if I wasn't leaving in such a rush."

Teri didn't attempt to suppress her sigh. She would never have believed that by middle age she would still be struggling with so many issues involving her mother. She could only imagine what she and Carly had yet to go through. She made a mental note to work on that when she entered therapy, something she'd decided she was finally ready to tackle. It was time to do the work: To dig into the impact of being the daughter—the only child—of a mother like Selia. Of having lost her father so young. Of feeling unfulfilled without a career, yet taking no steps to change. Of her marriage, her own mothering issues. On and on. And then, Elise. "Come on, Mom. You better get going." Teri held the carry-on in one hand and guided her mother's elbow with the other. At security, Selia stood on tiptoe and kissed Teri's cheek. "Don't forget about the beef stew in the refrigerator. You'll need to serve it tonight or freeze it."

"Mom?"

Selia halted.

"Thanks for being here. I love you. And please call that gerontologist Len recommended. I'll fly down and go with you, if you want. It's time to check things out."

She watched Selia move through the snaking security line, watched her remove her pumps and jacket, watched as she walked through the metal detector, watched until Teri couldn't see her anymore.

The older man was still sitting in his chair, but the seat next to him was empty. Teri considered asking if he needed assistance or even just wanted company. Instead, on impulse she dug into her purse, pulled out her cell phone and called DeDe. After one ring, it went straight to voicemail. She nearly hung up, but at the end of DeDe's message she left her own: "It's Teri. Berger. I need to thank you for, you know, um, for making me see what I couldn't see. As your niece may have told you, Carly is doing fine. Well, that's all. I'm taking tomorrow off but I'll see you Monday." She pressed end and stared at the phone, willing it to ring right back, to open the door to a new friendship.

Next she called Bud, left a voicemail that she needed one more day. Maybe when she saw him again, she'd even offer to spruce up his office decor, tell him she used to have an eye for that sort of thing.

She dropped the phone back into her purse and began the lengthy trek to her car. At the door to the garage, Selia's voice reverberated in her head. "Okay, Mom, okay," she muttered aloud as she spun on her heel and headed back toward the ticket counter to see where she and Len might go from here.

Acknowledgements

NEARLY TWENTY YEARS AGO, I began my first novel as part of my MFA thesis. My idea was to play with the fictionalized rippling effects of a fatal crash as it applies to the driver. Out of this grew *AFTER ELISE*, a book I wrote and rewrote numerous times throughout the past two decades. Ten years ago, I put the book aside to write and publish *THE MIDDLE STEP* (High Hill Press, fall 2015), only to return again last winter to a novel that refused to stay out of my head.

It's been a long journey leading up to the exciting call from the Ardent Writers Press publisher, Steve Gierhart, offering me a contract to publish this book. Along the way I've had many readers at various times, each of whom has contributed to the story, the characters and the writing. I want to thank my earliest readers who believed in the rough drafts enough to encourage me to keep going: David Carkeet, Allison Hunter, Janet Goddard, and Jonathan Bogard. As I continued to churn out new drafts, I benefited from the readings by Robin Kevrick Baker, Annie Silver, Perry Pattiz, Debra Finkel, Debbie Taryle, Susie Dykstra, Cheryl Silver, Vanessa Diaz, and David Greenblatt. And during the past year, when I was nearly finished with the novel, I received particularly helpful and specific feedback from Patti McCarty, Lise Bernstein, Linda Wendling, and Dr. Diane Rosenbaum. Also, a special thanks goes to Steve Gierhart for taking on this novel and sending it from manuscript to published book.

Even once "done," every writer needs an editor, someone who doesn't hold back from tough honesty and constructive criticism. I was fortunate to have two such readers. My Ardent Writers Press editor, Doyle Duke, read at least eight drafts and each time returned the book with suggestions that pushed me harder and further. I am so grateful for his wisdom and his concern.

MY OTHER "EDITOR" happens to be my husband, who is not only smart, insightful, and honest, he also cares enough to challenge me to be a stronger writer. In return, while the words on these pages are dedicated to my children and grandchildren; the words not on these pages are dedicated to my husband, best friend, and true partner in everything, Robert Bogard.

Denise Pattiz Bogard

About the Author

DENISE PATTIZ BOGARD, author of *AFTER ELISE* and *THE MIDDLE STEP*, has been writing professionally for more than 40 years. Her award-winning fiction and non-fiction have been published in, among others, *The Oklahoma Literary Review, Newsweek, Lady's Circle, The St. Louis Post-Dispatch*, and *Teacher Magazine*, and two of her essays have been anthologized. Denise earned her MFA in creative writing from the University of Missouri-St. Louis and her BS in journalism and history from Indiana University. Over the years she has been a journalist, a co-founding public relations partner, a certified secondary English/writing teacher, the founder of St. Louis Writers Workshop, and a novelist. Denise lives in St. Louis with her husband.

AFTER ELISE has been named a finalist in the Faulkner-Wisdom Creative Writing Contest, novel category.

94478940R00136

Made in the USA
Lexington, KY
30 July 2018